Mission Alch

Producer & International Distributor
eBookPro Publishing
www.ebook-pro.com

Mission Alchemist
Charlie Wolfe

Contact: Charlie.Wolfe.Author@gmail.com
ISBN

MISSION ALCHEMIST

CHARLIE WOLFE

PROLOGUE

In the chest of every real scientist beats the heart of an alchemist dreaming of converting base metals into gold, but even the wonders of modern technology have not managed to produce gold through transmutation.

The closest resemblance is turning cheap, inexpensive uranium into precious, almost priceless, weapon-grade plutonium. To date, this has been carried out only by a small number of states using nuclear reactors and deploying complicated chemical processes to extract the plutonium product. Strict safeguards are implemented to monitor production of fissile materials—plutonium and high enriched uranium—to prevent the proliferation of nuclear weapons.

The dreadful alchemist has devised a method to transmute thorium into uranium-233, a fissile material that is not closely watched. The process can be carried out in a clandestine facility, readily disguised as a regular chemical laboratory. With this material making an atomic bomb is as easy as lighting a fire, a fire that might engulf our entire planet.

CHAPTER 1

April 18, Barcelona

Oscar Gunar Axelsson, a fine looking man in his late twenties with typical Scandinavian features known to his few old friends simply as Ossi, strolled down the famous Ramblas promenade in Barcelona.

The regulars, including pickpockets, con artists, and wallet snatchers that made their living off the many gullible tourists, took a fleeting look at the tall, blond man and viewed him as a potential victim, but, a second look convinced them he was far from being a soft touch.

Perhaps it was the controlled way he moved his athletic body or the toughness in his weary facial expression, as if he had seen all this before.

Ossi sauntered along the Ramblas enjoying the living statues, the three-card-Monty shysters, and the vivacious crowds. Although the tourist season was just beginning, there were large swarms of people bustling in the shaded avenue, eating ice cream, admiring the street vendors with their meager merchandise displayed on a blanket ready to be folded in seconds if the police hassled them. The gathering of people around the street performers provided good opportunities for pickpockets with nimble hands and for those working in groups to make sure the victim was unaware of being robbed in broad daylight.

The instinct of the regulars to avoid Ossi served them well as his outward appearance was in sharp contrast with his real personality. In fact, after obtaining a bachelor's degree in mechanical engineering from the Faculty of Science and Technology of Uppsala University, he decided that spending his entire life in an industrial plant or a research laboratory would be boring and looked for more adventurous and challenging things to do.

He was initially drawn to Islam through some of his fellow students and later through a romantic involvement with a beautiful and exotic young girl. After a tragic accident that killed her on their wedding day, he had to leave Sweden in haste and seek refuge in the Middle East from the police in his home country.

Within a short time he drifted to more and more extreme factions until he became a full-fledged member of the Islamic State of Iraq and Sham (ISIS) movement and excelled in their murderous journey through Iraq and Syria.

He accepted their vision of establishing a new Caliphate— an empire that would encompass a vast area and include present day Iraq, Syria, Lebanon, Jordan, Israel, the entire Arabian Peninsula, and a broad strip along the southern shore of the Mediterranean Sea stretching from the Sinai-peninsula, through Egypt, Libya to Tunisia, Algiers, and Morocco—and like many converts was a fervent devotee of the Caliphate.

Ossi had recently returned from the battlefront in Syria

where he had led a death squad unit in charge of sowing terror into the hearts of the unbelievers and those Muslims not considered as true believers. For ISIS, the category of the unbelievers included practically everyone who was not a member of their faction or even their own men that showed compassion or hesitation before shooting old men, women, and babies who were unfortunate enough to be in the wrong place at the wrong time.

The leader of ISIS had designated Ossi to head the efforts to obtain the ultimate weapon—a nuclear device—that would bring the West and its allies to their knees and would ensure the removal of the last infidels from the holy territory of the Islamic State and the Arab Nation, the *Ummah*.

ISIS realized that the fundamentalist Shiite regime in Iran would not supply them with the fissionable material they needed. Even worse, the religious leaders of the Islamic Republic of Iran correctly saw ISIS as a threat to Shiites worldwide and, therefore, were willing to join forces with the U.S.-led coalition against ISIS.

The "black market," in smuggled or stolen nuclear materials that thrived after the demise of the Soviet Union had practically ceased to exist and offers of nuclear warheads for sale were now considered as no more than a hoax. This forced the ISIS leaders to devise plans to acquire the material through a different route.

Arabic-looking agents were bound to raise suspicion immediately, so the leaders chose to conduct a "false flag" operation with their agents posing as a European ultra-right-wing group. Ossi's Aryan looks, his unquestioned dedication to ISIS and its cause, his proven ruthlessness made him an ideal candidate to lead this effort.

Ossi knew that the best place to hide, and to lose a tail if he was being followed, was in a crowded area and the Ramblas avenue was ideally suited for this purpose. After strolling along the boulevard for several minutes and playing at being a tourist, he slipped in to the quieter Boqueria Street and made his way to the Travel Bar, famous for serving as the starting point for free walking tours led by excellent guides.

The tables in the shaded courtyard were almost fully occupied by tourists and a few local young men trying to pick-up unattached female and male tourists.

Ossi found a vacant table and sat down waiting for his contact to arrive. A dark, good-looking young woman asked him in rapid Catalan if the chair next to him was free. Ossi answered in English that he did not understand and the woman asked in slightly accented English whether she could join him as all other seats were taken.

Hearing the code phrase, "all other seats were taken," he answered with the prearranged, "please be seated and I'll buy you a cool drink."

She sat down and introduced herself as Ramona and he introduced himself as Ollie, short for Olaf Gunther Andersson, his current cover name, and asked her if she would be his guide in Barcelona.

This charade, straight out of a cheap spy novel, was acted out for the sake of anyone sitting nearby and listening to their conversation. After finishing their drinks, Ramona led the way to her car parked nearby and drove off without telling him where they were heading.

They passed by Catalunya Caixa, the square that had been the focal point for many popular demonstrations, then drove up the beautiful Passeig di Gracia through the modern Eixample quarter and then along the Avenida Diagonal taking a sharp left down Carrer de Berlin into Avenida de Madrid passing by the famous Camp Nuo the home of the Barcelona football and basketball teams and on to the Universidad de Barcelona.

Ossi kept glancing at Ramona and was impressed by the practiced way she handled the car and weaved through the traffic and told her so.

Ramona shrugged at the compliment and said that this was a prerequisite for survival in the crowded streets of Barcelona.

Ramona parked the car and, again, without saying a word, led the way to one of the buildings that housed several classrooms and laboratories. There was a large courtyard with many tables occupied by noisy students who were busy drinking coffee and laughing. On the second floor, Ramona knocked on the door with a sign indicating this was the office of Professor Matias Antonio Modena.

Ramona exchanged a few words in Catalan with the tall, thin man that appeared to be in his early sixties and then introduced Ollie as the emissary from Sweden.

The professor turned to him and in perfect English said, "I am pleased to meet you Ollie. You can call me Matias. Ramona told me you came from Sweden to discuss matters of mutual interest."

Ollie respectfully responded, "Professor, I am honored

to meet you and am sure we will find that we have similar goals. My organization has heard about your groundbreaking research in nuclear physics and engineering and it interests us."

"Unfortunately, no scientific journal has agreed to publish my work and the reasons the editor gave for rejecting it were based on peer reviews by narrow-minded, ignorant, and envious colleagues who do not believe what I did in my lab is possible. They do not accept my reported experimental results and even went so far as to write to the head of my department here that I should be audited for malfeasance and for fabricating results."

"I am not a scientist, Professor, but I understand this is highly unusual. What did you do to upset them and raise such suspicions?"

"I spent hours on end working alone in the lab. I did this because all my graduate students, except Ramona here, left me because they thought I was insane, or so they implied. Ramona participated in most of the work but for safety reasons I preferred she leave the lab when I performed some rather dangerous experiments. I must say that I have repeated the work several times and obtained the same results—thorium was transformed into uranium-233 without the use of a nuclear reactor or a standard neutron source, just by using an intense gamma radiation source. The scientific community is unwilling to face the facts and therefore I have been ostracized."

"Professor–" Ollie began but vas cut short.

"Please call me Matias."

"Okay, Matias. Could anyone repeat your experiments and validate your results?"

"Well, young man, this has such a large commercial potential that I left out some technical details. Therefore, anyone attempting to repeat my work was bound to fail and indeed they did. The basic physical principle is quite complicated but in simple terms you could say that I converted common cheap thorium into a very precious commodity—fissile material."

"May I ask how you gained access to a gamma source?"

"Very strong gamma sources are used in hospitals for radiation therapy or in facilities for sterilization of medical equipment and food products. Another application is in the chemical industry. Several sources are lost accidentally each year and they are called, "orphan sources." For my experiments, I got hold of two such sources and by combining the radiation from both sources I created a single, extremely strong source. I would rather not go into the details of the means I used to get these two sources but suffice it to say that with enough money and the help of Catalan patriots it became possible."

"Aren't these sources difficult to handle and dangerous?"

"If you keep them properly sealed in their protective containers they are perfectly safe for someone who knows what he is doing. I did need some manual help and proper equipment to transport them to my lab, and there I disguised them as items of standard laboratory equipment. Even the audit of my work, carried out by the head of the department and the faculty dean did not identify the sources as I made sure they were sealed and no radiation leaked out."

"Professor, sorry, Matias, what is the efficiency of the

transmutation you have achieved converting thorium into uranium-233?"

"Well, Ollie, my method exceeds, by far, the efficiency of neutron bombardment that occurs in nuclear reactors."

"This is very impressive, Professor. Can you tell me on what scale you have carried out your experiments?"

"So far only on a few grams of thorium, but scaling up should be simple, provided I can get enough gamma radiation sources. Purchasing thorium is very easy—several companies in India and China will gladly sell you as much thorium as you can pay for and ship it to you disguised as fertilizer or other innocuous chemicals for a fee, of course. High purity thorium is more expensive but can also be bought without the need to answer any questions."

"Do you mean to say that all you need to produce pound-quantities of uranium-233 are some gamma sources, a few hundred pounds of thorium, and a suitable laboratory?"

"Yes, Ollie. But then you need to separate the fissile uranium-233 from the parent thorium and this requires a small chemical laboratory and some patience."

"Why patience?"

"You need to wait about three months to allow enough time for the formation of uranium-233 from the intermediate product formed after irradiation of the thorium and nothing can be done to make this conversion occur faster."

"I understand that you need to wait a few months for that, but is it correct that this could be done in almost any chemical laboratory with a few additional safety measures?"

"Yes, indeed. I can produce enough uranium-233 to fuel

a nuclear power plant at a fraction of the cost needed to enrich natural uranium or to produce plutonium in a nuclear reactor."

"Professor, as you know, our movement is not too concerned with power plants and electricity production…"

"Ollie, please do not elaborate what other applications you have in mind. Given the proper utilities and a few months, I can provide you with pound-quantities of high purity uranium-233."

"Thank you, Professor Modena, for meeting me. I am sure that your scientific genius will soon be recognized by your peers and nomination for the Nobel Prize is only a matter of time once you show them the energy problems of the world can be solved without using fossil fuels. I need to present these exciting ideas to my organization and convince them to fund your project and lend you all the assistance you need. I will be in touch as soon as I can."

"Thank you, Ollie. It was a pleasure meeting such an enthusiastic young man."

CHAPTER 2

Uppsala University, Sweden, 3 years earlier

Young Oscar Gunar Axelsson, Ossi, was in the final year of his undergraduate studies of mechanical engineering and trying to decide what to do after graduation.

Despite his blond good looks he had not managed to form a lasting relationship with any of the many female students that also attended the university. Sure, he had been through several one-night-stands where each side just sought physical relief from pressures and by mutual consent took advantage of each other.

Seeing that his classmates knew exactly what they planned to do after leaving the university—some intended to go on and get an advanced degree, others wanted to start a bourgeois career with jobs in industry or government while a few enterprising souls wanted to start their own high-tech company—Ossi felt somewhat like an outcast.

His best friends were two dark-skinned second cousins students, Ahmed and Abdullah, who had immigrated to Sweden from Lebanon after one of the many civil clashes that ripped Lebanon. As devout Muslims, they refused to join him in his drinking binges and did not show any interest in the female students.

Although they were registered as students of political science at the university, they spent more time at the Islamic community center than in the classroom. A fact that explained why after 6 years at the university—courtesy of the Swedish taxpayers' money—they had yet to attain their bachelor's degree.

One evening when Ossi shared his doubts about the future with Ahmed and Abdullah, they asked him if he would like to travel and experience some adventures rather than just become another brick on the wall.

Ossi wanted to know what they had in mind and they invited him to meet their spiritual guide at the community center on Friday before the morning prayers. With nothing better scheduled for that day, Ossi agreed to meet them at the back entrance of the community center.

The two youngsters were waiting for Ossi at the appointed time, though such punctuality was not typical for them. When he arrived they knocked three times on the small side door. It was opened by a young woman wearing a long, black robe that covered her body and a chador that left only a pair of gleaming black eyes visible through the opening covered with a fine net. The way she carried herself and the mysterious power radiating from her intrigued Ossi but wisely he kept his silence.

Without saying a word, she dismissed Ahmed and Abdullah with a small hand gesture and signaled for Ossi to follow her. She led the way down a narrow, bare staircase to the basement and knocked on a metal door that bore no sign. When the door opened Ossi could see that a large Afghan carpet was spread on the floor and a lone old man was seated on a low, wooden chair surrounded by some cushions arranged haphazardly in front of his chair.

He sensed a strange odor purveying the basement but could not quite identify it. The girl bowed toward the old man, gestured for Ossi to sit on one of the cushions and left the room, gently closing the door behind her.

The old man spoke so softly that Ossi could barely hear him. He instructed Ossi to take a deep breath, hold it for as long as he could and exhale slowly. Doing as he was told, Ossi felt a strange feeling of peace and quiet come over him. The old man looked into his eyes for a long moment and Ossi felt as if all his thoughts were like an open book to the old man.

After a while the old man asked Ossi what he wanted to do with the most precious gift in the world—his life. Ossi was at a loss for words but then heard himself saying in a weak voice that he wanted to do something significant, something important, something that would leave his mark on the world. He felt that this was exactly the answer the old man expected.

The old man smiled briefly and said he would guide Ossi along the pathway for fulfilling his true wishes, but it would be a tortuous path with many physical and moral obstacles and that once he set foot on this path there would be no turning back. He invited Ossi to stay for a while and attend the morning prayers and sermon he would be leading shortly and asked him to meet again afterwards.

The old man pressed a small button next to his chair and summoned the girl, whom he introduced as his niece, Fatima.

In Arabic, he asked her to take Ossi to the small semi-concealed alcove above the main hall of the community center that served as a mosque during prayer time.

Once again, without uttering a word, Fatima motioned for Ossi to follow her. As soon as the basement metal door was closed behind them she offered Ossi her hand to guide him through the dark corridor. When he touched her, he felt as if he was jolted by a surge of electricity and had to let go of her hand. He did not see her veiled face but sensed that she too was stunned by the impact of the brief physical contact.

Still not saying a word she led the way up two flights of stairs, through a narrow hallway and into the small alcove overlooking the main hall of the community center. A beaded curtain separated the alcove from the hall so the people in the hall could not see who was in the alcove. Without a word, Fatima departed leaving Ossi alone in the alcove.

A few minutes later all the worshippers stood in straight lines facing the podium and Mecca. The old man slowly ascended the podium and led the prayer in Arabic. After the prayer, the old man delivered a sermon in Swedish, explaining that not all the worshippers spoke Arabic beyond the verses required for prayers.

Ossi could see that among the crowd below there were quite a few men of obvious African ancestry, some Scandinavian-looking fair-skinned men that were probably new converts but the majority of men were probably of Middle Eastern and North African descent.

He immediately noticed there were no women among the worshippers, unlike the service in the church he attended as a child and a young man.

The old man began his sermon by quietly praising the deeds of Allah and the cornucopia his true believers were promised and then started accounting the evils brought upon the believers by the infidels. As he continued with the sermon his tone rose in volume and intensity. As he mentioned the heroic acts of 9/11 when a small group of nineteen true believers sent three thousand infidels to Gehinem—hell—and the dastardly invasion of the Muslim countries of Iraq and Afghanistan that followed, his voice became exceptionally loud.

When he described the way the fraudulent colonialists bribed and bought the cooperation of Arab despots and coerced them to join the coalition troops invading Iraq, spittle sprayed out of his mouth. He went on to describe the defeat of the Iraqi army as a test by Allah to see if the holy warriors, the Jihadists, would carry on the battle.

Toward the end of his sermon, the old man clung to the podium, his face took on a crimson hue as he swore to avenge the deaths of the true believers. Suddenly his voice wavered and he collapsed on the podium. Two men rushed up and carried the old man down from the podium and then to his room in the basement.

Ossi wondered whether he should keep the appointment with the old man but before he could reach a decision, Fatima quietly entered the alcove and motioned for him to follow her. She kept her hands in the pockets of her robe to discourage any contact.

Once again she led Ossi along the hallway and down the

stairs to the basement. When the door opened, he could see the old man was seated in his chair holding a glass of water and a person, he assumed to be a doctor, was taking his blood pressure.

When he saw Ossi, the old man dismissed Fatima and the doctor and spoke softly to Ossi asking him what he thought of the sermon. Ossi hesitantly replied that he knew nothing of the injustices inflicted on the Muslims and had to learn the facts before answering. The old man smiled painfully and said that his niece, who was a history major at Uppsala University, could tutor him privately and show him the true facts, since the information he would find in the Internet was planted there by the American CIA and its collaborators.

Ossi barely managed to conceal his enthusiasm at the opportunity to spend more time with the enigmatic Fatima and agreed to proposed tutoring. Hearing this, the old man once again summoned his niece and told her she would be Ossi's tutor.

She answered in rapid Arabic that Ossi did not understand but he realized she protested the idea and this upset the old man.

He repeated his command in Swedish that she guide Ossi through the history of Islam and its relations with colonial forces, especially after the events of 9/11. Reluctantly, Fatima faced Ossi and set a date for their first lesson to commence the following Sunday at noon in the university library.

Ossi spent the time until their meeting trying to read as much as he could about the history of Islam from its inception in Arabia in the seventh century AD, through its period of grandeur in the Middle Ages until its present status in the twenty-first century. He was not able to fathom how the rift between Sunni and Shiites continued for over a thousand years, with each side doing its best to send the followers of the opposing sect to meet with Allah prematurely.

The more he read the less he understood how a proud nation, that during the dark Middle Ages in Europe, was at the forefront of science, mathematics, literature, poetry, culture, and architecture, and was a considerable economic power became a symbol of backward and murderous tribal rivalry among the Muslims themselves as well as against the Judeo-Christian world.

When he met Fatima at the university library on Sunday, she was wearing jeans and a closed top that could not hide the outline of her breasts that seemed to have a life of their own moving with every movement she made. Her face was the kind that came to mind when it was said that a face could launch a thousand ships, as attributed to Helen of Troy.

With a small smile, Fatima noticed Ossi staring as she asked him to sit down across the table from her. She inquired if he had tried to study the facts about Islam history and when he brought up his confusion and reservations she sighed slightly and told him they would need to cover a lot of ground. Ossi couldn't have been more pleased to hear the promise of many more meetings with this lovely young woman.

They spent the next two hours with Fatima doing most of the talking and Ossi drifting in to daydreams every so often. At two o'clock Fatima said she was famished and the two of them headed for the cafeteria, but when they arrived, there was a sign that it was closed on Sunday.

They found a nearby quiet restaurant that was open and ordered a light lunch of sandwiches. Ossi refrained from ordering beer and asked for a fish sandwich out of respect for Fatima's religion, forgoing his favorite meal of a ham sandwich washed down with a couple beers. Fatima noticed this and smiled her appreciation, which set Ossi's pulse racing.

After finishing their paltry lunch, they returned to the library and continued the tutoring for another couple hours. Fatima explained a custom he was not aware of, that as an unmarried faithful Muslim woman she could not meet in private with a man who was not a member of her immediate family but as she lived in Sweden she was permitted to meet with him in public places, even without a chaperon.

Much to Ossi's delight they agreed to continue the lessons at the library twice a week for two hours each time.

After approximately ten lessons Ossi was convinced of two things: the treatment of Islam and Muslims by the U.S. and its Western allies was unjust and he was infatuated with Fatima and would do anything to win her heart.

Fatima told him that the old man, her uncle, wished to see him again and Ossi gladly consented to meet him just before the Friday prayers. This time he made his way to the community center on his own and when he knocked on the side door it was opened by the robed and veiled Fatima.

Without a word she offered him her hand and led him down to the basement, giving him a small pat on the back as he opened the door and entered the carpeted hall.

The old man welcomed him with a smile and asked how his studies were going. Ossi answered that he now understood the injustices inflicted on the Muslims and said he would be ready for an advanced course on Islam if it were given by Fatima.

The old man frowned and said that Fatima could continue with the history lessons but religious teachings were not for women, so he would personally become his tutor.

Ossi was a bit disappointed but grasped at the opportunity to continue seeing Fatima and agreed.

The more time Ossi spent with Fatima the closer their relationship became. In no uncertain terms she indicated she would be willing to fully give herself to him if he converted to Islam and married her in a religious ceremony.

The lessons with the old man were more centered on politics than with religion and Ossi gradually became convinced he should contribute to the cause of Islam—the big prize being, of course, Fatima. So, after another three months of religious teachings on the one hand and growing fascination with unattainable Fatima, Ossi was willing to forego his atheist beliefs and convert to Islam.

On a beautiful Spring day, the old man performed the official ceremony of accepting Ossi into the folds of Islam and immediately after that the betrothal to Fatima was performed.

According to the teachings of Islam no alcohol was served or consumed at the modest wedding ceremony.

The young couple took off for their long-awaited honeymoon in Ossi's old Volvo. They left the outskirts of Uppsala and crossed the intersection leading to the A4 highway on their way to Gavle, where they intended to spend their honeymoon.

Suddenly a motorcycle travelling at a great speed entered

the intersection and hit their car on the right side crushing the door on the passenger side, severely injuring Fatima.

The Volvo spun around and Ossi was thrown against his unlocked door that flew open and he was tossed out of the car. His head hit the paved road knocking him unconscious. After a few moments Ossi recovered from the shock and ran back to the Volvo only to see that Fatima was being carried to an ambulance by two paramedics.

Ossi managed to get on the ambulance but was told by the paramedic that Fatima was not breathing and without a pulse because her rib cage was crushed and probably punctured her lungs and heart.

At the Uppsala University Hospital, Akademiska Sjukhuset, Fatima was announced as dead-on-arrival.

The funeral was arranged for the next day and attended solely by Fatima's friends and family as Ossi had gradually severed all contacts with his own family and few friends.

The local newspaper covered the fatal accident in detail and released the fact that the alcohol content in the motorcyclist's blood exceeded the limit of zero point two percent by a factor of five and that he lay unconscious in the intensive care unit of the same hospital.

The old man told Ossi that according to tradition it was his duty to avenge Fatima's death or he would not be counted a man by his Muslim friends. He used the term 'murder under the influence of the Satan's alcohol.'

Without hesitation, Ossi said his true love would be avenged. He found a uniform of the hospital janitorial staff, donned it, and walked into the hospital room where the unconscious motorcyclist lay.

He placed a pillow over the patients face, pressed down until he was sure the man was dead. He took off the uniform, nonchalantly walked out of the room and the hospital, returning to the Islamic community center.

The old man, knowing that Ossi would be the obvious suspect of foul play, told Ossi he had arranged for him to clandestinely board a ship that was to leave Stockholm the same evening, heading to Beirut in Lebanon. The old man gave Ossi an envelope containing five thousand dollars, a false passport with the name Olaf Gunther Andersson, and a letter of introduction to be presented to the captain once the ship entered the Mediterranean Sea.

When the ship docked at Beirut harbor, Ossi disembarked at night, wearing traditional Arab cloths that covered his blond hair and his Scandinavian features. He followed the captain's instructions and entered a small, noisy café a few blocks away from the harbor and asked for Abu Yusef, the proprietor.

Abu Yusef had been warned that a Swedish man called Ollie—short for Olaf Gunther Andersson—would be arriving and arrangements were made to take him across Lebanon to the Baqa'a Valley, where a Hezbollah training camp operated.

The Baqa'a Valley, 3 years earlier

Ollie was one of the many new recruits sent to the training camp that was run by Hezbollah; the Lebanese so-called Party of Allah that was a political party with a military arm, or as some people regarded it, a Shi'ite militia with a political party.

The instructors at the basic training camp were a motley collection of professional army officers, mainly from Iran, self-proclaimed experts, mainly from Syria and Lebanon, and some psychopaths with battle experience from Iraq and Afghanistan, as well as several others from all over the Muslim world.

The trainees were even more varied as they included volunteers from various countries in Europe, North and South America, and even Australia. Some of these were simply adventurers who were just looking for action, but most believed that Islam was the only true religion and were willing to persuade everyone else of that conviction, by whatever means necessary.

The training encompassed several activities. First and foremost was religious and political indoctrination meant to provide the recruits with a deeper understanding of the cause for which they were fighting.

The instructors used classic brainwashing techniques, including food depravation and endless repetition to convince them that Islam is the only truthful religion and Mohammad was the only real prophet and messenger of Allah. They were also told that dying while fighting for the cause would earn them a place in paradise where each will be served by seventy-two virgins. For the foreign recruits, there were also lessons in basic Arabic.

The second focus was installing ruthlessness and brutality. This was done by forcing the recruits to slaughter farm animals confiscated from neighboring farms with a blunt knife while soaking their hands and clothes in the blood. This method was considered effective since it was used to train the

Al Qaeda terrorists that seized control of the four airplanes used for the 9/11 attacks.

The trainees were encouraged to spy on their fellow recruits and report any indiscretion, such as drinking alcohol or blaspheming the name of Allah. These offenses were punished severely, by extra duties like cleaning latrines, whipping, solitary confinement, and sometimes even with a death sentence carried out by the fellow trainees.

Physical fitness was ensured by long marches lugging backpacks filled with sand, by jogging up to fifty miles and by carrying heavy telephone poles up and down the hills that surrounded the camp.

Weapons training included the use of handguns, rifles, rocket-propelled grenades or RPGs, small caliber mortars, as well as unarmed combat and knife duels. A special prize, proffered only to the most proficient trainees, was an advanced course in the use of explosives and demolition.

Finally, the trainees had to traverse an obstacle course that included climbing a stone wall, crawling under barbed wire, running on a narrow wooden plank that was set fifteen feet above ground and jumping down at the edge of the plank.

As if this was not enough, the final test was to pass this obstacle course under live fire. The instructors aimed just inches above the heads of the recruits and every so often the aim was a bit too low or a trainee lifted his head at the wrong moment resulting in one less able-bodied graduate. Several trainees dropped out and a few committed suicide but the graduates were tough, ruthless fighters.

Ollie, as he was called by all, excelled in all these classes.

He was highly motivated, had arrived knowing the basics of Islam from his tutor in Uppsala, and was physically and mentally in great shape. He was marked for promotion by all his instructors and was soon selected to lead a squad of the newly-anointed Hezbollah fighters.

With his squad, he was taken to a fortified outpost on a hill overlooking the border between Lebanon and Israel. From there he could see some of the villages on each side of the border and easily noted the difference between the modern agricultural techniques used on the Israeli side and the traditional methods on the Lebanese side.

He saw the patrols of the three armed forces that operated in the region: the white vehicles and blue uniforms of the United Nations 'peace keeping' force; the khaki vehicles and uniforms of the Israeli patrols that always travelled in pairs; and the camouflage uniforms of the Lebanese Armed Forces (LAF) with their American-made M-113s Armored Personnel Carriers. He also saw quite a lot of aerial activity by jet-fighters, helicopters, unmanned drones, and was told they were all from the Israel Defense Forces (IDF).

He was taken to one of the large villages on the Lebanese side and shown the primitive rockets and more sophisticated missiles hidden in bunkers and tunnels that were dug under the school and mosque and was told these were the insurance policy of the villagers that they would not be attacked by the IDF ground and air forces.

Ollie found the whole situation not to his liking for two main reasons: first, when he converted to Islam, it was as a Sunni Muslim like Fatima and the old sheik in Uppsala and not a Shi'ite like most of his Hezbollah colleagues. Second, he sought combat action not to be positioned in an outpost waiting for something to happen.

So, when he heard about the formation of a radical Sunni armed faction in Iraq and Syria, he found a way to desert from Hezbollah. On a dark night when no one was watching he left his post and travelled across the border from Lebanon to join the ISIS forces in Syria.

North-East Syria, one year earlier

The fierce fighting between the Islamic State forces and the poorly trained but determined Peshmerga Kurds near the Turkish border continued with no winner. But there were many losers: the civilian population on both sides of the border; the fighters that lost their lives; and even the Turkish regular army soldiers. They were ordered by their government to stay out of the fighting but to prevent fighters from either side to cross into, and out of, Turkish soil, but were often caught between the two sides.

Ollie, led a small but select unit that consisted of volunteers from Western Europe that had recently converted to Islam. This unit, soon became known as Ollie's Butchers, was feared for its ruthlessness and cruelty.

The new converts to Islam wanted to show the world and, particularly, their fanatic comrades in arms, that they were totally dedicated to their newly found faith. Members of this unit were seen on global TV networks beheading prisoners with a dull dagger. Not shown on TV, although they really wanted to be seen in the act, were the incidents of rape of women, men, girls, boys, and babies.

These acts were too much even for the most sensational TV stations and were quickly removed from YouTube due to their excessively graphic violence.

***

Ollie's cellphone rang once and a coded text message summoned him to the Supreme Commander, known only as El Kahiri, in reference to his original hometown of Cairo.

El Kahiri set up his headquarters near the front lines of skirmish so that he could watch his troops closely and make sure they carried out their duties per his 'shock and awe' to borrow the U.S. term—tactics. Ollie left his small unit under the command of his second-in-command, John the Beheader, also known as John the Jihadist. He was an ex-Briton, whose masked face was familiar to TV viewers globally as the executioner of Western prisoners and hostages.

Still wearing his blood-soaked military fatigues, Ollie mounted a motorbike that was 'loaned' from a local garage, and rode to the five-story house in which El Kahiri established his headquarters. He passed through the door guarded by two armed troopers, who frisked Ollie and removed his weapons and cell phone. He entered a windowless room on the ground floor with walls that were fortified by slabs of concrete as protection against artillery and mortar shells, as well as against the barrels of explosives dropped by Syrian air force helicopters.

El Kahiri was seated on a folding chair at a rickety table and looked emaciated with a nervous tick in his left cheek. In a low voice he asked Ollie to sit opposite him at the table and then ordered all others to leave the room.

After the door was shut, El Kahiri said, "Ollie, you know that we have reached a dead-end here in Syria. The world media refuses to screen our footage of executions, pillage, destruction, and rape. You are one of my best fighters and certainly a commendable leader of people into battle. You have shown your bravery, ruthlessness, and total commitment to the cause of the Islamic State. You have worked hard to rid the world of infidels, be they Christian or Jews who refuse to acknowledge the greatness of Allah and Muhammad his Prophet, or Muslims who are misguided and believe that they can co-exist with these *kefirs*, and our own brethren who do not recognize our leadership."

Ollie responded by saying, "Supreme Commander, you know that I have seen the light of the true religion and will follow you to the Heaven promised to the *shahids* who sacrifice their life for the greatness of Allah."

"Ollie, I wish to invest upon you the most important mission of our movement. A job that requires great responsibility and is our last chance to show the infidels the true way of Allah. This will involve a great deal of scheming and cunning, acting ability, and apparent denial of all you believe in. Are you ready for such a task?"

"Supreme Commander, I am ready and willing to sacrifice my life and that of many others, for our just cause."

"You are to leave the Middle East, return to Sweden under

a false identity, join the nationalist Swedish Resistance Movement (SMR) and pretend to be an avid Muslim hater. With your combat experience, natural leadership ability, and utter ruthlessness, you will soon rise among the ranks and assume a dominant position. You will then advance the use of extreme measures to 'encourage' non-Scandinavian residents to leave Sweden. When it turns out that conventional methods are not sufficient to force them to leave, you will suggest the use of unconventional action."

"How will I do this?"

"You will propose to get hold of a nuclear device that will be used to blackmail the Swedish government to expel all people that are not of pure Scandinavian descent. You will contact the Nationalist movements in all Western Europe and, together, with them will construct such a device. You will convince them to help you by offering the use of this nuclear threat to one country after the other. You will argue that one such device, not to be really detonated but only used for blackmail, will be sufficient to rid Europe of all its undesired elements."

El Kahiri continued, "However, your true mission will be to take this weapon to Jerusalem and detonate it at the center of the Old City, wiping out the holy sites sacred to the three false religions: the Wailing Wall of the Jews, the Church of the Holy Sepulchre where the Christians believe Christ is buried, and the Dome of the Rock mosque where the misguided Muslims worship Allah instead of going to Mecca."

Ollie could not believe his ears and asked, "Do you want to destroy the mosques on Temple Mount? The place from which Muhammad took off on his flight to heaven on his winged horse?"

To this El Kahiri replied, "I am glad to see that the religious teachings were taken seriously by you. Yes, I mean that these mosques must also be destroyed as this will start a religious war on a scale that will make World War II look like a minor skirmish. If you are fortunate enough to get another nuclear device, you will not hesitate to detonate it in the heart of the primary Colonialist nation—the City of London—causing as many casualties as possible."

"The plan sounds plausible but where will I get hold of such a device?"

"Ollie, my son, one of our supporters who has studied physics in Spain informed us about a professor of physics in Barcelona who is a rabid supporter of Catalan independence and claims to have developed a method to produce fissile material. I do not understand the scientific principles, but my advisors tell me he does not require a nuclear reactor or a facility to enrich uranium. You, with your background in mechanical engineering and Scandinavian looks, can contact him as a leader of the Swedish Nationalist movement and offer to help him develop his technique. You can convince him that having a nuclear device and threatening Madrid with it is the best way to guarantee Catalan independence. You can also play on his inferiority complex derived from the fact that the scientific community effectively shuns him and that his articles were rejected by every scientific journal. Offer him the means to complete his project and to show the whole world what a great innovator he is."

"I hope I am up to the challenge."

"One last thing, my son. Remember that no members of our ISIS council are aware of this plan. When you leave Syria, the council will be informed only that you were sent by me on a personal top-secret mission for the cause of true Islam. So you will have to go into deep cover and will not be allowed to contact me or any known member of ISIS. You will operate independently and will have no access to any of our funds, bank accounts, and supporters."

"Supreme Commander, I am honored to have such an assignment and will do my best to succeed. Praise Allah."

Ollie left the house, retrieved his weapons and cell phone from the bodyguards and got on his motorbike to return to his unit. As he approached their location, he saw a column of black smoke rising from a large smoldering crater. The stench of smoke, blood, and bodies was so strong he had to wrap his *keffiyeh* over his nose and mouth.

Through the dense smoke he could barely see body parts and twisted weapons scattered all over the crater and realized he was the sole survivor of his unit. Looking up he saw three women from a nearby demolished building standing on the rim of the crater and raising their hands toward the sky and blessing the Syrian pilot of the helicopter that threw the bomb that killed his whole unit. An uncontrolled rage swept through his body at the sight of his dead comrades and the gloating women and without a second thought he aimed his AK47, set the selector to automatic, and with one long burst cut the three women in half.

CHAPTER 3

Stockholm, 6 months earlier

When he returned to Sweden, Ollie resumed the name and identity he had used when fleeing Sweden a few years earlier, so he continued to call himself Olaf Gunther Andersson, known in short as Ollie.

He decided to stay away from Uppsala, where he might be recognized and established himself in Stockholm as an unemployed, disgruntled young man. He started frequenting seedy bars in which cheap beer and bootlegged whiskey were sold and within a few days he made friends with some like-minded young men.

He loudly complained about his fate and the fact that he could not find suitable employment and blamed it on the Jews that controlled the economy and on the Arab immigrants that got all the jobs as they were willing to work for a very low salary. He tried to pick fights with anyone with dark skin who dared enter the bars he visited, but made sure to avoid being questioned by the police for fear of being recognized as the person wanted for involvement in the death of the motorcyclist that killed Fatima a couple years earlier.

One or two of the young men that were present at such

brawls occasionally joined him in beating up the suspected Jews or Muslims, or any other foreigner that happened to be unfortunate enough to be near them.

Ollie, was soon invited to attend public rallies and private meetings in which the crowd called for the expulsion of all foreigners from Sweden labelling them parasites that sucked money and health benefits from the social security system. In fact, most of the protestors and demonstrators themselves lived on social security money while most of the immigrants were gainfully employed and paid their taxes regularly. But these facts were irrelevant since prejudice and xenophobia were dominant.

Ollie soon organized a gang of racist hooligans and initiated raids on neighborhoods in which immigrants lived. They used firebombs to ignite and burn cars and apartments and beat up anyone who tried to stop them. The police responded slowly to calls for help in these neighborhoods as they had often been pelted with rotten fruit and stones by the residents. Some of the police even sympathized with the hooligans and had no interest in detaining them.

Ollie became known as a reliable participant in any brawl that involved immigrants. In one case, three of his colleagues beat up a skinny youth who unfortunately for him could not speak Swedish fluently. When he lay almost unconscious on the sidewalk, Ollie happened upon the scene and without hesitation kicked the boy in the head with his heavy boot murmuring inaudibly Allah Yerahamo—Allah will have mercy on his soul.

His friends were too shocked by this act and did not ask

what he had whispered. Word soon got around that Ollie was a fearless bully without any inhibitions when it came to beating up immigrants. On this particular case, the newspaper reported the unidentified young man suffered irreparable brain damage and would spend the rest of his life in a vegetative state.

Soon after this incident, Ollie was standing at the counter of his favorite bar sipping a beer. He was approached by a blonde girl whose arms were covered with tattoos depicting gory scenes of fierce Viking warriors torturing and raping dark-skinned women. The blonde snuggled close to Ollie and introduced herself as Alva asking him if he would like to buy her a drink.

She then removed her shirt, leaving her with a barely-there vest and Ollie could see additional tattoos with even more garish scenes spread over her torso. Ollie, who had not spent time with female companions since Fatima's death, not counting the women he raped and then killed in Syria, was slightly at a loss for words. But her open face, her smile, and the invitation in her eyes convinced him that she presented no danger to his clandestine cause and he asked her what she would like to drink.

Alva said she would have whatever he was drinking and suggested they move from the crowded bar to a quiet table. Ollie recalled his days in university where free sex and one-night-stands were common and wanted none of that but followed her to the table.

When they were seated, Alva said that she was sent by Andreas who was the notorious leader of the Street Brigade of the Nationalist SMR militant organization. While the movement itself was above board and careful not to cross the line between legitimate speech and actions and illegal activities, the Street Brigade was the paramilitary arm consisting of enforcers and bullies very much like the Nazi Sturmabteilung (SA) Brown Shirts in prewar Germany.

They protected the Nationalist SMR rallies and brutally disrupted meetings by opposing parties. Their leader, Andreas Harald Nordholm, a Viking giant six foot five inches tall weighing three hundred and ten pounds, was known as the "head cracker," due to the walking stick he wielded and used freely when the cameras were not rolling.

Ollie knew that by gaining the attention of Andreas he had achieved an important step of the plan concocted by the Supreme Commander. What he now had to do was gain Andreas's confidence and present him with the grand scheme of manufacturing a nuclear device as well as forming an alliance with likeminded Nationalist and racist movements in Europe.

After finishing their drinks, Alva told Ollie to hug her and pretend they were just going out for some private time together. Once outside she disengaged herself from his grasp and beckoned him to follow her to a modern apartment building nearby.

She entered the access code on the keypad at the entrance to the building and led the way to an elevator. Inside the elevator she took a small key out of her pocket and inserted it in the lock that allowed access to the penthouse on the top floor of the building.

The elevator door opened and Ollie was frisked unprofessionally by two bodyguards. This reminded him of the very different and thorough search he had undergone before meeting the Supreme Commander in Syria a few months earlier.

Andreas was seated in a comfortable leather recliner with a snifter of cognac in his hand. Alva approached him and tried to sit on his lap but Andreas slapped her gently on her back and told her to wait for him in the bedroom. He then welcomed Ollie.

Ollie knew that the following minutes would be crucial for the success of his plan and prepared himself for the questions bound to follow.

"You must be Ollie. I heard a lot about you and was especially impressed by the way you kicked that boy in the head."

"Andreas. I heard a lot about you as well. I am sorry I couldn't finish the job but your men were so shocked by that little friendly kick I gave the boy that I felt they would throw up if I continued and finished the job."

"Yeah, these softies are only good when they are three to one against a lone boy. They have a soft core. You, on the other hand, are probably the real thing. Tell me about yourself."

Ollie now had to use his acting skills. "I had a perfectly normal life until I was fifteen and joined a football club at my hometown of Malmo. Most of the other players, and the coach, were Muslim immigrants who saw an opportunity to advance in society by excelling in sports. After each match we used to go to the shower together to wash ourselves from the perspiration of the game. One day, two of the kids made sure that none of the other true Swedes were in the shower and grabbed my arms and then called the coach who tried to rape me. I was quite big and strong even at the age of fifteen and managed to kick one of the kids who held my right arm, punch the kid who held my left arm and then free myself and run naked out of the shower. The coach and kids hesitated for a moment and I got away. When I tried to lodge a complaint with the police, it was my word against the three of them. So, I decided to hunt them down one by one and do justice myself. I caught the first boy just outside his home and broke his right leg so he would never play football again. I waited for the second boy near his school and when he was alone, I caught him and punched him silly several times on his head until he collapsed. He, too, did not return to the football field. The coach, in a typical cowardly Arab fashion, left Malmo and disappeared. Ever since, I have hated foreigners and particularly Muslim Arabs."

"How old are you, Ollie? Where have you been since that incident?"

"I was in and out of schools and correctional institutions. I got a partial education attending a local college but never got a degree. I am now twenty-seven and have nothing: no job, no girl, and no future. Only if we can rid our nation of these parasites will I have a chance for a real life."

"Would you like to join our Street Brigade as a group leader?"

"There is nothing I would like more. I believe we can make a bigger impact on the good people of Sweden by doing unexpected things. Just beating up immigrants hardly makes the headlines anymore and vandalism of public property loses favor in the eyes of the conservative Swedes. We need to do something really big and I have some ideas."

"Ollie, we should meet again after you prove yourself as a worthy member of our Street Brigade. I noted that you said you had no girl and I assume you are not interested in boys after your shower experience."

Andreas laughed to show he meant no offence, and continued, "I wonder if you would like to spend some quality time with Agda? Who is Alva's twin sister. She really likes rough guys who don't use sweet talk."

"Thanks for the offer. I'm sure we'll get along, if that is what she likes."

"I'll send Agda to your apartment shortly."

Ollie left Andreas and returned to his small apartment. Fifteen minutes later he heard a knock on the door and when he opened it, he did a double take as he saw Alva standing there with a large smile on her face. A second glance told him she looked different as Alva's blonde hair was now dyed red and he realized he was looking at her twin sister, Agda.

Ollie knew she was sent by Andreas to test him, yet started to feel aroused, knowing she could give him pain and pleasure. Without a word Agda took off her jacket and he saw the gory tattoos that Alva had were substituted by even more garish ones.

When he looked down at her hands, he saw long, red nails and wondered if she was aware of the damage they could inflict. Agda noticed his look and her knowing smile grew bigger and in a hoarse voice she asked Ollie if he had something to drink.

Ollie, who as a devout Muslim did not consume alcohol in private, although in public he was a beer drinker as part of his cover, said that he had just finished the last of the alcohol and offered to go out and buy some.

Agda looked him up and down and moved in very close to him so she could feel his body. Without a word, she removed his shirt and caressed his muscles, starting with his bare neck and shoulders, slowly working her way down over his hardened stomach. In a low throaty voice, she said she didn't really need alcohol to get into the proper mood.

Ollie felt she represented everything he hated about the corrupt, decrepit Western society, so different from the pure way Fatima had behaved. In frustration, he slapped her face with his open hand.

Agda's breathing became rapid and she moaned. "Not on my face." She tried to grab him. Ollie responded by pulling her up and giving her a bear hug that crushed the air out of her lungs and almost cut her breath and held her like this for what seemed like eternity.

On the verge of passing out she managed to stick her nails into his upper arms forcing him to release her.

Suddenly she started to shake uncontrollably, and her eyes rolled in their sockets and she stopped moving. Ollie, beyond himself with passion and rage, could not let go of her throat until he realized she was no longer breathing.

He immediately sobered knowing he would have to account to Andreas if Agda did not call Alva. He let go of his stranglehold and gently touched her throat, finding a very weak pulse. He started mouth-to-mouth resuscitation blowing air into her lungs and massaging her heart until she groaned weakly.

Her eyes opened and she stared at him and slowly started to smile and said she had never experienced such a strong orgasm.

Ollie was embarrassed as he too had not had such a pleasurable physical response with any of the women with whom he had slept during his university days or with any of the women he had forcefully taken in Syria.

Ollie and Agda looked at each other and then at the physical damage they had caused each other. Thankfully the scratches, bites, and wounds were superficial and stopped bleeding after they took a hot shower together in his small bathroom.

They then got in his bed and fell asleep only to be woken up by their cell phones ringing simultaneously. Agda received a call from her sister while Andreas wanted to know how Ollie enjoyed his night and summoned him back to his apartment in the evening.

That evening Ollie returned to the apartment building and with one of Andreas's bodyguards entered the penthouse. Andreas was sitting in the same recliner smoking a cigar and once again holding a cognac snifter in his other hand.

Alva was nowhere to be seen but the smile of Andreas's face told Ollie he had already received a detailed account of the affair with Agda and of their sexual escapades. Andreas told Ollie he was relieved to hear that things had gone so well as he was concerned Ollie had not had any female companion since he reached Stockholm. He also told Ollie he had tried to check the story Ollie had told him about the reasons for his hatred of Muslims and foreigners but although he could not find any direct corroboration he tended to believe the story because the emotions were so convincingly described. Finally, he said he wanted to know what plans and ideas Ollie had on his mind.

Ollie described his plan in detail. The idea of getting hold of fissionable material, making an improvised nuclear device, and using it to blackmail the Swedish government to expel all foreigners, Jews, and Muslims. Or, at the bare minimum, force those that had acquired citizenship or legal residence into labor camps where they would serve as cheap laborers for the benefit of the true Swedes.

Andreas considered this for a moment, then said he liked the idea but did not know how to obtain the fissionable material.

This was the opening Ollie had been waiting for, so he explained how all true Nationalist movements in Europe should join forces to obtain the ultimate weapon to convince their respective governments to cleanse their countries from 'undesirable elements.'

This was the term that all the movements could adopt because in addition to Muslims and Jews who were hated by all European Nationalist movements, Polish workers were regarded as foreign invaders in the United Kingdom, Rumanians were unwanted in Poland, Albanians were disliked in Rumania, and so on.

In addition, there were several separatist movements all over Europe—Basques in Spain and France, Catalans in Spain, Northerners in Italy, Scotts in the Britain, Flemish in Belgium, and many others less vociferous minorities. All these could be enlisted to promote the true cause of the Swedish movement.

***

Ollie then said he had very specific plans how to implement his idea, but he needed help from Andreas. The first step would be to convene a meeting of the leaders of the Nationalist and Separatist movements under the auspices of the Swedish movement.

The messages were not delivered to the official leaders, those who appeared in the media, and were seemingly respectable public representatives of legitimate political parties, but to the real power wielders—the industrialists that secretly funded the movements and particularly to the leaders of the brutal arms of hooligans like the Swedish "Street Brigade."

To minimize the risk of exposure of the plan, couriers were to be sent from Sweden to these leaders to deliver the message in person since they were all aware of the capability of the intelligence services to eavesdrop on all electronic communications with the help of the U.S.-NSA and the Echelon network.

These couriers were only to be trusted with a short message requesting the presence of each leader in a meeting of 'vital importance to the purity of Europe.'

Those that responded favorably were then to be given details of the meeting venue and time—at an elk farm at Bjurholm, a small village near Umea, Sweden, on March 15.

The attendants were to appear as cross-country skiers meeting for a joint trip into the lovely forests of the area to observe the majestic elks in the wild.

CHAPTER 4

March 15, near Umea, a month earlier

The leaders of nationalist and separatist movements from several European countries arrived around noon after flying into the small Umea airport via Stockholm.

With their cross-country ski equipment, they blended in with other tourists. Some of them travelled alone, others brought their spouse but, as instructed by the courier, none of them brought their bodyguards.

Most of them were not recognized by the public and did not know each other, as the real leaders preferred to keep a low profile in order to avoid unwanted attention from the local press and police force.

A few of the well-known men, not to say infamous ones, that had other priorities, sent their second in command. A minibus with the prearranged sign saying, 'Elk tours' waited at the exit from the airport building. At two o'clock, after checking the list of participants, the minibus left for the forty or so mile trip to Bjurholm, where rooms were booked in a small bed-and-breakfast place run by one of Andreas' supporters.

The participants were welcomed by the proprietor and Andreas who offered them schnapps and some elk meat sandwiches and told them the meeting would convene at seven in the evening over dinner. All vocal or visual recording devices were banned from the meeting and the participants were asked to leave their cell phones in their rooms.

Dinner was held in the small dining room and two tables were arranged next to a wood burning fireplace. Andreas started by introducing himself and presenting Ollie as his chief strategist.

Introduction of the participants was according to the pre-set rules of the low-profile meeting. Therefore, each leader introduced himself by his first name or nickname and country, so their true identity was known only to Andreas.

Although there were conflicts between the declared objectives of some of the different movements, the leaders came to hear the proposals and ideas that Andreas hinted at in his cryptic message and all differences of opinion were put aside for the duration of the meeting.

After all of them had enjoyed their dinner, once again based on elk meat, and were sipping their digestive drinks consisting of Andreas's favorite cognac, Ollie stood up and presented his plan for constructing an unconventional weapon, preferably an improvised nuclear device, that would be used to blackmail the government into accepting the demands of each movement.

The leaders applauded the brilliant idea but then some questions were raised. The leader of the paramilitary extension of the British National Socialist Party (BNSP), a ruffian with a thick neck and low forehead, asked if fissile materials could cause brain function impairment.

The leader of the Flemish separatist movement, an intelligent looking thin man with round eye glasses, answered him that he personally should have no fear of that. This caused a short burst of laughter that was wasted on the Briton who raised the question.

The Hungarian representative asked if Gypsies would be affected by nuclear radiation because he had heard that low, life forms, like cockroaches, were not affected by it. This comment brought smiles to the faces of those few representatives who understood the cynicism of the comment.

More serious questions were raised including the means needed to acquire the fissile material and Andreas asked if anyone had an idea about obtaining the materials needed to implement the plan. Andreas estimated that a considerable sum of money would be needed to acquire fissile material on the 'black market,' if there were any sellers and even more for manufacturing a crude improvised nuclear device.

He proposed they should all establish a fund for that purpose and each organization should contribute to the joint venture. The leaders did not want to make any financial commitments on the spot but consented to go home and consult with their financiers and wealthy backers.

Andreas now realized that disclosing the plan to so many people with conflicting interests could lead to a disaster and wondered if the whole idea should be aborted when help came from an unexpected quarter.

The Catalan representative, cynically known to his colleagues by the name of Delgado—thin man—despite his impressive girth, stood up and declared he may have the answer to their problem. Everybody paid attention as Spain was not one of the countries that possessed the knowledge, far less the actual means, for producing fissile materials.

Delgado said that one of the dedicated members of his support group was a professor at Barcelona University and in one of their clandestine meetings he claimed he had developed a novel technique for producing a unique fissile material. The professor tried to explain the scientific principles underlying his invention but Delgado, who had finished his schooling at the age of fourteen when he was sent to help his father in the field, did not understand anything beyond the fact this material could be used to make an atomic bomb.

This revelation changed the dynamic of the meeting and the leaders that had already stood up, prepared to leave the room returned to their seats.

Andreas and Ollie suggested they all meet again after some background checks were carried out about the technical details of the invention. The specifics of that meeting would be delivered once again by courier to the representatives who were willing to contribute financial aid and technical support in return for gaining access to the nuclear device and permission to use it against their governments in order to further their specific cause.

Ollie was relieved the idea of approaching the Catalan professor did not come from him, as that may have given the whole plan away. So, pretending to be surprised by Delgado's suggestion, he asked him to stay after the meeting adjourned and obtained the name and address of Professor Modena.

With the help of Delgado, a meeting was set up for the

middle of April. Delgado said he would arrange the meeting and his representative would be in the Travel Bar on April 18.

When Ollie asked who would meet him, Delgado said he would be met by Ramona, a graduate student of the professor. Ollie asked how they would recognize each other to verify their identity and Delgado said she would say, "all other seats were taken" when he will invite her to join him by saying, "please be seated and I'll buy you a cool drink."

May 5, Corfu

Once again the leaders of the separatist and national-ist movements convened after receiving a message from Andreas. This time they met in Corfu Town, a bastion of the Greek Golden Dawn movement that provided the security for the meeting. They all posed as early season vacationers that wanted to take advantage of the low prices and yet enjoy the sunshine, beaches, and good food.

They took over a small hotel located just above a popular restaurant and close to the town center and the pedestrian streets. Andreas and Ollie were glad to get away from gloomy Stockholm, especially as they felt they had achieved a break-through for obtaining fissile material and were anxious to share the good news with their like-minded colleagues and to start carrying out practical steps toward their goal.

The delegates checked in and were offered a refreshing cocktail of Ouzo and mint-flavored red-grapefruit juice. They all gathered in the small breakfast room on the second floor and waited for Ollie's presentation.

Ollie, who thus far had managed to hide the fact he had a bachelor's degree in mechanical engineering and a better understanding of the physical principles on which Professor Modena's idea was based, presented the idea in very simple terms so everyone, except the British delegate of course, could understand.

The participants discussed the matter and tried to decide on a safe place in which to establish the laboratory. Delgado, the Catalan separatist, proposed they use a remote semi-deserted village in the Pyrenees Mountains. Other delegates each suggested some uninhabited area in their own country, hoping to control the production of the fissile material and thus have priority access to it.

The debate had gone on for half an hour with each delegate feeling he had to make his own claims until Ollie, who had anticipated this, stood up and waved his hand. Everyone fell quiet waiting for his words. He proceeded by asking them a rhetorical question: "Where is the best place to hide a book?"

Books were not the forte of most of the delegates, so he had to give the obvious answer: "In a library or a bookstore, of course." Not seeing looks of comprehension he asked them, "Where would you hide a stolen car?"

This time, smiles lit up their faces, and in unison they said, "In a crowded parking lot." So Ollie said, "We'll hide the production laboratory in an industrial high-tech park where people come and go at all hours and trucks carrying scientific equipment are a common sight."

Once again every participant offered their local facilities but Ollie and Andreas overruled these suggestions and said northern Italy would be ideal due to the fact that it was centrally located in Europe, had advanced high-tech companies, and the local authorities could be easily steered away from the site.

The delegates accepted this decision and the Italian delegate promised to make the necessary arrangements as quickly as possible. Before he could name the locality of the site, Ollie told him that from now on they would all operate on a need-to-know basis and the exact location was not to be mentioned.

They then moved on to discuss practical matters. Each movement was asked to contribute one million Euros to the joint fund and to try to get hold of as many gamma radiation sources as possible. Ollie directed them to the prime locations where such sources could be found—mainly hospitals that performed radiation therapy and industrial facilities that used such sources to test the integrity of pipe welds or measure the level of liquids in closed holding tanks.

He told them the sealed sources were safe but heavy because of the protective radiation shielding. If they did not care about the safety of the people handling and transporting the sources, and if removing a heavily shielded source was impossible, then the bare sources could be taken, risking external radiation exposure to the people close to them.

In order to keep the location of the laboratory secret, all stolen sources were to be brought to an address in Milan and from there they would be taken to the clandestine laboratory by the two drivers who knew its exact location.

Goals were set for each participant according to the technological development of their country, their access to the sources, and the number of trustworthy members.

A cover story was established claiming that the radioactive materials would be used to make a radioactive dispersion device known in short as RDD, or to the public as a 'dirty bomb.' This would seem plausible enough for the underground movements and yet make them aware of the necessity of keeping the activity in secret.

July 10, Padova

Ollie suggested the joint venture receive the codename Astraea, after the mythological goddess of innocence and purity often also associated with justice and this was supported enthusiastically by the Greek Golden Dawn faction and accepted by the other members.

Professor Modena, with the help of Ollie and a few hand-picked technically skilled people from the European countries that participated in the project, started acquiring the equipment needed for the laboratory and moving the personnel and materials to the vicinity of the famous Botanical Gardens of Padova.

They rented a warehouse with a large, deep basement and converted the street level floor into offices that served as the front of the high-tech company they named Astraea. It was presented as a research and development company involved in development of innovative industrial chemical processes.

On the first-floor level they constructed a small dormitory and rigged a couple bedrooms to serve as the lodging of the small workforce. They also converted some space into a kitchen and dining area as they did not want to be seen frequently in restaurants in the neighborhood.

This well-travelled section of town provided excellent cover for the handful of international scientists, engineers, and technicians involved in the clandestine project.

The acquisition of the raw materials needed for Professor Modena's plan was quite easy as none of them were closely scrutinized. Thorium oxide was purchased from India through a fictitious front company and quantities of beryl mineral were shipped from Argentina, enabling the chemists to produce beryllium oxide on site. Other common multi-purpose chemicals such as mineral acids, ion exchange resins, lead bricks, and organic solvents were acquired mainly from China and from several companies in Europe.

In the deep basement, the walls were lined with the lead bricks that served for radiation shielding. Four irradiation tunnels from the same materials led from the corners of the largest room in the basement to the center, where a large stainless steel reactor vessel was placed.

As the stolen radioactive sources arrived at the laboratory site from all over Europe, they were moved to the basement and placed in the center of the four lead-covered tunnels.

Measurements showed that only a very small amount of radiation reached the surface level. Due to the twenty-seven point five days' half-life of the protactinium-233 intermediate radionuclide, the irradiated thorium oxide needed to be stored for three months before the uranium-233 could be efficiently extracted. For this purpose, a storage space shielded with lead bricks was constructed in an adjoining room of the basement.

In the same room, a chemical pilot plant was constructed to dissolve the "cooled" irradiated thorium oxide targets and to separate the uranium-233 produced through the sequence of nuclear reactions from the thorium and beryllium oxides. The thorium and beryllium were then recycled by precipitation as a mixed oxide and returned to the central reactor vessel for another irradiation cycle. The U-233 product was to be transferred to another section of the basement where it would be further chemically purified by solvent extraction and ion-exchange.

In the final stage, the uranium was to be converted into a metallic form through a few well-known chemical conversion steps. The uranium metal product was to be stored in a sealed vault, also coated with lead bricks, until processed into the shape and dimensions required for the core of the improvised nuclear device.

By the end of July, all the parts were set in place. Stocks of thorium and beryllium oxides were admixed and ready for placement in the reactor. A sufficient number of gamma radiation sources had arrived and they were placed in the lead tunnels.

The staff had practiced using the separation and purification equipment with thorium and natural uranium that were only slightly radioactive and managed to produce high purity uranium metal.

According to the calculations, overseen by Professor Modena, every week each batch would produce about one pound of U-233, so the critical amount needed for a simple improvised nuclear device of thirty-five pounds could be completed within about eight months of continuous operation of the facility.

After the production of the uranium metal it had to be cast and shaped to enable it to produce a fast chain reaction that would release enough energy to obliterate every living being and structure within a radius of a few hundred meters.

It was assumed this would take another couple months to complete or somewhat less time if an experienced scientist would be put in charge of this stage. Professor Modena intended to ask Ollie to try and enlist a suitable candidate for this or at least obtain detailed blueprints of the device.

The irradiation of the first batch took a little longer than one week due to some minor hitches, but then they had to wait for several weeks before uranium could be extracted from the irradiated thorium oxide.

Extensive chemical and isotopic analyses showed that the U-233 produced did contain only a small amount of the highly radioactive isotope of uranium-232, which made handling of the product more hazardous.

August 12, Vienna

At the headquarters of the International Atomic Energy Agency, the IAEA, in the section responsible for tracking radiation sources, a flurry of activity started when an unexplained increase in the number of 'orphan sources' was noted.

Numerous reports of missing radiation sources were received from Sweden, Germany, France, Belgium, Italy, and other European countries. These included gamma radiation sources of all kinds—Cobalt-60, Cesium-137, Iridium-192 and a few others. Strangely there was no change in the number of reports on missing sources for other types of radiation, like beta or alpha sources.

The Section head, who was a political appointee from a South American country with financial ties to the president of that country, could not care less about this. However, Doctor Eugene Powers, his permanent deputy, a professional health physicist from the United States, became deeply concerned about these missing sources. He contacted his Russian colleague, who was also his opposite number in the Safeguards Section, Dr Vassilly Nomenkov, and proposed a private meeting over lunch.

They met in the IAEA employees' cafeteria and Eugene described his concerns about the increase in the number of reports of missing gamma sources and they both discussed the implications. Vassilly asked if this could just be a coincidence but Eugene told him the extent of reports and their geographical distribution made this an unlikely explanation. Vassilly then suggested that perhaps some international conspiracy aiming to detonate several 'dirty bombs' simultaneously in different European capital cities was involved.

The immediate suspect was a terrorist organization with a global network of supporters and naturally El Qaeda was the first one that came to mind. They decided to consult with an expert on global terrorism to try and get to the bottom of this. They both knew that Colin Thomas, a former counter-terror department head at the British MI6, was now a member of the UK delegation to IAEA and arranged to meet with him on an urgent matter after dinner.

Thomas heard them out with growing interest and looked very worried when they expressed their fear of coordinated 'dirty bomb' attacks in several cities. He explained that although the expected number of direct casualties from each of these attacks would be very small, involving mostly people injured from the detonation of the conventional explosives used to disperse the radioactive material, the disruption of normal life that would follow could upset the global economy.

In addition, the financial costs of cleaning contaminated areas could be extensive, particularly if the most expensive commercial real estate areas were selected as targets. Another aspect to consider was the panic factor—people who were nowhere near the incident site would overcrowd the hospitals demanding to be examined and this could lead to a collapse of the medical services further enhancing the public's panic.

With these sobering words, the three people each went their own way. Eugene immediately called his contacts at the U.S. Embassy who in turn sent an urgent message to the White House, the State Department, and the director of the CIA.

Vassilly went directly from the meeting to the FSB Resident who represented the Federal Security Bureau (FSB) of the Russian Federation and Colin Thomas used a secure line to phone the duty officer at Thames House. In addition, Eugene made sure that all the major security services in Europe received warning that a terrorist plot to deploy unconventional radioactive dispersion devices was suspected.

August 25, Stockholm

The result of the actions of the European intelligence services and police forces was exactly what Ollie had hoped for—increasing security in the centers of the major cities, drawing troops and police forces from the countryside and smaller cities.

Furthermore, Ollie had advised Andreas to invest most of the funds contributed by the different movements in companies that manufactured radiation detectors. The stock value of these companies jumped fivefold within two weeks, just as they had after the Fukushima accident.

The manufacturers of personal radiation detectors, especially those that could be worn on a person's wrist like watches, could not meet the huge demand and opened new production lines in China. Ollie cashed in the stock holdings and the coffers of the Astraea joint venture increased accordingly.

Professor Modena flew from Padova to Stockholm to report the progress of the project and to explain the small delay in production of the first batch. Ollie and Andreas took advantage of the opportunity the professor was in Stockholm for a strategy discussion.

The three of them debated whether to disclose the existence of their improvised nuclear device after completion of the first one or to wait until they had a second device so they could demonstrate they meant business by detonating one device and using the other for blackmailing the governments.

They could not reach an agreement on this point as the professor wanted an early demonstration to prove to the world his genius while Andreas and Ollie said they were afraid they would not be believed until they used one device for a demonstration and in that case a second device had to be held in reserve to make their threats credible and their demands acceptable.

At this early stage of the project there were only a dozen or so people who knew where the laboratory was and what its true purpose was. These included Andreas, Ollie, Professor Modena and his team of seven professionals—three scientists, two engineers, and two technicians—the administrator responsible for the purchasing and running of the laboratory, and the executive head of the Italian separatist party involved in setting up the laboratory.

The two local drivers in charge of transporting the gamma sources from Milan to the laboratory knew where it was but not its objective, and then there were the several delegates and the top people in their organizations who knew the alleged purpose of the Astraea project but not the location of the warehouse.

Nobody was aware of Ollie's real purpose that had nothing to do with blackmailing European governments to dispose of 'undesirable elements.'

The small size of the production workforce in the laboratory meant they could only work two shifts a day with each shift consisting of a scientist, an engineer and a technician. The third scientist and the professor shared the responsibility for overseeing the other employees.

Andreas and Ollie asked the professor whether they should not enlist a few more people in order to expedite the production of uranium-233, but he said that finding professionals who were dedicated to the cause would be difficult and could detrimentally affect the strict security measures, while taking in dedicated, unprofessional people, would increase the safety risks.

The direct result of this situation, the three of them realized, was that the production of the fissile material might take a full year.

CHAPTER 5

North-East Syria, December 28

El Kahiri lay mortally wounded after his Toyota Jeep was attacked by a crowd of angry women on the way from his headquarters to the front lines.

Apparently, he had received a distress call for help from one of his units that was in charge of controlling the local population in a small village, mainly by using intimidation and random brutality intended to induce fear by exemplary punishment of innocent bystanders.

He travelled with three of his bodyguards in a lone Jeep as he did not expect any real resistance from a bunch of women. However, when he reached the small village he saw that perhaps one hundred women were encircling his fighters, shouting and pointing at the small blood-covered bodies of what looked from a distance like dead dogs. When they got a little closer, he saw that the bodies belonged to three babies. His men were holding their weapons pointed at the angry mob but hesitated to fire.

At a glance, El Kahiri took in the situation and immediately drew his own AK47 and started shooting at the closest group of women, cutting them down. His bodyguards joined him and within seconds there were three dozen dead and injured protesters.

Instead of running away in panic, the remaining women stormed the Jeep with short daggers and kitchen knives they drew from the folds of their chadors. Some of them got close enough to El Kahiri and his bodyguards and managed to stab them before being mowed down by the combined firepower of the encircled unit and the bodyguards.

The area looked like a scene from hell with dozens of bodies of dead women scattered around a handful of dead uniformed men. The cries of anguish and pain from the wounded fighters were the only sounds but they called in vain as there was no one left to aid them.

An old Kurdish woman wearing a black chador and veil crawled towards El Kahiri and with her last breath stuck her kitchen knife through his left eye into his brain and collapsed dead over his body. All the women who were still able to run, fled the spot as fast and as far as they could.

Fifteen minutes later, three Toyota Jeeps carrying machine guns arrived at the site of the massacre. The Islamic State fighters on board could not believe their eyes. In front of them their Supreme Commander lay dead, obviously killed by the old woman lying on top of his body with the handle of a kitchen knife in her right hand and the blade buried deep in El Kahiri's head.

They picked up his body and the bodies of his fighters, loaded them all on one of the Jeeps and set out to take revenge. They entered every house in the village, forced the inhabitants that comprised old men, women, and children out into the village main square next to the mosque. They forced all of them to lie down along the mosque's wall and summarily executed every living soul by a single shot to the head.

***

During his life, El Kahiri made sure that no one could replace him or threaten his position as the Supreme Commander. He did this by nominating several unit leaders that answered directly to him alone and kept shuffling them around so they could not develop a cadre of loyal followers.

As a result, after his death, brawling among the unit leaders broke out, with each trying to gain control of the entire Islamic State forces. This led to withdrawal of troops from the front lines and loss of ground to their enemies—the Iraqi government forces, the Peshmerga Kurds, and the coalition forces. Even the Turks and Iranians managed to gain ground and control some of the Iraqi and Syrian territories formerly held by the ISIS forces.

January 1, Stockholm

Word of the fate of El Kahiri and the Islamic State movement reached Ollie just as he was about to leave for Padova.

The TV news stations displayed cell phone photos of El Kahiri's body with the dead old woman on top of him. These were taken by ISIS fighters in order to incite the troops to avenge the disgraceful circumstances of their Supreme Commander's death but were sold to the networks once the leadership in-fighting broke out.

Adding insult to injury was the fact, known to all radical Islamists, that dying in the hands of an inferior person, like a woman, would prevent El Kahiri from reaching the seventy-two virgins awaiting him in heaven.

In between showing these gory photos on all TV channels and the internet, the New Year celebrations all over the globe were broadcasted. Many of the revelers made the V sign for victory and cursed ISIS and its dead leader—a sight that further enraged Ollie.

Ollie now had second thoughts on the Astraea project. He was not sure whether any of the current ISIS chieftains who were still fighting amongst themselves had any knowledge of the project, as he had not contacted El Kahiri after leaving for Sweden to reduce the likelihood of being discovered. He had also not tried to contact the old man in Uppsala for the same reason and now had no way of knowing what was going on in Syria and Iraq except what he saw on TV.

In the end, Ollie decided he could not avoid going on a trip to that region in order to find out if a new leader had emerged to take over the role of Supreme Commander.

Ollie estimated he would need at least one week for this mission and wondered how to explain his sudden disappearance to Andreas. He thought the best cover story would be that he needed to travel to Greece to meet with the heads of the Golden Dawn movement now posing as legitimate politicians, in order to discuss their reneging on the financial commitments to the project.

He planned to leave Greece and cross over into Turkey and

then sneak in to Syria. Andreas accepted the story but was a bit suspicious about this sudden need to travel to Athens and suggested that Agda should join him. This would provide some cover, he added, as a young, handsome Scandinavian couple pretending to enjoy a vacation in Greece was less likely to draw the attention of the counter-terror forces.

Ollie did not like the idea but could not decline the suggestion. He started to think of a plan that would turn Agda's presence from a burden to an asset and came up with a win-win idea.

January 3 and 4, Athens, Greece

Ollie and Agda arrived in Athens on a direct flight from Stockholm and checked in to one of the hotels near the National Archeological Museum, since their meeting with the Golden Dawn contact was set for noon the next day at the main entrance to the museum.

Agda was in a very romantic mood brought about by leaving cold, dark, snow-covered Stockholm behind for what she expected to be a vacation in the sun with a little time devoted to business meetings.

A couple drinks in a nearby tavern enhanced her mood, while Ollie was preoccupied with thoughts of executing his plan to disengage himself from Agda for a few days.

Nevertheless, after they had returned to their hotel room, when Agda slowly undressed and as he once again saw the garish tattoos that covered most of her body he stopped worrying about the future.

The next day, after having a late breakfast, they sauntered over to the museum. The sun was bright in the sky and the temperature fifteen degrees warmer than in Stockholm, so that the sun and warmth made them happy.

As they started ascending the stairs to the museum a handsome young man approached them and asked them in English if they had seen the dawn and the rising sun. This was the code for the meeting and they responded by saying they liked the purity of the air—which, of course, was not quite true for Athens, even in winter.

The young man introduced himself as Niko and jokingly asked them whether they were really interested in archeology or were ready to follow him to the meeting. Ollie smiled and said that if the exhibits in the museum had waited for over two thousand years to be viewed by them then they could wait another few years.

Niko led them to a car in which a driver was waiting and directed them to the back seat. They drove out of the congested center of town towards the marina in Piraeus.

They entered a small building on Akti Moutsopolou and Niko signaled for Ollie to go up to the second floor while asking Agda to sit down at one of the small tables near the entrance and offering her some Greek coffee.

Adga realized he could not take his eyes off her and was quite flattered by the attention of this handsome, dark man. She felt that the energy radiating from him was like that emanating from Ollie, but the two men were like negative and positive images on film.

On the drive to the marina, Ollie had felt the mounting

tension between Agda and Niko and saw that it perfectly suited his plan for leaving Adga in Greece for a few days while he continued his journey to Syria. So he was quite glad to leave them alone drinking coffee on the ground floor while he climbed the stairs to the second floor to take care of the business for which he had allegedly come to Athens.

On the second-floor Ollie saw an open door leading into a small conference room. A large oak-wood table occupied the center of the room and many marine ornaments such as a small anchor, a yacht's steering wheel, a folded sail, and many photographs of large fish lined the walls.

Two men sat on chairs arranged around the table. The senior man with a full head of white hair and an aristocratic look invited Ollie to sit down. The other man was the person that had attended the meetings in Umea and Corfu as the representative of the Golden Dawn and he made the introductions between Ollie and Guido—no last names given.

Ollie gave them a short progress report and told them that the project was short of funds and the Greeks were expected to contribute their share of one million Euros as promised in Corfu. Guido outlined the dire financial situation in Greece, which was nothing new, and offered to help by sending two of their own people to work on the production of the fissile material instead of paying cash.

Ollie said they needed qualified professional people that could keep a secret and safeguard the location even from their own bosses. Guido said he was well aware of this and the people he had designated complied with these qualifications. Both were engineers with experience in handling radioactive materials as they had worked in the Greek National Radiation Protection laboratory until they were fired three months earlier. Furthermore, Guido said the Golden Dawn movement and he personally could vouch for them.

Ollie said that funds were a priority, but he understood their predicament and was willing to have Professor Modena interview the two candidates, so he asked that they be sent to Milan the next day and he would arrange for the professor to meet with them.

Before parting he said he had to go away on business for a few days and asked if they could provide someone to escort Agda and show her around Athens until he returned. Guido said that Niko was available and if they all agreed he could play host to Agda.

Guido descended the stairs to the ground floor and in Greek briefed Niko on his new assignment while Ollie told Agda that he had to leave Athens for a few days but that if she wished she could stay and be entertained by Niko.

A brief look was exchanged between Agda and Niko and they both agreed to the new plan. Ollie said he had to leave shortly and asked to be driven back to the hotel to collect his things, so they all got back in the car and returned to the hotel in the center of Athens.

On the way, Niko outlined a program for Agda's visit to Athens that included seeing the main tourist sites and getting a taste the nightlife in the famous tavernas where Greek food was served, and folk shows were performed. They all liked the plan—each for their own reasons.

Before leaving Athens, Ollie called the professor and told

him to meet the new candidates for an interview in Milan
the next day, and that adding them to the small workforce
could enable them to work three full shifts and increase their
output. This could enable them to get back on schedule for
production of the fissile material.

January 5 to 7, border between Turkey and Syria

Once again Ollie donned local clothes to hide his Scandinavian features and blond hair and as dusk set in, he followed
his guide down the narrow streets of a village through which
ran the unmanned border between the two countries.

After crossing the virtual border, they avoided the Peshmerga fighters and made their way deeper into the Syrian
controlled area. They passed through deserted villages and
along dusty roads now covered with a thin layer of snow that
had turned into ice in many places. After marching for five
hours, the guide told Ollie he had to continue on his own
as they had reached an area controlled by the Islamic State
troops.

Ollie paid the guide and asked him to meet him again at
the same place after forty-eight hours promising to double his
fees if he returned on time.

Ollie found a ruined house, spread his thin blanket on the
floor and lay down waiting for the sun to rise as he feared that
approaching the ISIS held territory in the dark would be too
dangerous.

At dawn he rose and for the first time after almost a whole
year bowed towards Mecca and prayed. At this stage he was

not sure if his dedication to Islam was as strong as it had been while he fought with the ISIS troops but the memory of Fatima and his promise to the dead Supreme Commander kept him going.

He exited the ruined building and waving a white rag tied to a stick continued his way south until he saw the black flag of ISIS flying on a Toyota Jeep with four-wheel drive.

Slowly approaching the Jeep, he took off his *keffiyeh* exposing his blond hair and shouted in Arabic that he wanted to speak with their leader. He was answered by a short burst from an AK47 aimed at the ground near his feet.

Without flinching he shouted that he was the head of the fabled Ollie's Butchers unit and the firing stopped. He was ordered to come closer with his hands raised.

The troops he saw were nothing like those he remembered. Instead of a group of self-confident, fearless warriors, dressed in battle fatigues and armed to the teeth, he saw a group of disheveled troops, poorly dressed, with lifeless expressions.

They all appeared to be red-eyed and under the influence of hashish or some other drug. Nevertheless, one of the older soldiers recognized his name and volunteered to take him to their local commander.

Ollie followed the soldier to the Jeep, and they drove a few miles back to another village that was only partly destroyed. He was led to the largest house in the village and although the front door was missing, the house was occupied by the local ISIS commander and some of his troops.

The smell of cooked food reminded Ollie that he had hardly eaten since leaving Athens two days earlier. A tall, haggard looking, bearded man invited him to have some soup, bread, and water and to join him in prayer before sitting down to eat. He introduced himself as Abu-Alli, the commander of some two hundred and fifty ISIS fighters in charge of one of the sectors closest to the border. He told Ollie his troops were holding back the Peshmerga forces but the air attacks by the coalition air forces made this increasingly difficult. He added that every day he lost some of his soldiers in battle and others through desertion.

The air raids by the Syrian air force, that had recently received support from Iranian and Western forces, were decimating his troops and although they had a few Russian-made Strela, and U.S.-made Stinger shoulder fired, anti-aircraft missiles which tried to keep away low flying helicopters and aircraft, the damage from the aerial raids was still severe.

Ollie inquired as to who was now in the position of Supreme Commander and Abu-Alli told him that ISIS had effectively split into two main factions; one was led by Ahmad Nuseirat and the other, smaller and more extreme group, by Ibn Tutta.

Nuseirat was willing to cease fighting and reach an agreement with the governments of Syria and Iraq if they promised amnesty and allowed him to remain in control of a small area bordering on both countries.

They were inclined to agree if the fighters would lay down their arms. Ibn Tutta, on the other hand, had sworn to continue fighting until the new Caliphate was established and the whole world acknowledged that Islam was the only true religion and accepted it or until the last of his men became a *shahid* and earned his place in heaven.

Abu Alli then explained that he supported Ibn Tutta, who saw himself as the new Supreme Commander, and that he was, in fact, his top lieutenant. He said this was the main reason so many air raids were directed at his unit.

Ollie asked to meet with Ibn Tutta as soon as possible and Abu Alli offered to take him to his hiding place. The U.S. had placed Ibn Tutta at the top of their most wanted list and had posted a reward of fifty million U.S. dollars for information on his whereabouts so he had gone into a safe haven deep in a cave in the hills east of Ar Raqqah, the unofficial capital of ISIS controlled areas.

The trip from the border vicinity to Ar Raqqah took over five hours as they had to avoid roadblocks set up by other opposition factions. By the time they arrived, the sun was setting.

Before being allowed into the presence of Ibn Tutta, Ollie and Abu Alli were frisked by the bodyguards that ensured they empty their pockets and left them almost undressed before they admitted them for their audience with the new self-proclaimed Supreme Commander and Caliph.

The room in which Ibn Tutta sat was actually a large excavated space inside the cave that provided shelter from aerial attacks.

Ollie felt uncomfortable about discussing the secret project in Abu Alli's presence but could not think of a way to get him to leave the room without offending him, so solemnly said what he had to say to them both was for their ears only. He asked Ibn Tutta to send away everyone else and waited until the bodyguards left them alone.

In a low voice, Ollie revealed the plan concocted by the dead Supreme Commander without divulging the status of the project and its exact location. He knew there was no point in going into technical details with the two Arabs whose scientific background was practically nonexistent. He emphasized that the ultimate objective was to initiate a religious war between Christians and all Muslims, especially the moderate regimes that were corrupted by the Western culture, precipitating this by exploding an improvised nuclear device in the heart of the Old City of Jerusalem.

The plan was that first the Jews would be blamed for clearing the way to build their Third Temple on the site where mosques and churches prevented this construction. Then the Christians would suspect the Muslims were willing to sacrifice their third most holy shrine to destroy the place where Jesus had set foot on his way to the cross and where, according to the tradition of most Orthodox Christians, he was buried before being resurrected.

The Muslims would naturally suspect Christian extremists who had relatively easy access to nuclear weapons and soon a global religious war would begin. In the aftermath, the Muslims would claim what was rightfully their place as the dominant force, imposing their own version of world order. Ibn Tutta and Abu Alli were speechless and impressed by the magnitude and sophistication of this plot.

After a few minutes Ibn Tutta, who although he had little formal education did have political savvy, shrewdly asked if the Chinese would not seize the opportunity and take control of the world themselves. Ollie stated frankly that they had thought the Chinese would also be drawn into the global conflict but would be in no position to be an active player, but that was a speculative unknown factor.

Ibn Tutta offered financial assistance as he had gained control of most of the monitory assets confiscated from banks by ISIS when it was at its prime, but Ollie was afraid he would not be able to explain to Andreas where these funds had come from and declined the offer.

However, Ollie made a request that when the stage was getting set for the final act—detonation of the device in Jerusalem—he would need cooperation from Palestinians loyal to the cause and willing to sacrifice their lives for it.

Ibn Tutta told him that as that time approached, he should contact Sheik Khalil, the head of an extreme Islamic movement in Israel in Umm al-Fahm and use the code word *al tahrir al Islami* (freedom of Islam). Meanwhile Ibn Tutta would make sure that Sheik Khalil received instructions to assist Ollie with anything he requested, even to the point of sacrificing his own life and the lives of his disciples if necessary.

Ollie thanked him for his support and said he would not be in touch and that his actions would speak for him.

After they had concluded their meeting, they all prayed together, had a modest dinner, and went to sleep in Ibn Tutta's secure cave.

For Ollie, a full night's sleep was a luxury he had almost forgotten. The next morning Abu Alli drove him back toward the Turkish border where he was to meet his guide in the evening. The trip was uneventful, and Ollie reached the meeting place an hour ahead of the scheduled time so he was able to verify that no unpleasant surprises awaited him when the guide arrived. They crossed back into Turkey without being challenged, the same way they had left it two nights earlier.

January 9, Athens

As soon as Ollie crossed back from Turkey into Greece, he called Agda's room at the hotel. He was not really surprised when a male voice answered the phone and upon hearing Ollie's voice pretended he had the wrong room number.

He called the hotel exchange again and asked for the same room number and this time the phone was answered by Agda who said she had just stepped out of the shower. Ollie told her he would arrive at the hotel three hours later and that she should start packing her things as they were flying back to Stockholm later that night.

Agda motioned to Niko to take off the clothes he had just put on as he had begun to get dressed after hearing Ollie's voice on the phone and said they had time for a short farewell party.

In fact, Agda did not see much of Athens during the last four days but saw quite a lot of Niko and managed to teach him to satisfy her needs in the way she liked most. Niko was reluctant at first to use violence to enhance her pleasure but gradually got into the same game himself and started to enjoy it too. Their farewell party almost led to mutual mutilation as they sought their last share of elation, but as the clock advanced, they quickly showered separately, got dressed, and Niko left the room while Agda packed her clothes and checked out of the hotel.

When Ollie arrived, he found her sitting in the hotel lobby with a long drink in her hand and an enigmatic smile on her face.

He asked her if she'd had a good time in Athens and her smile broadened, so he too smiled and said they had to fly back to Stockholm, but they could return to Athens another time if she wanted.

January 10, Stockholm

Upon reaching Stockholm late the previous night Agda and Ollie returned to their separate apartments and agreed not to discuss their vacation with anyone—each for their own personal reasons.

In the morning, Ollie called Andreas and updated him on the arrangements he had made with the Golden Dawn people. Andreas informed him they were now indeed on a three-shift schedule and that production had increased accordingly.

Ollie broached the subject of strategy and said he had been convinced that the longer they waited before sending out the blackmail demands the higher the risk of exposure, so they should plan to reveal their demands secretly to the relevant governments as soon as they had the first device and not wait until they had two of them.

The true reason was, of course, that for the ISIS plan to successfully detonate a nuclear device in Jerusalem only one device was required, and any delay in carrying this out was undesirable and risky.

Andreas considered the proposed change in strategy and said he had to study this for a little longer.

January 10, Vienna

While Ollie and Andreas met in Stockholm, Eugene and Vassilly were summoned to meet the IAEA Secretary General, Doctor Javier Augustin Marcos, known for short by his initials JAM.

The honorable Argentine who held a doctorate in political science, with emphasis on the first part of the subject, disliked this nickname as he felt that it was disrespectful, but people kept calling him by this nickname behind his back.

When Eugene and Vassilly entered his vast office, they saw that their section heads were also present. They were not invited to sit down and JAM proceeded to read them the riot act: blaming them for raising a false alarm and causing panic in the IAEA and within the intelligence communities. He mentioned that the number of orphan gamma sources had barely changed since last August and there was no evidence terrorists were trying to produce 'dirty bombs' for sabotage in European capital cities.

He demanded that they cease and desist from all their activities and focus on their designated jobs or else they would be dismissed from the IAEA. Furthermore, pointing at the section heads, he said they would be closely watched and supervised to make sure that his directive was followed verbatim.

Eugene felt like a child being reprimanded in front of his whole class and friends by the teacher. He stole a sideways glance at Vassilly, whose face had turned crimson red. Both were then sent away and left the room with their heads down.

Eugene's certainty that there was a concerted effort to steal radioactive sources to be used for an act of terror deepened. He decided to continue his investigation of the matter but to do so while keeping a low profile. He was disappointed by the response he received from MI6 and the CIA, and the lack of reaction that Vassilly got from the FSB and decided to approach the one security organization he trusted would not participate in a cover up, the Israeli Mossad.

However, he did not know any Mossad agents, so he asked for a meeting with the security officer of the Israeli delegation to IAEA. It turned out that this officer was actually a young woman, who introduced herself as Orna Cohen and heard him out patiently but then bombarded him with astute questions.

Apparently, she had already heard the story of the mysterious increase in the number of missing radiation sources and read the analysis that it had no real significance but stated she herself had a gut feeling there was more to this than met the eye.

Eugene asked her to convey the detailed information he gave her to Mossad contacts and this she promised to do so.

January 12, Tel Aviv and Haifa

The coded message from Orna in Vienna attracted the attention of the Deputy Director of the Mossad, Haim Shimony, and he convened a meeting with his experts in the technology department to discuss the possible implications of the orphan radiation sources.

The group of experts included an interesting mix of older scientists and engineers with a lot of operational experience, and several young and bright graduates of Israel's top universities.

The Deputy Director presented the statistics of missing gamma sources he had received from Vienna and then opened the meeting for discussion. Unlike similar institutions in the world, in this type of meeting Mossad employed the same principles used in the Israeli air force when debriefing air crews after an exercise or operational mission.

In these sessions everyone could freely express their thoughts and ideas regardless of rank or seniority. Often, the person chairing the meeting asked the younger and junior participants to speak first so they would not be influenced by the opinions of their bosses.

A lively discussion commenced with the consensus being the most probable explanation for the missing sources was someone planned to use them for the construction of 'dirty bombs.'

In view of the fact this occurred all over Europe the likely culprits were, as usual, the racist, extreme-right movements that planned to terrorize their governments. One of the participants, the descendent of holocaust survivors and a great believer in conspiracy theories, suggested it could be a provocation by the extreme-right trying to place the blame on Muslims as a means of inciting public opinion against foreigners and immigrants.

The youngest member of the technical group, David Avivi, a fresh physics graduate of the Technion in Haifa, said the number of missing sources and the broad geographical spread of the incidents was an overkill for just deploying an RDD and that they should not limit themselves to this explanation but should consider other possibilities. Furthermore, he said, the fact that only gamma sources were missing raised his suspicion because for an RDD including both alpha and beta emitters, especially if inhaled, would be more effective since monitoring exposure would be much more difficult. This would enhance panic and terror in the population, overloading the public health services.

David Avivi came from a family of scientists who had worked in two of the renowned Israeli government research institutes. His father, who held a doctorate in chemistry, was a senior research scientist at the Israel Institute for Biological Research (IIBR) and was head of the department of analytical chemistry at the institute. David's mother held a PhD in physics and specialized in the development of electro-optical devices at the Soreq Nuclear Research Center (SNRC).

The family lived in Rehovot, a city in which a large community of top-notch scientists and engineers resided in a small tightly linked community. David's childhood in this community was well-suited for a boy with his natural gift for computers, mechanical devices, and mathematics.

As a child he was fascinated by the Sidney Pollack's movie, *Three days on the Condor*, starring Robert Redford and Faye Dunaway. The hero, played by Redford, worked in a clandestine section of the CIA that scanned books, newspapers, and magazine articles looking for new weapons, military tactics, political intrigues, and unconventional ideas. The whole section, except Redford who was out for his lunch break, was murdered and he had to seek refuge while trying to figure out what had happened and who was responsible.

David didn't care too much about the plot of the movie but liked the job description of reading exciting thrillers and suspense stories for a living, and hoped that one day he would have such a job in Mossad, Israel's improved version of the CIA. He sought a challenging and adventurous career in his compulsory military service and finished the tough course in the elite unit of the Israel Defense Force (IDF) as commander of a small squad and as a commissioned officer.

He specialized in all forms of unarmed combat, intelligence gathering, special weapons, and tactics. After his army service, he studied physics and graduated top of his class and then applied for a job with Mossad, seeing it as a step to fulfill his dream.

Mossad recognized his talent and after completing another rigorous training course, David was assigned to a special technical unit that dealt with threats to Israel's security. There, too, he excelled and managed to foil a couple of schemes that could have caused serious damage in Israel.

So, in his late twenties, David had combat experience in

the military, technical and scientific skills, and some knowledge of the way the intelligence community operated. His physical appearance fit the description for the leading actors in the Hollywood films from the 1950s and 1960s—tall, dark, and handsome—so he was sought after by many women who were attracted to his good looks as well as to his intelligence and keen sense of humor. Yet, he felt that the demands of his job did not allow him the luxury of having a family or even engaging in long-term relationships and settled for good sex with no serious commitment.

The Deputy Director thanked the participants and dismissed them, but asked David to stay. He then told David to hand over all his tasks to colleagues from his department and to devote his entire time to pursuing his idea that there may be another rationale for the increase in the number of orphan gamma sources.

He asked David for a preliminary report within two weeks and told him he had free rein if he needed to travel to Vienna or elsewhere. David said he would first like to meet some of the Israeli scientists, particularly those with expertise in health physics and nuclear science and asked the Deputy Director for permission to share the information with them and divulge the problem. Shimony told David he should use his own judgment for that but warned him panic may spread if the information reached the media so he should caution them to be discreet.

David left Tel Aviv and headed north to Haifa to meet with one of his former instructor at the Technion who was a well-known nuclear physicist. Professor Alex Kaufman was happy to see his star student once again, and although he was not told specifically that David now worked for Mossad, he knew how to put two and two together, and guessed that David's visit involved some matter of national security.

David described the problem of the missing gamma sources and asked the professor what possible uses such sources could have with regard to illegal, clandestine activities.

Professor Kaufman deliberated for a while and then switched on his computer and started to scan his e-mail messages looking for something. David suddenly heard the professor saying, "Aha, that is what I thought." He turned to smile at David.

He then told David that two years earlier he had been asked to review a manuscript submitted for publication in Physics Review Letters, a leading journal in physics. In that manuscript a weird scientist from Barcelona University claimed he had managed to produce a fissile material using gamma radiation.

Professor Kaufman said he did not remember the exact details but that still had a copy of the manuscript and said it was rejected unanimously by him and two other reviewers due to an insufficiently detailed description of the experimental conditions. In addition, the whole idea was contrary to all accepted physical principles.

He then searched through his files, found the manuscript but said that as the peer-review process was "blinded," he did not know the name of the author though he could surmise his affiliation from some of the details in the manuscript.

David thanked the professor and felt he had a lead to

an alternative explanation for potential uses of the missing gamma sources.

He then returned to Tel Aviv and booked a flight to Barcelona for the next day.

January 13, Barcelona

David Avivi arrived in Barcelona in the afternoon, rented a car and headed to the university. He had prearranged to meet Professor Gardino, the head of the physics department at Barcelona University after Professor Kaufman had called his colleague there and asked him to meet his ex-student.

David told Professor Gardino he was interested in continuing graduate studies in nuclear physics and particularly wanted to spend some time in the thriving city of Barcelona, thus combining business and pleasure.

Professor Gardino told him that Professor Kaufman had described him as his most brilliant student and there were several scholarships he could apply for.

David said he would first like to meet the faculty members in order to learn about their research activities and find areas of mutual interest.

Professor Gardino agreed that was a good approach and assigned one of the department's post-doctorate fellows, Fillipe, to escort him through the offices and research labs that worked on nuclear physics and related fields.

They walked through the corridors and spoke with the senior staff members. David was impressed by the friendliness of the people with whom he talked—apparently his reputation as a brilliant promising scientist preceded him, probably after a warm introductory phone call from the department head.

Fillipe and David entered all the offices and labs and David was convinced that none of the people he met could be the person he was looking for. They then reached a laboratory that was closed and locked with several signs cautioning against radiation hazards.

David asked Fillipe who worked there and was told the lab had belonged to a staff member, Professor Modena, but was now locked up because the professor had taken an indefinite leave of absence. David enquired about the research interests of the missing scientist and Fillipe said no one in the department really knew what he was doing as he behaved like a true recluse.

He further informed David that all the professor's graduate students had left him, except for Ramona Guerro Vidal who shared an office down the hall with two other graduate students. David asked if he could meet Ramona and hear more about Professor Modena's research interests and Fillipe took him to the office and introduced Ramona and David to each other and then said he had to get back to his work and left them.

Ramona looked at David with suspicion and appeared to be skeptical after hearing his cover story. She was far from being forthcoming but agreed to discuss her own research project in brief and said it involved transmutation induced by radiation.

David asked her which elements she was trying to

transmute and was answered that at this stage she was only doing a literature survey and had not yet selected her target. David smiled at her and told her he was in a similar situation—trying to decide on a subject for a thesis and surveying the field before committing himself to an advisor and a research topic.

As dinner time was approaching, he asked her if she could recommend a restaurant, and on second thought if she would join him as he was alone in the city. Ramona looked at him, liked what she saw, and said she had no plans for the evening and she knew a fine restaurant nearby.

David said he just had to thank Professor Gardino on the way out and they left the university campus together.

Over dinner that consisted of several small plates, with a lot of red wine, at a typical tapas bar, Ramona seemed to thaw a little and their conversation became more personal. David told her he was a bit older than the typical graduate student as he had served four years as a junior officer in an elite unit of the Israeli Defense Forces and started his studies after his military service.

Ramona said that she had grown up in a small village near Girona and her grandparents from both sides were murdered by the Franco regime because they supported the Republic and Catalan right for independence.

However, David's attempts to discuss Professor Modena and his whereabouts failed. Ramona was becoming more interested in David as a young man and less and less willing to talk shop, particularly about Professor Modena.

Naturally, she did not mention the meeting she and the

professor had had with Ollie and certainly refrained from telling David about her own ties with the Catalan separatist movement.

David told Ramona he had to go to his hotel as he had had a very long day and she said she hoped they could meet again.

At this, David said he had to leave Barcelona the next day but hoped he would be back soon for an extended period and they could then resume their relationship.

CHAPTER 6

January 14, Vienna

David left Barcelona after partially accomplishing his mission—he now had a prime suspect involved in the disappearance of the gamma radiation sources, and more importantly, some indication these were to be used in a more dangerous way than in a 'dirty bomb.'

If, indeed, Professor Modena was the culprit, and was intending to pursue his seemingly groundless theory of producing fissile material by irradiating thorium, then the world was facing a very serious problem.

David decided that a discussion with the people at the IAEA in Vienna, who had informed the Israelis about their concerns, would help clarify the issue and was necessary before he returned to the Mossad Deputy Director with his report and conclusions.

That afternoon, Orna Cohen, the security officer of the Israeli delegation to the IAEA, met David at the Wien-Schwechat airport. She had a lovely round face with bright blue eyes and a full figure that reminded David of the statues of fertility goddesses he had seen in museums of ancient arts.

She told him she had arranged a meeting with Eugene

and Vassilly in a small discrete coffee shop after dinner and suggested they go to his hotel to check him in and then have dinner. David was impressed with her efficiency as well as with her vivacious good looks and liked the way she handled the car through the crowded highway into town.

On the way to the hotel he found out she was recently divorced, with no kids, and was bored with her own lack of social life in Vienna. David thought she was very young for the responsibility as security officer but was wise enough to refrain from saying so.

Orna waited in the hotel lobby while he checked in, took his hand luggage to the room, and freshened up. She liked the fact that he did not try to hit on her and invite her to his room while he was getting ready for dinner and the meeting.

They left the hotel and drove to the restaurant located in a central plaza near the meeting venue. Both were famished and ordered a large plate of the traditional Wiener Schnitzel, made from veal, of course, with Sachertorte for dessert.

Once the meal was finished, they walked across the plaza to the café and sat down in a small booth in which Eugene and Vassilly were already having a Vienna lager.

After an introduction was made using first names only, Orna asked for a glass of white wine while David joined the men for beer.

Eugene went through the story of how he had come to suspect that the increase in the number of missing gamma sources was not a coincidence and his report was dismissed by his department head and by the Secretary General himself. He also explained that when he was ordered to stop his investigation, he became slightly paranoid and that was why he contacted the Israeli delegation.

Vassilly then told them that Federal Security Bureau of Russia, was also not very concerned about this, while he personally agreed with Eugene there was more than meets the eye.

David was impressed by their frankness and by the fact that they were willing to take a personal risk to continue with the investigation. He decided to share with them his own suspicions about Professor Modena and his research objectives, particularly of producing fissile materials through gamma irradiation of thorium.

Vassilly and Eugene remained open-mouthed as he finished his story and for a long time did not utter a sound. After recovering from the inferences of the story, Vassilly asked Eugene if he thought that there was a scientific basis for Modena's idea and the scientists remained deep in thought as they pondered the issue.

David told them he did not expect an answer immediately but asked them to discreetly present this as a theoretical question to the nuclear physics experts in their national laboratories, without disclosing their concerns about an actual attempt to carry out the project.

They agreed to meet again the following week to discuss the information they obtained and their findings. Orna was to serve as their contact as they did not want to be overheard talking to a Mossad agent in Israel.

By the time the Eugene and Vassilly parted it was close to midnight but there was so much adrenaline flowing through the veins of Orna and David that they decided to stay a little longer and have a nightcap of schnapps.

This was followed by another couple of shots of schnapps that got them even more wound up. As they were too intoxicated to drive and could not find a taxi, they slowly walked aimlessly through the quiet streets of Vienna. It was very cold but there was no rain or snow, so they huddled closer and continued talking quietly as they strolled along the Danube banks.

Orna said they were very near her apartment and invited David up for a cup of coffee. In Israel, when a woman invites her date to 'come up for a cup of coffee,' it very seldom ends after drinking coffee, if coffee is served at all.

This time was no different, and, as soon as Orna and David shut the apartment's door behind them, they fell into each other's arms and exchanged a long passionate kiss which enhanced David's impression of her as a fertility goddess. Sleep, certainly sleeping alone, was far from their minds and they found themselves in her comfortable bed seeking warmth and security in each other's body.

Orna had not had a close companion since her divorce and David still remembered Ramona's implied invitation from the previous night that he had to decline. Their lovemaking reflected this—both were hungry for human contact so it was over quickly, but after settling down quietly for sleep, they woke up an hour later and very slowly aroused each other until they climaxed almost simultaneously.

In the morning they took a taxi that dropped them off near Orna's car. She drove David to his hotel, where he checked out without using the bed and they headed back to the airport.

David promised Orna he would be back in Vienna to meet with Eugene and Vassilly after they received feedback from their scientists.

January 18, Padova

Professor Modena paced back and forth in the basement adjacent to the gamma irradiation chamber.

He was quite pleased with the current rate of U-233 production but was worried about the quality of the product. The concentration of the bothersome intensely radioactive U-232 was increasing from batch to batch and was now at a level that posed a safety hazard for the crew in charge of separating the uranium product from the feed materials that consisted of a mixture of thorium and beryllium oxides, as well as from the small amount of highly radioactive fission products.

Cynically, he thought, that all the engineers and technicians would become "disposable" once enough fissile material was produced, so he decided not to worry too much about the health and safety of the personnel.

On the other hand, what did concern him was that the high radiation would complicate the construction of the improvised nuclear device. He had, therefore, called Andreas and Ollie for an urgent meeting and was expecting them to arrive at the lab later that afternoon.

He deliberated with himself how to present these problems as he knew their technical and scientific acumen was not sufficient for them to appreciate these fine points. He worried they would blame him and perhaps even try to replace him by some other physicist or, God forbid, by a chemist or an engineer.

**

Andreas and Ollie arrived smiling since they had received regular progress reports and were pleased with the amount of U-233 that had already accumulated but seeing the look on Modena's gaunt face their smiles faded away.

The professor tried to explain the problem in simple terms and realizing that Andreas, in particular, had a hard time understanding, he used a quote attributed to Harold Agnew, familiar mostly to people involved in nuclear terrorism. *If someone thinks making a plutonium implosion weapon is easy, he is wrong, and if someone thinks making an improvised nuclear device using highly enriched uranium is difficult, he is even more wrong.*

He then gave them an overview of the technical problems of making a plutonium implosion weapon and emphasized that using U-233 for that purpose would be even more difficult as there was much less public information available.

The professor explained that though it was possible to produce a primitive "gun type" device, which would be like the U-235-based "Little Boy" the Americans dropped on Hiroshima, this would require a much larger amount of U-233 and constructing a device of this type would delay their project by at least one year.

Ollie understood that getting enough fissile material was

a prerequisite for making the improvised nuclear device and that additional expertise was required to actually build the device.

He told Andreas they needed to convene another meeting of their supporters, particularly from the countries that had nuclear weapons in order to enlist such an expert.

Modena was pleased he managed to convey the message but his apprehension about his own fate grew when he realized they would have no use for him once enough fissile material had accumulated. He feared he would not fare any better than the "disposable" technicians and engineers when they reached that stage and he started planning how to obtain an "insurance policy" against such an event.

January 20, London

Ollie travelled to London to meet with his British and French contacts from the Nationalist movements.

These two were selected by him as in each of those countries there was a thriving nuclear industry as well as established laboratories in which nuclear weapons were produced.

They met in a small hotel on Cartwright Gardens close to the St. Pancras railway station where the Eurostar cross-channel train from Paris arrives.

Instead of the thick-necked ruffian, the delegate from the British National Socialist Party, Paul Dooley, was an aristocratic gentleman, a graduate of Trinity College in Cambridge, with a law degree. The French counterpart, Ettiene Brune, was from Marseille, a stronghold of extreme racists, and an engineer by training.

Ollie described the progress in production of the fissile material and explained that they now had to manufacture the actual nuclear device, and this called for expertise Professor Modena did not possess.

He asked them to help in enlisting a suitable engineer or scientist from one of their national weapon labs—someone who was willing and able to work clandestinely in support of their cause. He emphasized there would be no moral qualms or issues because the device would not be detonated but only used for blackmailing the governments that gave in to immigrants while forfeiting the rights and welfare of the true citizens.

Brune was skeptical if such a person could be found but Dooley said that he had someone in mind who might be persuaded to join them, and he would set up a meeting with him and Ollie at noon the next day.

The Frenchman had nothing further to contribute to the project so booked a return journey to Paris by the Eurostar and continued on the TGV train to Marseille.

The Briton returned to his office in the City of London, and Ollie went to an excellent Italian restaurant in nearby Bloomsbury for dinner on his own.

The next day Ollie met with Dooley and his friend in a private room inside a pub near Dooley's office in the City. Dooley was welcomed by the pub owner and they exchanged a secret signal that did not escape Ollie's eye.

Without consulting his table guests, Dooley told the pub owner to bring his regular lunch for the three of them and a jug of pale ale. The private room was lined with fine wooden walls and Union Jack flags and British National Socialist Party (BNSP) blood flags. When he saw the reaction of awe and reverence of Dooley's friend, Ollie's mind was set at ease, since he realized the man was a dedicated fanatic member of the BNSP and would probably not have qualms performing the task at hand.

Dooley introduced his friend only as Doctor Jay and commended his knowledge and experience in designing and manufacturing what he termed "special devices."

It seemed to Ollie as if Dooley was afraid of surveillance at this known meeting place of BNSP supporters and quietly wondered why Dooley had chosen to meet there.

Dooley quietly whispered that MI6 suspected him of illegal activities and occasionally followed him, so he preferred to meet right under their eyes and not to try evasive actions that would alert them he was up to some mischief.

Ollie understood the rationale but did not like it and suggested they just enjoy lunch and then he could meet with Doctor Jay privately somewhere else without fear of being followed by Paul Dooley's "babysitters."

After having their lunch and talking about sports, films, and politics, Doctor Jay and Ollie left the private room in the pub and went to a crowded café and sat at a corner table.

The background noise was at a high level so they could speak quietly without fear of being overheard. Ollie asked Jay about his background and learned he had earned a doctorate in physics, *summa cum laude,* from University of Manchester Institute of Science and Technology (UMIST), and had worked for several years at the very center of British nuclear weapons production in the Aldermaston Atomic Weapons Establishment (AWE) near Reading.

However, he had recently been fired for abusing a co-worker who happened to be a British-born chemist of Pakistani descent. Jay expressed to Ollie his hatred for Muslims, blaming the government for allowing "fifth columnists" to penetrate the most sensitive center for development of nuclear weapons. He explained that after publicly stating the Pakistani scientist would probably steal atomic secrets like A Q Khan had done, he was reported to the authorities. He was ordered to leave the building immediately, and informed he was to be fired without compensation, and lucky to escape charges.

Jay said he was willing to do anything to speed up the process of expelling all foreigners from England and said he did not care if they went to Scotland or swam into the North Sea as long as they left his country.

Ollie asked him if he could lead a small team in production of a nuclear device based on U-233 and Jay said he believed there were few differences between that and the plutonium-based weapons he had manufactured. Furthermore, he said, he was privy to the most advanced designs that had not even been tested but were accepted as the latest word in nuclear weaponry.

Ollie did not like the idea of untested designs, but Doctor Jay claimed the new designs were tested computationally and completely foolproof and their manufacture was simpler than the older models.

Ollie insisted they did not have the means to produce anything except the simplest device and Jay said he had no problem with that approach. Jay said Dooley had roughly outlined the project and he was willing to travel abroad as nothing now tied him to the UK, especially after his wife left him and he no longer lived with his boyfriend who was the main reason his wife divorced him.

Ollie said he didn't care if Jay liked women, men, or both and told him to prepare to leave for Italy two days later and they arranged to meet at Heathrow airport for the direct flight to Venice Marco Polo airport, a short drive from Padova.

January 23, Padova

Ollie and Doctor Jay left their hotel without even having breakfast and went straight to the warehouse in which the secret laboratory was located.

Professor Modena was initially a bit reluctant to share his knowledge and concerns with Doctor Jay, but Ollie convinced him that their jobs complemented each other, and Jay was not about to replace him or take over the production and separation of the U-233.

In order to restrict the number of people who knew the true purpose of the Astraea project, they were not to exchange ideas or discuss the project in front of the other people. The only exception was one of the older technicians from the production facility that would work with Jay on the fabrication of the device.

Doctor Jay was asked to prepare a list of the equipment

and materials he needed for the device and hand it to Ollie personally in the evening. Ollie was pleased to see Jay and Modena have a professional discussion of the modifications needed for use of U-233 as the fissile material for the device.

When he realized he was being virtually ignored because the two scientists were already arguing about this very issue, he bid them farewell after arranging to meet them for dinner.

Doctor Jay told the professor they should adopt the classic, well understood, and tested design for their improvised nuclear device since they would not be able to conduct any actual trials. He said the most foolproof design was based on a solid core of the fissile material, U-233, that would be transformed from a subcritical configuration to a supercritical one by the tremendous pressure of the implosion of a few hundred pounds of conventional high explosives.

Professor Modena asked him if he meant to deploy the "Christy gadget" configuration and Doctor Jay answered that although more fissile material was required than in other more advanced configurations such as the hollow sphere model, it was more reliable and easier to manufacture even with the primitive machining equipment they had in the lab.

He also explained that with this simple configuration the implosion could be triggered by simultaneous detonation of high explosives from thirty-two points arranged evenly around the sphere.

Ollie felt he needed to clear his head and strolled through the famous Botanical Gardens in search of the renowned Goethe's palm tree he hoped would give him inspiration as it had to Goethe when he wrote about plant metamorphosis.

He had seen many palm trees growing naturally outdoors in Syria and Iraq, where they were very common and served as an important source of food, so he was disappointed to see the tree was situated in a greenhouse inside the *Ortus Spheari-cus* and not out in the open as he had expected. Nevertheless, he was thankful for the serenity the garden induced.

He hoped the combination of the racist Doctor Jay and the Catalan independence supporter Professor Modena would not lead to political altercations, but there was little he could do trying to re-educate these two grown men with huge egos.

Later that evening they reconvened for a meal. The proprietor of the restaurant was glad to have three tourists dining on a quiet Thursday evening in mid-winter, especially as they ordered two bottles of his most expensive wine.

Doctor Jay gave Ollie his shopping list and the three of them talked quietly about it. Ollie glanced at the list and stated there were only two items that would be difficult to purchase: the special explosives and the thirty-two detonators needed for simultaneously timing the implosion. He realized those would only be needed at the very final stage of the construction of the device but was very worried about their acquisition.

Doctor Jay said that almost anything could be bought for the proper price on the nuclear black market or in China.

Ollie noted that since the network of the Pakistani A Q Khan had been practically closed down and the Chinese were extremely careful about exporting items of this type, the best option was to discreetly approach the North Koreans. He hoped they wouldn't refuse an offer of a large sum of hard currency with which they could buy food for the masses, or what was more likely, increase the foreign bank accounts of the country's elite leaders.

The scientists had no idea how to contact the North Koreans so Ollie said he would be responsible for obtaining these materials, while the lab's administrator could take care of acquiring all the other items, including those that were considered as "dual-use" and their sales were somewhat restricted.

Jay and Ollie returned to their hotel and Modena to his small room above the laboratory. Arrangements were made for Doctor Jay to move to the dormitory above the laboratory as a long stay at the hotel would raise suspicion.

January 24, Vienna

David arrived at Vienna airport on the evening flight and once again Orna met him at the airport and they exchanged a short hug and warm, welcome kiss and immediately headed to the same café where Eugene and Vassilly were already waiting.

Both had grim looks on their faces and appeared to be deep in thought so they barely acknowledged the presence of the two young Israelis. Eugene started speaking excitedly even before Orna and David were seated and summarized the insights he had gained during his discussions with the scientists from the national laboratories.

He had asked them if theoretically it was possible to produce U-233 through bombardment of thorium with gamma radiation. Their unanimous spontaneous reply was that it was not possible but after giving the matter some thought they said, in theory, if the gamma radiation could somehow induce generation of neutrons they may be captured by thorium atoms and produce uranium-233.

They were skeptical if this would be practical because of several physical considerations including the efficiency of neutron generation by this method, the energy of these neutrons, and the uncertainty in the capture cross-section of these neutrons by thorium. In conclusion, the scientists did not rule out the possibility this could be done and also raised a question about the availability of suitable gamma radiation sources.

Vassilly said the Russian scientists with whom he consulted agreed with these observations and conclusions. He also stated that one of the experts he had talked to, took him aside during a tea break and in confidence told him he had been one of the reviewers of the manuscript submitted to the journal—he did not know it was written by Professor Modena—and was familiar with the idea. He said that at the time he thought the whole scheme was in contradiction of basic physical principles and ridiculed the idea, recommending rejection of the manuscript on those grounds, but he now had second thoughts it may not be impossible to generate neutrons using gamma irradiation of thorium.

Eugene then said he had obtained access to declassified files from the Manhattan Project that described the efforts of the U.S. Atomic Energy Commission to produce and test uranium-233 as the "fuel," or fissile material, in a fission atomic bomb.

He said the theoretical idea of producing U-233 from thorium in a nuclear pile—as a nuclear reactor was then called—was first proposed as early as May 1943, but not seriously investigated until after the war.

By 1950, about one pound of U-233 were produced at the Hanford reactors in Washington State and separated from thorium at Oak Ridge, Tennessee, by a chemical process called Thorex that he said was quite similar to the well-known Purex process used to separate plutonium from irradiated uranium fuel.

After a long debate within the U.S.-AEC, an actual test of a bomb core consisting of a mixture of plutonium and U-233 was carried out only in 1955, as part of the TEAPOT Operation and the explosion had a yield approximating the atomic bomb dropped on Nagasaki.

However, by the late 1950s, the U.S. increased the production of plutonium and enriched uranium sharply curtailing the requirement for U-233, though a few more tests were carried out until completely abandoned in 1968.

Vassily smiled when he heard this detailed account and proudly stated that the Soviet Union had tested a primary core containing a blend of U-233 and U-235 even before the 1955 U.S. test.

When David asked them if configuration of a bomb based on U-233 was more complicated than using the more standard U-235 or plutonium, both scientists agreed there were some differences but, on the whole, the technical details were the same.

David was not surprised by these reports as he had already

discussed this again with Professor Kaufman and with experts from the Israeli Atomic Energy Commission.

He felt it was time for the three of them to jointly write a memo and to inform their respective governments about the potential of terrorist groups clandestinely producing fissile materials that could be used in an improvised nuclear device.

He suggested this should not be restricted to their three countries but that the information should also be passed on to the United Kingdom and France. He also proposed they set up a task force to locate Professor Modena and his whereabouts as well as find out where all the radiation sources were shipped to and if there was a clandestine laboratory in which work for producing U-233 was being carried out.

Eugene expressed his concern that if the IAEA got word of this, it would disclose the plot and the source of information thus driving the perpetrators into deep cover.

They deliberated whether Spain should be included in the loop as Professor Modena was officially a Spanish citizen but were afraid he would be warned by some sympathizer of Catalonia in the Spanish establishment.

Vassilly was not too happy about informing the UK and France but accepted the proposal to include them in the task force.

The participants knew they could not make these decisions without approval from their governments as they were not high enough on the totem pole. However, they were all aware of the historic precedent set by the letter sent by Albert Einstein and Leo Szilard to president Franklin Delano Roosevelt on August 2, 1939, which eventually set in motion the

Manhattan Project that produced the first atomic bombs.

They could only hope their memo would produce similar results. In their memo they tried to explain the difference between an improvised nuclear device (IND) and a radiological dispersive device (RDD) in a simple language that would be understood, even by politicians.

They explained that the IND is usually made clandestinely by non-government organizations for the sake of producing a nuclear explosion that can cause instant death and damage by radiation, burns, heat, and blast overpressure within a radius of several hundred meters, or more, depending on the size, or yield, of the explosion.

In addition, radioactive fallout would lead to many more casualties that would suffer from radiation sickness and may develop cancer which will cause further deaths and disabilities over a period of a few decades.

The two atomic bombs that were dropped on Hiroshima and Nagasaki at the end of World War II had demonstrated the lethality, even of crude nuclear weapons.

Compared to the effects of an IND, the RDD is not much more than a terrorist weapon that can cause mass disruption rather than mass destruction. In RDD a standard explosive is used to disseminate radioactive materials, usually over quite a small area.

The immediate effects due to the conventional explosives are no worse than that of a regular terrorist bomb, but the psychological effects may be disproportionally larger, as panic is sure to spread among the public. In addition, decontamination of property may be prohibitively costly, especially if the RDD is detonated in a high value commercial area.

In the memo, they also pointed out that any government that suffered from the effects of an IND or even an RDD would have to react against the perpetrators and do so rapidly to appease its citizens. An instant response, based on preliminary evidence, might be directed against the wrong culprit and invoke an unbalanced rejoinder which could further escalate to an all-out confrontation.

The participants believed that this terse memo would serve as a wake-up call for their governments and agreed to meet again in Vienna two weeks later, hopefully as members of a formally sanctioned task force, with the full support from their respective governments.

David and Orna returned to her apartment—this time David had not even bothered about booking a hotel in Vienna as he knew he had a much better arrangement for the night in Orna's bed. Although they yearned for each other, their lovemaking was performed as a purely physical exercise for relaxation as both had other things on their minds. They both felt they were getting closer and their relationship was well beyond a one-night, or two-night, affair.

CHAPTER 7

January 25, Tel Aviv

David set up an urgent meeting with the Deputy Director at Mossad headquarters.

Present at the meeting were several senior people including the heads of the intelligence gathering division and the operations division. David summarized his findings and concluded by saying he thought an international task force should be formed with the objective of locating Professor Modena and the clandestine laboratory, if it existed.

The division heads were not pleased with the fact that David's actions had exceeded his authority and criticized him for taking unauthorized steps without consulting them.

However, Shimony came to his aid and told them that David had acted with his authorization and they should all be grateful for his insight and should now focus on solving the problems facing them.

The mild rebuke did not placate the division heads, but they knew for the sake of the country they should forget their ego and turf wars and join forces.

The head of the intelligence division said they needed to find out what the intended target of the improvised nuclear device would be and whether it concerned Israel.

David pointed out that in order to do that they had to first locate Modena and the people, or organizations, that supported his project and knew its objective.

The Deputy Director asked if any of the participants had any information regarding the acquisition or construction of unconventional weapons intended for use in major terrorist operations. The only concern raised about this was the capture of Syrian army camps in which chemical weapons were stored by the rebels including Islamic State forces. None of them had heard anything, even rumors, about the existence of an improvised nuclear device or a radiation dispersion device in Syria.

Shimony summarized the meeting by saying he would present the problem to the Mossad chief and to the Prime Minister and ask for their support for the international task force (ITF). He continued by saying he believed Mossad should create its own team and not solely rely on the ITF, because its operation might be hindered by political considerations. He assigned David to be Israel's representative in the ITF and Gabi Golan from the operations section to head the independent Israeli team.

February 22, Stockholm

Ollie was more and more concerned his finely constructed plot would be exposed.

He had two major problems to worry about. First that the laboratory in Padova would be discovered and closed down by the local authorities or by agents of Western countries, and second, that Andreas and his colleagues would find out that his real target was not to promote the Nationalist and separatist causes but to strike at the heart of Western society and Judeo-Christian civilization in the name of Islam. In either case, his plan would fail and be terminated.

He wondered if there was a way to expedite the construction of the device and decided to visit the clandestine laboratory in Padova and see whether Doctor Jay was making headway.

He was aware the special explosives and timing mechanism were on their way from North Korea, disguised as heavy agricultural machinery originating from South Korea. They were due to arrive at the port of Venice the following week.

Using the connections with Swiss bankers with a Eurocentric hatred of foreigners provided by Andreas and his Swedish movement, a senior North Korean, Kong Kwak Kim—called by his Swiss bankers simply KKK—with a large account in Zurich was contacted and made an offer he could not refuse of several million dollars for a few hundred pounds of explosives and a handful of precisely timed fast detonators.

KKK even suggested that for a substantial additional fee the explosives could be configured to any shape and size according to blueprints that would be supplied by the anonymous client. The blueprints of Doctor Jay's design were then delivered to KKK, who was glad to receive the additional information and extra money.

The North Korean quickly understood these were to be used in an improvised nuclear device and that only increased his motivation as he expected it to be exploded in a Western European city. He almost suggested he would halve the price or that he would supply them with double the amount they requested but was afraid this would show he understood the objective, which may put him at risk.

KKK was not a simple greedy North Korean but was, in fact, a senior operative of the Ministry of State Security—MSS—the primary counterintelligence service in North Korea reporting directly to the First Chairman or Supreme Commander, to mention just two of the titles of the Leader of North Korea. KKK, who valued his life and his family's welfare more than the commendable sum of money he was offered by Andreas's associates, reported the tender that had been made and was directed by his supervisors to proceed with the deal.

In fact, he was told the explosives and detonators were supplied from the stocks held by the North Korea Nuclear Program and was also assured the merchandise was perfectly suitable for its intended use.

CHAPTER 8

March 1, Padova

One of the drivers brought the shipping container marked "agriculture machinery" to the clandestine laboratory. Ollie helped Doctor Jay and Professor Modena supervise the downloading of the packages and together they moved them into the closed street level parking garage above the laboratory.

With great care they unpacked the shipment, removed the boxes of shaped explosives, the detonators, and carried them downstairs to the chamber where Doctor Jay had started making preparations for the construction of the improvised nuclear device.

He placed the detonators inside a metal cabinet that had been grounded in order to prevent the build-up of static electricity that might cause the detonation of these sensitive devices. The storage area also had temperature and humidity control.

After seven months of operation, close to twenty pounds of purified metallic U-233 had been produced, with approximately three more pounds currently being processed for extraction, purification, and separation.

This was below the goal of one pound a week but was a

pretty good achievement considering the fact they had some start-up problems and worked only in two shifts until the reinforcement from Greece arrived in mid-January. In addition, they had to wait several weeks for the build-up of the Uranium-233 from decay of the Protactinium-233.

Ollie convened the two scientists and asked them once again about the minimal amount of the fissile material required to ensure a successful nuclear detonation. He emphasized that a fizzle, or partial detonation, was unacceptable. Furthermore, he said that in order to demonstrate how serious they were with their blackmail threats, they would have to provide blueprints of the design and a sample of the fissile material.

The scientists pointed out that in this case they did not really have to construct the complete device as they could already show the design blueprints and supply a sample of U-233.

Ollie could not tell them he needed a real operational device for his true objective, so he explained they needed the real thing since the plan included bringing a representative of the government blindfolded to a secret location where he would verify the device existed and was operational.

Ollie then contacted Andreas and brought him up to date on the situation and said they urgently needed more funds as the deal with the North Korean official had completely exhausted their monetary reserves. He suggested they reconvene all their European supporters and raise more contributions, promising them that construction of the device was on schedule and delivery was due in the summer.

He further proposed this time they only summon the

representatives of the movements fervently dedicated to the cause with the ability to contribute significant funding. Ollie emphasized the urgency of the meeting and proposed they meet again in Umea, Sweden.

March 4, Umea, Sweden

Once again, the handpicked guests made their way to the small bed-and-breakfast place in Bjurholm, an hour's drive from Umea airport.

After dinner they all gathered by the fireplace and Ollie gave a concise presentation, in which he described the progress of the project, once again without disclosing the exact location of the laboratory.

He discussed the timeline and the expenditures and told them that more funding was crucial for the rapid conclusion of the project since the chances of exposure increased with every passing day.

The delegates applauded and congratulated Ollie and Andreas on a job well done and said they should now start planning the order in which their respective governments would be notified of the nuclear device and blackmailed into passing laws for 'cleansing' their countries of 'unwanted foreign elements of inferior races.'

The delegates from the separation movements did not like this blatantly racist phrase and proposed something more moderate and ambiguous like 'achievement of the declared goals of all the movements.'

Ollie could not be bothered with this semantic nitpicking

as his own objective was completely different and he let Andreas chair the discussion while he himself tuned-out and thought about his own logistical problems.

The heated debate came to an end without an agreement, but they all realized they were fighting about, *dividing the bear's skin before she was taken*, to quote a old Irish proverb.

Then, with untypical consensus for such an opinionated gathering, they agreed this discussion could wait a few months until the device was almost ready for deployment.

As for contributing more funds, they were all enthusiastic and agreed to double their contribution in order to expedite the production of the device.

The next day they returned to their home countries and Ollie and Andreas headed back to Stockholm.

March 5, Vienna

The first meeting of the international task force (ITF) with delegates from the U.S., Russia, the UK, and France was chaired by David Avivi.

The British representative, Colin Thomas, a senior member from MI6, said they had a strong suspicion a disgruntled former employee of the Aldermaston Atomic Weapon Establishment had disappeared from his home in London about six weeks earlier.

He announced that Doctor Jason Smalley was fired from his job because of racist comments and unacceptable behavior toward his dark-skinned colleagues of Muslim origin. He was also known as an avid supporter of the British National

Socialist Party's cause and contributed funds to them for which he tried to claim tax deductions.

Furthermore, he said that Doctor Smalley was a physicist with experience in the design and construction of nuclear devices and advanced warheads. David saw this as a highly relevant piece of information and asked if there was any evidence Doctor Smalley may have left the UK but Thomas said it was practically impossible to track travel within the European Union.

David asked if they could trace Doctor Smalley's credit card transactions and Thomas said this had been done and the last known transaction was in January, shortly after he was fired from his job. Doctor Smalley withdrew a large amount in cash—thirty-two hundred pounds and five thousand Euros.

The only other irregular use of the credit card was one day earlier on January 20, in a small café in the City of London, quite a way from his residence in Reading.

MI6 followed up on this and showed his photo around to the café's staff.

The owner did not remember anything and suggested they show the photo to the waitresses that served customers. Surprisingly, one waitress saw the photo and told them she remembered Doctor Smalley only because she noticed the handsome blond man who was with him.

When asked to describe the other man she said he had a typically Scandinavian look with blue eyes and blond hair but had a deep tan that looked a bit strange to her for mid-winter in London. She also noted that when he gave his order, he had a slight foreign accent.

Thomas had then asked her to come over to construct a picture of him with the help of a police artist and showed them the image she had constructed.

He said that running the image on Interpol's database produced no certain hits but there were several dozen people who resembled the image. The list was too long, so it was impractical to try and locate each one, even after eliminating those who were known to be presently serving time in jail.

The other delegates had no useful information that would help locate the clandestine laboratory if it existed. David then asked the American and Russian delegates if they could provide some physical and engineering data on a possible design of a nuclear device based on uranium 233. They refused to provide classified information for reasons of 'national security' but referred the participants to Professor Google, a nickname given to the know-all internet website.

According to Doctor Wikipedia, it was believed the U.S. produced over two tons of U-233 at Hanford and Savannah River at a price estimated as two to four million U.S. dollars per pound and there was scant public information about its potential use in a nuclear weapon.

The same source noted the presence of uranium-232 complicates its use in nuclear devices as well as posing a health hazard, so that very high purity, freshly produced U-233 is needed for a construction of a nuclear device.

They also estimated that producing thirty pounds of U-233 would cost sixty to one hundred twenty million U.S. dollars according to the estimate given above. However, if indeed Professor Modena developed a different process for

producing U-233 then these cost estimates might be irrelevant and there was no data regarding the level of U-232 in
such a process.

David then brought forth the problem that had been on his
mind ever since he revealed that Professor Modena was missing and was probably trying to produce U-233 on a larger
scale than in his laboratory experiments.

He asked the delegates representing the four countries that
were the first to produce atomic weapons if they thought their
governments would support a crash program for testing the
feasibility of Modena's idea. He then looked at the delegates
but all avoided eye-contact.

David, who knew a thing or two about human behavior
despite his young age, suddenly recognized the fact that these
people were first and foremost patriots of their own countries
and that the ITF was only their secondary commitment. He
smiled and said, "Okay. Don't go into specifics but tell me
what your scientists think about the feasibility."

The U.S. delegate responded, "They do not rule out that
the process may be feasible but have doubts about its efficiency and production rate."

David asked what the production rate would be if all
missing gamma sources that 'disappeared' between last May
and August were used in the clandestine laboratory and the
Russian delegate said grudgingly that his scientists estimated
it would be between three to six pounds a month. David did
a quick mental calculation that in the time since Modena's
disappearance in July and the present time they could already
have enough for a critical mass with the higher estimate and

not far from it even with the lower estimate.

David did not take into account the cooling period of three months before the first batch of irradiated thorium would be ready for extraction of U-233 because he assumed a 'worst case scenario.'

David summarized the meeting by emphasizing the need to locate the whereabouts of Professor Modena and Doctor Smalley as this would be the key to finding the laboratory and eliminating the production of fissile materials that could serve for making an improvised nuclear device.

He suggested approaching the Spanish authorities and requesting their help in finding Modena and the northern European countries for tracing the origin of the mysterious blond man as he probably came from one of those countries. He also called for more help from Interpol in an attempt to reduce the number of suspects.

Finally, he set a meeting in ten days' time. The others did not respond immediately, saying they would need to consult with their governments.

Over a meal that Orna cooked for them in her apartment, David shared the new information from the meeting and asked her to continue to be his local contact with the task force.

They enjoyed a couple bottles of good Israeli wine he had purchased at the Duty-Free store at Ben-Gurion airport in Tel Aviv and then went to bed.

Orna slowly undressed David and told him to close his eyes and lie still on the bed with his hands behind his head while she tended to his stress and worries.

March 5, Tel Aviv

The Israeli task force also met on the same day.

Gabi Golan, who coordinated the small team of Israeli Mossad agents, asked them to present their findings and conclusions. All the agents noted there seemed to be a strong buzz in the Nationalistic racially prejudiced movements that something big was about to happen, but details were not available.

The political leaders of these movements appeared to be more confident and vociferous than usual, making promises there would be a great change and support for their nationalist causes would grow immensely.

The rank and file of these movements increased their provocative acts against Muslims and Jews and the streets were becoming more and more unsafe for the immigrants. Even tourists were frequently harassed if they could not speak the language like the locals.

Gabi thought this may relate to the information David provided about the possibility of the manufacture of a nuclear device or a 'dirty bomb.' There were more reports on attacks of synagogues by racists that also painted swastikas on windows of Jewish-owned businesses.

The Mossad agents could not find any connection between these activities and Israel but feared that the increased xenophobia and the rise in anti-Semitic incidents may endanger the local Jews.

The next day, David returned to Israel and met with Gabi and the Deputy Director. Both agents updated Shimony and each other on their findings.

Shimony introduced them to Gideon who was a representative of the Israeli Security Agency (ISA) also known by its Hebrew acronym as Shin Bet.

Gideon said there was no change in the noticeable level of terrorist activities in Israel, except for the Jerusalem area in which incidents involving Palestinians were on the rise. For example, he mentioned confrontations where Palestinians tried to drive their cars into groups of Israelis on the sidewalks, cases where young Palestinian men and women drew knives or even screwdrivers and tried to stab soldiers or Jewish civilians and the rising number of stone-throwing incidents by Arab youth targeting private cars and public transportation.

He noted that this appeared to the result of local initiatives in response to the prevailing feeling of hopelessness in the Arab community rather than an organized effort by a central command. The ISA knew of no rumors of something big that was about to happen.

March 15, Vienna

The ITF met again in Vienna. All the delegates had been very busy working on the items discussed in their last meeting.

The U.S. delegate, Doctor Eugene Powers, informed the meeting, emphasizing it was off the record, that the scientists at the Los Alamos National Laboratory had managed to produce trace amounts of U-233 through gamma radiation and that meticulous isotopic analysis showed the level of U-232 was around fifty parts-per-million.

He said this was significant as it ruled out the possibility of making a simple "gun type" device like the one used with enriched U-235 to bomb Hiroshima in 1945, and a more complex implosion type device was needed. He added that in any case a "gun type" device would require much more fissile material than the implosion type apparatus.

He also said the opinion of the scientists was that this would be an almost insurmountable task for amateurs but if an experienced person was put in charge, and detailed blue-prints were available, it could be possible.

The Russian delegate, Doctor Vassilly Nomenkov, said their experts had recalculated the critical mass and believed that even twenty-five pounds might be sufficient but a device with that amount of fissile material had a fifty percent chance of a fizzle unless experimentally-tested designs were available, further supporting the assessment of the U.S. scientists.

The French delegate, Doctor Nicolas Berrard, reported that the French nuclear organization had no experience with U-233 and nothing to add to the scientific estimates. He mentioned that the unrest in the streets of all the major cities in France, especially those with a considerable immigrant population, was at a very high level and street riots were erupting in some mixed neighborhoods.

Thomas, the British delegate, said they were investigating Doctor Smalley's connections with known BNSP activists, focusing on those that had business in the City. They had managed to find out that Paul Dooley was one of the people lending a respectable and legitimate front to the BNSP.

Dooley had been under MI6 surveillance for quite a while and they had even managed to install a microphone in the private room of his favorite pub where he often held meetings pertaining to the Party activities. They checked specifically the recordings just before January 20 and found that Dooley met with two unknown people that day.

No suspicious conversation was recorded but it was noted that one of the people had a foreign accent and appeared to be the 'guest of honor' as Dooley deferred to him.

In the recording, the listener heard that the two guests arranged to go elsewhere for coffee after lunch and this was a bit odd as the pub was known to serve very good coffee. In addition, the pub in question was just a block away from the café where Doctor Smalley and the blond guest were recognized by the waitress.

All this established a probable link between Dooley, Doctor Smalley, and the mysterious blond man. Thomas said they could not summon Paul Dooley for questioning without plausible cause, but they could try to get a court order issued to continue the surveillance and add permission to monitor his landline telephone, mobile phones, and e-mails.

David told them that Mossad had noted the rise in race related crimes not just in France, as outlined by the French delegate, but all over Europe. He also mentioned that the political leaders of the nationalist parties seemed invigorated as if they were expecting some very good news soon. He reported the news received from the Spanish authorities regarding Professor Modena that marked him as an activist in the Catalan separatist movement but had no idea where he went after leaving Barcelona the previous July.

David said he had visited Modena's closed laboratory in Barcelona University without discovering his whereabouts and said he felt it was time to pay Barcelona another visit and try to locate Modena through his friends and connections.

The information received from the northern European security and police agencies concerning the blond man were inconclusive as there were literally millions of men that fit the general description and the image constructed based on the waitress's testimony.

The Greek police responded there were rumors the Golden Dawn was up to something big, but no definite plans were revealed.

The meeting adjourned with an increasing sense of frustration they could not identify the threat they knew was lurking below the seemingly tranquil surface.

The one dramatic step they considered, but refrained from implementing, was to publish the photos of Professor Modena, Doctor Smalley, and the blond man on all TV networks and national newspapers, as well as the major internet networks. If such an approach were to be adopted the request would say these people were suspected of some heinous crime, such as white slavery or distribution of laced drugs that caused the death of several addicts and request the public's help in tracing them.

They knew the risk involved—it would show their hand and warn the suspects to go underground—and, therefore, they decided to use this appeal to the public only as a last resort.

They set the deadline for the decision for May 1, as they estimated that by then a critical amount of U-233 could be produced.

March 18, Barcelona

David returned to Barcelona University and tried to find Ramona in her office at the physics department only to discover she had not been seen in the university recently.

He then found Fillipe, the post-doctoral fellow that had shown him around when he visited the university in January, under the pretense of looking for an advisor for a graduate study. He told Fillipe he had to abandon those plans because of a family crisis and asked him about Ramona saying he had to see her again about a personal matter.

Fillipe believed that David had been charmed by Ramona, as had several other men, and told him she had a studio apartment on Carrer d'Arago close to the famous Casa Mila.

He gave David the address but said she could be abroad as she hadn't shown up at the department since the beginning of the month.

David thanked him and headed toward the address he was given. It turned out to be a nice building near the corner of Carrer del Bruc but the entrance door to the stairwell was locked.

David sat in café on the corner, ordered a beer, and watched the building. After a while he saw an old lady leaving the building with a shopping bag in her hand. He quickly rose from the table and managed to grab the entrance door before it closed. The old lady looked at him suspiciously but did not challenge him as she knew that several apartments in the building were rented on a temporary basis to tourists and believed he had forgotten his key.

David thanked her with a smile and entered the building. He quietly climbed the eighty-eight stairs up to the fourth floor and found the apartment number Fillipe had given him. He waited outside for a moment listening for any sounds and when he heard some chatter from a TV or radio in the apartment, he knocked gently on the door.

A woman's voice enquired who was at the door in Spanish and he answered in English he was David and had to see Ramona. The door opened immediately, and he was welcomed with a shy smile. She didn't ask how he had found her and invited him to join her for tea. She said she had been down with the flu and subsequently absent from university but was now almost fully recovered.

David sat down and told her he had returned to Barcelona for a vacation and had hoped to see her again. Her smile broadened and she said they should finish their tea and then go out for an aperitif before dining out. She suggested they go to the sport's bar a block away for a drink and then dine at the Hungarian restaurant on the same block before turning in for the night at her apartment.

David was taken by her forwardness and thought all the strategies he had prepared to enchant her were no longer needed.

Both were laughing as they returned to her apartment building after consuming a couple bottles of good Rioja red wine with their excellent Hungarian goulash meal. They climbed the stairs making quite a racket, earning complaints from the neighbors but were too laden with expectations about the night to worry about that.

As they entered the apartment, Ramona turned to David and told him she had hoped for his return and was disappointed it had taken him two months to do so.

David held her close and said he was sorry that his plans for spending a few years at Barcelona University had not worked out and he had wanted to return to Barcelona sooner.

They headed for the bedroom and Ramona came near him. They hugged and kissed deeply for a long moment. She told David to take off his shoes and socks and then kicked off her own shoes. Next, she shyly unbuckled David's belt and removed his pants looking very closely at his now fully erect manhood and started laughing.

David was so surprised at her reaction that he quickly covered himself with his cupped hands while his manhood began shrinking.

Her laughter grew so much louder that David started worrying the neighbors would start banging on the walls.

Ramona realized how embarrassed he was and barely managed to control her laughter as she pointed at him and said she had never seen a circumcised penis before, and the sight amused her.

David looked down at himself, saw nothing particularly strange and said it worked just like any other organ and she was welcome to compare.

At this, she pulled him to bed and said she would be the

judge of that.

For David, the experience with Ramona was passionate as she had no inhibitions and was willing to try anything to fulfill his fantasies.

While lovemaking with Orna in Vienna could be compared to an autumn day in Vivaldi's Four Seasons—tranquil, quiet, and cuddly—Ramona was full of dramatic twists like Stravinsky's Rite of Spring. Then another comparison popped up in David's mind: making love with Orna was like travelling downstream on a barge slowly floating with the gentle flow of the river while sex with Ramona felt like an Olympic kayaker negotiating the rapids without knowing which direction he would be tossed the next moment.

When they were done and exhausted, and trying to catch their breath, David asked her if she could now deliver her judgment. Ramona pondered the question for a few moments and said she would need another sample and rolled over to closely examine the member in question, turning it fondly in her hand and tasting it until it transformed in size and texture and ready for action.

This time David was more patient and willing to play along with her fantasies pretending to be a lecherous stranger robbing the innocence of a pure Catholic maiden.

Ramona barely suppressed her screams of joy and finally collapsed on his chest and with a large smile said he was wrong—for her it worked better than any organ she had encountered before, especially with older men.

David seized the opening and asked her if Professor Modena was one of those men, but she evaded the question by saying it was irrelevant as he was now in Padova. She then realized that she had let this piece of information slip and tried to cover this up by starting to stroke him again.

David was so pleased with the lead to the whereabouts of Modena he pretended not to notice anything and willingly played along with Ramona. This time they were both already fully satiated and did their best to pleasure each other gently before falling asleep with their limbs entwined.

March 21, Tel Aviv

David gave his report to the Deputy Director and Gabi, head of the Mossad team in charge of following up on the gamma sources and potential improvised nuclear device. They now had a substantial lead and discussed the strategic options for tracking Modena in Padova.

Working in a foreign country, even a friendly one like Italy, always involved risks for Mossad agents, as they had learned the hard way time and again in operations that were exposed in Norway, Switzerland, Cyprus, and New Zealand to mention a few examples.

They debated the pros and cons of updating the international task force in Vienna about this and discussed sharing the information with the Italian government. Shimony said that due to the potential risk of an international scandal the decision would have to be made by the Prime Minister and he would update the director of Mossad and request a private audience with the PM.

They then called in the head of the Italian desk and his

boss, the head of Mossad's international relations, and asked for a detailed description of the assets that would be available for finding Professor Modena and the rogue British scientist, Doctor Smalley, in Padova, if indeed they were together.

The head of the Italian desk told them that Padova itself had slightly more than two hundred thousand residents, but it served as a center for the surrounding area with a total population of over one million five hundred thousand. Going about it with brute force would be like finding a needle in a haystack. There were about seventy-five hotels in the area, a manageable number for a door-to-door search, but he said that for a long-term operation involving a workforce of a dozen or so people, it would be more likely they would rent an apartment or two.

Carrying out a search for rentals of this sort would be feasible but he believed that they were more likely to rent a large villa in the area surrounding Padova, with enough grounds to establish a laboratory of the type required for producing U-233.

He suggested they focus on this target area and screen all recent, long-term rentals of such villas, and look for large purchases of food supplies delivered to the suspect villas.

David stated they shouldn't confine themselves to preconceptions and must also look for any newly registered companies in the high-tech part of the area.

After the larger meeting, David and the Deputy Director privately discussed the actions that should be implemented after the laboratory and personnel were located.

Eliminating the people involved and the laboratory would

not suffice as they needed to discover the intended target of the device as well as the people, or organizations that had supported and financed the project in the first place. This meant some of the key personnel had to be captured alive and interrogated.

If the Italian government was not privy to the plan, this act of kidnapping would have to be done discretely, preferably without crossing international borders and raising an alarm.

Alternatively, they could smuggle Modena and Smalley out of Italy by plane or ship and bring them to Israel for an 'active interrogation.'

Based on previous experience, exposing this, even after the fact, could cause a major diplomatic furor. So this option, too, had to be presented to the Prime Minister.

CHAPTER 9

April 15, Padova

Ollie returned to Padova to monitor the progress of Astraea project. The last six weeks had been very productive and the accumulated amount of U-233 had reached thirty pounds.

In addition, Doctor Jay had manufactured a model of the device that included the arrangement of the special explosives around a core consisting of metallic natural uranium that had been machined to the dimensions of the real device simulating the core that would consist of U-233.

Modena told Ollie that some of the workforce members were getting restless after so many months of being practically confined to the warehouse and its immediate neighborhood and Ollie responded that in view of the progress they could close down the laboratory for a week, starting on Monday, and let everybody take a short vacation.

He then gathered all the employees and told them he was pleased with the progress made and they all deserved a well-earned break. He then gave each a cash bonus and warned them to keep their mouths shut and not disclose or even discuss the location of the lab and the activity taking place in it.

He suggested they pair up and not go individually so they

could supervise and look after each other and keep out of trouble.

Ollie had received word from Paul Dooley, hand delivered by courier, that he felt his phone was tapped and his computer and e-mail were scrutinized.

In the note he referred to the meeting with Doctor Jay as the event that may have set off this enhanced surveillance. Dooley also said he was now staying clear of any activity that may connect him with Doctor Jay, Ollie, or with other European nationalist movements, but would continue his usual meetings with the BNSP, as he feared an abrupt change of his normal routine would also look suspicious.

Ollie realized time was running short and the authorities in the UK, and possibly also in other countries, were getting suspicious.

April 19, Padova

The Mossad agents were frustrated after two weeks of looking for long-term apartment rentals in Padova and at villas in the surrounding area. They had found nothing that looked like the clandestine laboratory they were seeking, although they did find two farms in which illegal activities, such as growing marijuana and distilling contraband whiskey took place but refrained from informing the Italian authorities about these.

They carried photos of Modena and Jay in their cell phones but did not show them around in order not to raise the suspicion of the locals. One of the agents managed to bribe an employee at city hall and get a list of all the newly registered chemical firms. He started checking them, moving from the periphery to the center, but had not yet covered all of them.

One of the last on the list was called Astraea and located in a busy area near the Botanical Gardens. When he arrived there, he found a large warehouse with a notice pasted on the front door saying the place was closed for a week and would reopen on the following Monday. The place did not look like a clandestine laboratory but like a legitimate business. Nevertheless, he decided to return the following week and take another look.

In the evening, Gabi Golan arrived in Padova and gathered the team for debriefing. The feedback he got was discouraging as there was no positive evidence of the lab or the wanted people. Gabi said he would contact the Deputy Director and ask for further instructions and then decide whether to terminate the search and return home or to continue the quest. He told his team to take the evening off and meet again in the morning.

April 22, Vienna

As instructed by the Mossad director, David briefed the members of the international task force and told them that Mossad had found evidence that Professor Modena may be in Padova. He did not tell them the Mossad team had come up empty handed and had been recalled from Padova. The members of the task force were deeply disturbed by the news.

They all knew northern Italy was a stronghold of several

separatist political movements and political parties in the Veneto region and although they were not inherently racist, they may have formed an alliance with other militant European movements.

David suggested they contact, Umberto Stefano, the head of the Italian Internal Security Agency, who was known for his uncompromising war on corruption and whose life had been threatened several times because of his stand on that issue.

Thomas, the British former MI6 employee, said he was a personal acquaintance of Umberto and he could be trusted, so David asked him to arrange an unofficial meeting as soon as possible.

April 24, Padova

Professor Modena welcomed his workers back and asked them if they had enjoyed their vacation. He was pleased to see they had all returned and seemed to be invigorated by their time off the job.

He told them they had almost accomplished the goal of producing thirty pounds of U-233 and he estimated that working three full shifts, without any setbacks, they would have enough material within five or six weeks.

In a private conversation, Doctor Jay informed Modena the mock-up model he had constructed was ready for insertion of the real core of fissile material once that was made available. He also said the practice run with natural uranium increased his confidence in their ability to quickly construct the real fissile core. The only problem was a pretty high uncertainty about the U-232 content because each batch had a slightly different concentration.

In addition, the analytical methods used to determine the true U-232 content were inaccurate and could result in an underestimate by a factor of two. The practical implication was that the yield of the device would be uncertain.

Professor Modena assured Jay he thought it would never be tested as the plan was to use the device for blackmailing the governments and all they needed was to convince the official representatives that it existed and was the real thing, and they had the intent and determination to use it if their demands were not met.

Doctor Jay agreed with the professor but said that his sense of professional pride would not accept a failure, if for some reason the device was to be used.

Jay took in the professor's appearance and noticed he had lost some weight and his face was quite pallid, but when he asked him if he was feeling well the professor just grunted he was fine and probably did not get as much time in the sun as he had been used to in Barcelona.

May 2, Artena near Rome

The meeting between Umberto Stefano and the two members of the ITF had finally been arranged. Umberto Stefano's busy formal schedule had made it difficult to set an earlier date for a discrete, off the record meeting. So, they agreed to meet in his villa near Artena about one hour's drive from

Rome city center.

Colin Thomas made the introductions and David then briefly described the information they had about the missing gamma radiation sources, Professor Modena's rejected manuscript, his disappearance from Barcelona, and finally about the unknown whereabouts of Doctor Smalley.

He told Umberto there was some evidence Modena was in the Padova area and may have set up a clandestine laboratory for production of fissile U-233, and that expert scientists in the U.S. and in Russia could not rule out the possibility of constructing a nuclear device from U-233 produced by gamma irradiation.

David added that the task force had discussed the possibility of going public and requesting help in finding Modena and Smalley but were afraid such an act would drive them in to deeper cover. Finally, he asked the Italian what he thought about the whole affair and what his recommendation would be.

Umberto said he was shocked by the story and needed some time to digest it before proposing further action. After some thought, he said he had formed a counter-corruption elite police unit that had the same training as the most advanced special forces in NATO countries and they were the first-line intervention force deployed in the most dangerous situations. He asked their permission to call in the unit's commander, Piero Adriano, and consult with him.

David and Colin Thomas were not too happy about bringing in another person and suggested they make up a cover story about a radiation dispersion device rather than disclosing their suspicion they were dealing with an improvised nuclear device.

Umberto insisted he could vouch for the commander and he would perform better if he knew exactly what was at stake. In order not to alienate Umberto they agreed. Adriano was asked to come over to Artena as quickly as possible.

Adriano told Umberto he was spending the weekend north of the city and it would take him two hours to get there. Umberto told him to hurry. He then suggested to David and Thomas they go and have dinner while waiting for Adriano to arrive.

The three of them drove to a local restaurant and had a fine Italian dinner.

By the time Adriano arrived they were having coffee and he joined them for dessert. They did not want to discuss the matter in the restaurant although they were the last diners there, so they returned to Umberto's villa.

Piero Adriano received the news without any outward reaction but when he started talking the strain in his voice revealed he was distressed by the implications of a nuclear device in Padova, especially if an accident were to occur.

He said that he would move his unit to the north, discreetly enlist all the informers he had in the area giving them a cover story about a 'dirty bomb' manufactured by a 'mad professor', but would not try to ask the local authorities for help as he did not trust them not to leak the story to the press.

He asked for photographs of Modena and Smalley so his informants would know who to look for. He also requested as much technical detail as possible about the required laboratory facilities and if special large items of equipment were required.

May 5, Stockholm

Andreas was starting to feel uneasy about Ollie's dedication to the cause, as he had avoided participating in street brawls and had not attended the meetings of the movement. He suspected that Ollie's fervor was fading, and he was too preoccupied with the work in Padova.

Andreas noticed that Ollie even neglected Agda, or so he had been told by her twin sister, Alva, and that he kept pretty much to himself. He summoned Ollie but was told he was busy and could not come over until the next day.

Andreas was not used to being rejected and called upon Agda to find out what Ollie was going through. Agda said it had been quite a while since she had spent time with Ollie and had no idea about his life or love life. This disturbed Andreas even further and when Ollie arrived the next day, he told him about his concerns with Ollie's well-being.

Ollie tried to allay his concerns and said the device was rapidly approaching completion and he was now planning how to best use it for their objective. He thought moving it around could be difficult because of its weight, size, and the possible leakage of radiation that might be picked up by gamma radiation detectors.

Andreas was still worried because those plans should have been made months ago but Ollie said he had not been certain the device could be constructed until his last visit to Padova.

Furthermore, he said, only after seeing Doctor Jay's mock-up model could the planning reach a practical phase.

He also explained to Andreas that Doctor Jay said the presence of the U-232 impurity made it necessary to create a thicker radiation shield than he had originally planned, and this added significantly more weight to the device, encumbering its transport.

Andreas thought a truck equipped with a crane could be used without causing suspicion since many of them were seen in the streets of Europe and the device should be no bigger than the 'fat man' nuclear bomb used in Nagasaki that weighed under five tons and was ten feet long by five feet wide—he had checked that in Wikipedia.

Ollie informed Andreas that during his last visit to Padova, Doctor Jay assured him the device would weigh much less than 'fat man' and be significantly smaller so although it would weigh six hundred pounds it would be transportable even by a pick-up truck. Ollie, of course, did not tell him that he needed to transport the device by sea as there was no open ground connection between Italy and Jerusalem.

CHAPTER 10

May 15, near the old border between Syria and Iraq

ISIS troops brought a bulldozer to eliminate any sign of the old border between Iraq and Syria claiming that the 1916 Sykes-Picot agreement between the British and French colonialist nations was null and void and the whole region was now part of the new Islamic Caliphate.

The ultimate dream of the Islamists was to unite the entire Muslim world, including Iraq, Syria, Jordan, the Arabian Peninsula, Lebanon, Palestine, and Israel, as well as a large part of North Africa, and rule it according to strict Islamic code, and removal of the old border was the first step.

Ibn-Tutta himself was present at the ceremonial event and was just getting ready to deliver a fiery speech encouraging his troops to continue on the holy journey, when an unmanned drone fired a well-aimed rocket that hit the improvised podium on which he stood, blowing Ibn-Tutta and his bodyguards to smithereens.

Ibn-Tutta's last prayer to Allah making a wish that the drone had not been directed by a female returned unanswered, so he would be denied the pleasures in heaven promised to all *shahids* that died fighting Allah's holy war.

Captain Jannette Lewis, sitting in a bunker in Nevada, almost ten thousand miles from the border, received an ovation from her colleagues in the control room for her accurate strike.

Ibn-Tutta's second in command, Abu Alli, immediately seized the vacant position and asserted himself as the new Supreme Commander of ISIS forces. The irony that this had occurred on the same date the country of Israel became independent did not escape Abu Alli.

After arranging a traditional funeral for what was left of Ibn-Tutta and his entourage, he swore to avenge the death of his commander in a way that the world of *kefirs*, those people who rejected Islam and its prophet Mohammad, would not forget.

His problem was he had no indication about Ollie's progress or even where he was and had no way of contacting him. His only hope was that Ollie had completed his mission and would resurface soon and be in touch with Sheik Khalil, the head of the extremist faction of the Islamic movement in Umm al-Fahm, Israel.

May 17, Padova

Ollie had watched the TV news the previous evening and saw the video footage filmed by the drone of the disintegration of Ibn-Tutta and his podium.

He had to grind his teeth when he watched the celebration in the control bunker, especially as he understood the significance of the festivity surrounding the female Captain who handled the drone and fired the rocket.

His resolve to detonate the device in the heart of Jerusalem and instigate a global war among the *kefirs* grew stronger, and he hoped his next planned trip to Padova would be successful.

Ollie and Andreas arrived at the laboratory in the evening after being urgently summoned by Professor Modena. The professor informed them that thirty pounds of U-233 had been produced and converted into metallic form. He noted this was due to the extra effort made by all members of the workforce after their vacation, so they were slightly ahead of schedule.

Doctor Jay said the fissile uranium core had been cast and was now cooling. He expected it could be shaped to the proper dimensions early the next morning and inserted into the center of the device. He said that if no unexpected problems arose the device would be ready by noon and could be transported.

Ollie was taken by surprise at this announcement as he had anticipated it would be at least one more week before the device was ready.

Doctor Jay explained that the detonation mechanism of the improvised nuclear device was quite like the mechanism used on the 'fat man' atomic bomb dropped on Nagasaki, August 9, 1945.

The conventional explosives were arranged in a spherical configuration surrounding the sphere-shaped core of the fissile material. Several fast detonators were purchased from the North Korean collaborator and thirty-two slots were drilled in the shaped segments of the explosive charges.

Doctor Jay further elaborated that for safety reasons these detonators were kept separately in a steel box that was locked with a combination lock.

Ollie asked what steps were needed to be taken to detonate the device.

Jay and Modena looked at him and then at each other, as they had thought the device would only be used for blackmail purposes and not detonated.

Andreas also thought that Ollie's inquisitiveness was out of place but was also curious about the detonation mechanism.

Doctor Jay eventually answered that one needed to insert all the detonators into the slots drilled in the explosives, connect the prearranged wiring to the detonators, then attach the two main wires to the timer that was battery operated. When the device was ready to go off, the detonators would be inserted in the slots, and the trigger would simultaneously set them off. The detonation would compress the fissile core to a critical mass.

The battery used in this improvised nuclear device was a standard twelve-volt car battery and the timer was a simple mechanical alarm clock from which the minute's dial had been removed. The hour dial served as a terminal so that whoever set off the device would have up to twelve hours to get away from the explosion, just in case they needed to use it.

Ollie, who had seen many films in which the explosive devices had tamperproof protection and the 'good-guy hero' had to make a dramatic decision whether to cut the red wire or the black wire was surprised their device had no such sophisticated mechanism, but was glad it could be armed and rendered safe without any special skills or training.

Ollie realized he had to quickly arrange for moving the device to the secure location he had prepared in a small farmhouse near San Giorgio delle Pertiche, about ten miles northwest of Padova.

Only Ollie and Andreas knew about this place and they thought the two of them could rent a self-drive truck with a crane to transport the device there without any of the workforce knowing their destination.

Ollie had considered 'taking out' the entire workforce, including Professor Modena and Doctor Jay. Then he thought that none of them knew what his real objective was, so if they were apprehended and questioned they would only be able to disclose the plan to blackmail the governments into expelling immigrants and 'unwanted elements,' which would distract the authorities away from himself and his true target. He knew he would have to eliminate Andreas once the device was safely stored in the farmhouse but there was no hurry to carry that out.

So, Ollie congratulated everyone on the excellent job, announced they would gather for a modest celebration at noon the next day, and promised them all a fat bonus.

He then called Andreas aside and asked him to go and pick up the truck he had booked from a local rental company. He told Andreas to use a false name, pay cash, and try to avoid having his driver's license photocopied. He said that could be done with a few additional bank notes slipped quietly under the counter.

They decided the two of them would take the completed

device to the new hiding place immediately after the little party. Andreas quietly asked him if it was safe to allow everybody to just walk away but Ollie convinced him that as they did not know where the device would be hidden there was less risk in letting them go unscathed than in leaving a mess and a mass of dead bodies.

He also told him the rumors about some big and unconventional terrorist act would make their blackmailing job easier. Andreas was still skeptical and went as far as quoting Stalin, the infamous dictator who executed many of his own countrymen, and quoted the saying attributed to Stalin, *no man no problem.*

Ollie was a bit surprised Andreas made such a dramatic proposition but finally convinced him to bring the truck with the crane at noon and not to worry about the loyal workforce.

May 18, Padova, noon and afternoon

At noon, the entire workforce gathered in the front office where tables were laden with good Italian food and bottles of French champagne.

After everyone held a flute of champagne in their hand Ollie, Andreas, Professor Modena, and Doctor Jay raised their glasses together and Ollie delivered a toast praising them all for their exceptional achievement.

He then addressed the professor and asked them all to have a drink honoring him and wished him luck in gaining the long-deserved recognition of his genius by his colleagues and by the Nobel Prize committee.

Next, he toasted Doctor Jay and acknowledged his great contribution to the cause and told him he would be remembered by history as the man who had constructed the device that would purify Europe of all inferior races.

He then faced Andreas and thanked him for his leadership in the unification of the European racist—he used the term 'true nationalist'—movements under one common cause.

He also wished all separatists success in achieving their goals, particularly the Catalan movement heralded by Professor Modena.

He opened his large duffel bag and removed several envelopes stuffed with large denomination Euro notes and distributed them among the workers. He asked them all to stay in the warehouse for another hour and then leave quietly in groups of two or three and return to their home countries without raising suspicion, or to take a well-deserved vacation in their favorite location.

He sternly warned them not to say a word to anyone about the project, its objective, the laboratory, nor their colleagues.

With the help of several men, the device was moved to the garage where a standard shipping container marked as 'agricultural machinery' was waiting on the platform of the truck he had rented.

Assisted by the crane, and some manual force, the device was loaded inside the container, and the steel suitcase with the detonators, and the car battery were also placed in the container, then its doors were sealed with a stamped optical tamper-proof seal.

Ollie took the duffel bag that still contained a lot of cash he figured he would need and then he and Andreas got in the truck's cabin and slowly backed out of the garage. The doors of the garage closed behind them and they headed on the short drive toward the farmhouse.

They drove slowly in order not to attract police attention and within less than thirty minutes were at the cattle gate of the farm. Ollie got out of the cabin and opened the gate while Andreas drove carefully on to the farm grounds.

Ollie closed the gate and got back in the truck which was then driven into the empty barn where the container was unloaded with the trucks winch and placed on the ground.

Ollie locked the barn door and directed Andreas to drive back to Padova while he remained at the farm to keep an eye of the device and container.

They had arranged for Andreas to return the rental truck and come back to the farm with a regular car.

Then Ollie entered the farmhouse to prepare a 'warm welcome party' for Andreas.

An hour later Andreas returned to the farmhouse and found Ollie sitting on the porch, enjoying the last rays of the setting sun and a bottle of Chianti red wine.

Ollie held up his full glass and invited Andreas to join him in celebrating the great success of the Astraea project. Andreas sat down and Ollie poured him a glass of wine from the open bottle.

Andreas and Ollie took large sips of their wine and a couple minutes later Andreas's head dropped to the table as he passed out.

Ollie pulled him out of his chair, and dragged him into

the living room where he awkwardly lifted the unconscious man to sit him in a solid wooden chair. This was no easy feat as Andreas weighed over three hundred pounds and tied his hands and feet to the chair with strong plastic manacles.

Two hours later Andreas slowly regained consciousness and shook his head. When he tried to move his hands and feet, he realized he was restrained to the chair.

Ollie faced him and proceeded to tell Andreas what his real objective was and that he had manipulated the most chauvinistic fanatical and xenophobic movements to support the *Jihad*, the holy war of Islam against the European colonialists and racists.

Andreas was so shocked by these revelations he almost forgot to fear for his own life.

Ollie was extremely pleased by this reaction and for a moment he even considered letting Andreas live in shame. Then cold logic prevailed and he reckoned that if Andreas lived to disclose his plan, it would make it more difficult to smuggle the device out of Italy and to Jerusalem.

In comradeship, he told Andreas he would allow him to choose his mode of death—quickly by knife or to starve slowly.

Andreas looked him in the eye, spat at his feet, and said he did not care one way or the other.

Ollie coolly pulled a commando knife from his boot and with the serrated edge cut Andreas's throat, leaving him tied to the chair, and walked away.

Ollie entered the barn with a radiation detector. As he approached the sealed container, the detector clicked more and more rapidly the closer he got. He then moved away and out of the barn and noted that the reading of the detector, the background level, was below one count per second.

Thirty feet from the container there was only a very slight increase in the reading, at fifteen feet it already increased to two counts per second, and at five feet was near fifty counts per second.

This bothered him as he realized two things: first, the radioactivity might trigger an alarm if the container was monitored by a radiation detection portal when it was loaded on a ship in Italy or after being unloaded in Israel. Second, this meant the U-232 level was higher than expected, which could cause failure of the device.

While he knew he could alleviate the first problem by adding another layer or two of radiation shielding material such as lead or even depleted uranium, there was nothing he could do about the second problem.

Even dissolving the U-233 core and purifying it would not remove the U-232 isotope, so all he could do was pray to Allah and hope for the best. The fact that the radiation outside the barn was at the background level assured him that unless someone opened the barn door and entered with a radiation detector the device would remain secure and protected from detection. If someone would see the container in the barn, he would assume it was just some piece of agricultural equipment unless he had a radiation detector or broke the seal and opened the container.

He left the farm in the car Andreas had rented and headed toward the Rijeka port in Croatia, where he expected security to be much less rigorous than in the Italian ports of Venice or Trieste he had earlier planned to use.

He also assumed there wouldn't be any radiation detectors and monitors there. He recognized that this change of plans would involve crossing international borders but also knew arrangements could be made to evade a close examination of the container's contents by bribing the customs and border people.

He would tell them the 'agricultural machinery' was a shipment of smuggled electronic commodities he intended to sell in Zagreb. In Rijeka, he would say he was smuggling the same commodities to the Palestinian Authority via the Haifa port in Israel.

In both cases, he would make sure the generous payment would keep their eyes closed and their mouths shut for at least a month.

For a short while he regretted Andreas's death as he knew the Swede had connections in Italy and Croatia that could smooth the way, but the remorse did not last more than a moment.

May 18, Padova, late afternoon

The Italian anti-corruption unit, headed by Piero Adriano, had combed the area in and around Padova looking for sources of gamma radiation.

Handheld radiation detectors were distributed among the troops and they had meticulously scanned every farm, villa, or secluded residence in a vast area.

In addition, unmarked vehicles specially mounted with highly sensitive detectors had traversed the many gravel roads in Veneto province around Padova, travelling at very low speed causing traffic delays and giving the impatient Italian drivers cause for silent complaints and not-so-quiet verbal abuse.

The only positive responses the radiation detectors attained were from discarded smoke detectors that contained americium.

David was given a daily report of the lack of progress and growing frustration but could not reveal the fact that a search on a smaller scale by the Mossad team also yielded no results.

He gradually became convinced the clandestine laboratory had to be in a central location so the unexplained burst of activity would not be noticed by local authorities and residents.

He advised Piero Adriano that they should focus on finding a group of foreigners that resided and dined near the center of town and, although not really expecting successful identification of the two scientists, asked him to check the hotels and restaurants in the vicinity.

He consulted with Umberto Stefano and Piero if the time was right to permit the agents to use the photos of Modena and Smalley and the police artist's image of the blond man when questioning staff at the hotels and restaurants.

He emphasized they were running out of time and needed to take a chance that word of the ongoing intensive search would reach the suspects.

The Italians agreed they needed to use more decisive measures and all the agents were sent to inspect the tourist areas in the town itself.

Umberto said people trying to keep a low profile would probably shy away from the large tourist hotels as those insisted on registering the guests and photo-copying their passports and were usually paid with credit cards whose transaction records could be traced.

In addition, a group of men staying for an extended period in a large hotel was bound to raise suspicion that something irregular and perhaps illegal was taking place.

On the other hand, the small bed and breakfast places often 'forgot' to register guests and preferred cash deals, so there would be no record that could attract the attention of the tax authorities.

He figured there would be a couple dozen of these places near the center and promised to send the agents to cover these with a top priority. Within twenty-four hours the proprietors at all these small B&Bs were questioned.

After being promised no information would be passed to the tax authorities, the owner of a small pension recalled that two men, one who looked like Doctor Smalley and one like the blond man, stayed at his place for one night a few months previously.

He remembered them because very few tourists came in winter and these two arrived at night, without a reservation, paid cash, and checked out early the next morning without even having breakfast.

They did not appear to be interested in the tourist attractions but did not look like businessmen. When the information was passed on to David, he asked Piero if he could find out if the date of that stay was at the end of January—coinciding with the approximate date that Doctor Smalley met the mysterious blond man in London.

The owner did not remember the exact date but thought it could have been near the end of January. In one of the restaurants they also got a positive identification of all three suspects.

The proprietor noted the three men had a quiet but intense discussion in English. He remembered they ordered two bottles of his most expensive wine, a fact that pleased him as there were very few tourists at that time of the year. He also noticed that whenever he came close to their table to serve them their discussion ceased and was renewed after he was out of earshot.

When asked again about the language they were speaking, he said they placed their orders in English but two sounded like foreigners and the third had a British accent.

David and the Italians marked the two places on a large-scale map of Padova and saw they were not far apart and quite close to the Botanical Gardens.

Piero called all his agents and divided the area in question into small sections and assigned a team to meticulously comb each section.

The teams were briefed to pay special attention to newly established firms that presented themselves as involved in the chemical industry, according to the list obtained from the municipal authorities under the guise of searching for a clandestine laboratory for drug manufacturing.

Given the number of agents, the small area on which the

search focused and the guidelines, it was no surprise that within less than an hour the warehouse was found.

The two agents saw the name Astraea on the front door and a quick inquiry of the neighbors told them the company was allegedly involved in research and development operations in the chemical industry.

They immediately called Piero, who summoned Umberto and David to the site. The front office of Astraea was closed and as far as they could tell there was no one in the building.

They brought their most sensitive gamma radiation detector and noted the reading was slightly above the background level and the source appeared to be in the warehouse.

Even though it was early in the evening, they managed to obtain the floor plan of the building from the municipal archives and discovered it had a vast basement area.

Without waiting for a court order, Umberto instructed Piero to cautiously break down the door and enter the premises. He alerted them to use the radiation detectors to make sure people were not exposed to radiation.

They carefully entered the building and found the first floor had been converted into a dormitory that appeared to have been abandoned in a hurry. David counted twelve bunks, which confirmed the estimate of the size of the workforce. They also found a small kitchen and dining area in which unwashed dishes were scattered indicating people left the place without bothering to tidy up and probably with no intension to return.

Going down the stairs to the basement the radiation intensity grew so that even the personal detectors with their relatively low sensitivity registered significant levels.

David and Umberto told the rest of the people to remain at the street level office area, while the two of them slowly went from chamber to chamber in the basement looking at the equipment in the three main rooms.

The radiation monitor clicked like crazy when they entered the largest chamber and saw the lead bricks that lined the walls. David took one look at the four channels that led from the corners of the room to the middle of the chamber and saw the stainless-steel vessel in the center and immediately understood that Professor Modena had carried out his plan to irradiate thorium.

In the next chamber, they found the chemical processing equipment and realized the U-233 must have been successfully separated and purified there. The radiation level in this chamber was also high and they noticed a few stains on the floor that indicated some liquid had been spilled. These stains emitted particularly intense radiation and David thought this could have been due to the uranium, thorium, or fission products.

In the third chamber, they found a lathe that had probably been used to shape the uranium core and some metallic shavings.

Umberto called David's attention to a spherical object on a side table that consisted of two solid hemispheres with a diameter of about four inches. The radiation emanating from this sphere indicated it consisted of a radioactive element, but it was not as intense as the levels measured in the other rooms.

David surmised it was the mock-up core made from natural uranium that had probably been used as a model for the real fissile material core and for practicing the shaping of the uranium hemispheres.

David told Umberto he had to urgently inform the international task force of these findings so the two of them left the basement and ascended the stairs to the street level.

Meanwhile, Piero had put his team to the task of searching for documents and papers that could help identify the people who had worked in the facility. They did not find anything specific but the food products in the kitchen implied the workforce came from several nationalities, or at least a varied taste for food and drinks.

Piero also said there were many plastic bags with the name of one of the major local supermarket chains and he had already sent one of his agents to the closest store to try and enquire who did the shopping for feeding a dozen people.

Umberto asked Piero to seal the warehouse and place guards outside until a scientific survey could be carried out. David said he would ask the members of the ITF for assistance from their most advanced nuclear forensics analysts to evaluate the quality of the improvised nuclear device based on the forensic evidence that could be gathered in the warehouse.

He called Eugene, Vassilly, and Thomas and without going into great detail on the unsecure phone line set an appointment for an urgent meeting in Vienna.

Piero followed the money trail and tried to find out who had rented the warehouse and within minutes got the name of a local firm that belonged to a prominent businessman with known ties to the separatist party, Liga Veneta Repubblica, also recognized as a racist stronghold.

The businessman said he had been asked to rent the warehouse as a personal favor by a local politician and claimed he had no idea what the warehouse was used for.

An interrogation of the politician quickly led to the Italian delegate who participated in the Corfu meeting. He was forewarned and by the time Piero's agents got to his home, they were informed he had gone on vacation to an undisclosed location.

Umberto and David were extremely aggravated since this was their strongest and most direct lead to the organization that was behind the project.

It was obvious to all of them the device had been moved from the warehouse recently and the top priority was to locate and neutralize it. This could be done if they could determine the target by finding the key people and the organization that had built the device.

Umberto wanted to immediately post the photos of Modena, Smalley, and the blond man on all media channels and appeal to the public to help in locating these dangerous 'drug dealers.'

David asked him to wait a little longer until he consulted his colleagues in the international task force. He was particularly concerned that panic would spread if word got out that an improvised nuclear device had been produced by a group of fanatics and was now at large somewhere in Europe.

They already knew that Doctor Jason Smalley was a racist who believed in expelling all foreigners of inferior races from

England and that Professor Modena was a Catalan separatist. They did not know who the blond man was and what connection he had to the others but after he had been seen in London with Smalley and in Padova with Modena; suspecting Smalley as one of the major players in the project.

Umberto suggested they focus on identifying the mysterious blond man and proposed circulating his photo image through all the airports around Padova in the hope that someone would remember him.

May 19, Vienna and Padova

In the morning, David flew back to Vienna and was met by Orna Cohen at the airport.

The ITF members were already gathered in one of the conference rooms of the IAEA headquarters and received David's report about the events and findings in Padova with ashen faces.

The American delegate, Eugene Powers, was the first to recover from the shocking news, and said they should discuss the ways and means needed to transport the device from the warehouse to the target area.

Assuming the device consisted of a U-233 fissile material core and was not manufactured by a fully equipped advanced workshop it would probably be quite cumbersome as it would have to be a primitive implosion type device. He speculated it may be as large and as heavy as the 'fat man' plutonium bomb dropped on Nagasaki at the end of Second World War and would require a crane to lift it and a truck to carry it. He suggested they first look for trucks and cranes in the Padova area that may have been used to transport the device.

Vassilly interjected that if an expert such as Doctor Smalley was involved then perhaps they could do with a much smaller and lighter design. He also emphasized that the Nagasaki atomic bomb had to be transported and dropped by an airplane, requiring an additional protective shell of heavy metal while the improvised nuclear device would be transported on land, and perhaps by sea, and would not need this heavy shell.

The British member of the task force, Colin Thomas, said he had closely examined Smalley's qualifications and found he had no access to anything but quite primitive designs so Eugene's assumption the device would be large and heavy was probably correct though Vassilly's point was also valid.

David added that if a truck was used to transport the device it could be hundreds of miles from Padova as at least twelve hours, and possibly even twenty-four hours, had passed since the device left the warehouse.

He then excused himself, left the conference room, and called Umberto with the new information and speculation, asking him to find all companies in the Padova area that had cranes, trucks, and especially flatbed trucks equipped with cranes. He asked him to investigate sales and rentals of such equipment and then returned to the conference room.

The discussion now focused on the wisdom of contacting Interpol about these developments and the consensus was it would only cause panic all over Europe if news of an unsupervised nuclear device got out.

They then talked about involving the Secretary General

and the IAEA and decided to wait before alerting the agency because of the same reasons.

They agreed that regardless of the exact location of the target they had to alert the friendly intelligence agencies of the European countries, especially those in which strong racist and separatist movements were active and strengthen the radiation monitoring network on the major highways and in ports, in case its target was a large harbor town.

Just after noon time, David received a phone call from Umberto telling him his people had located a local car rental agency in Padova that had rented a truck with a crane to an exceptionally big person who looked like a Viking.

There was no written record of the rental but after some short questioning one of the employees admitted he had carried out the transaction but had not had time to complete the forms as the truck was returned the same afternoon and the large Viking exchanged it for a regular passenger car.

The employee said that this deal was also done without a rental agreement for the same reason. When asked if he had made a photocopy of the Viking's driver's license, the employee said the copying machine had a malfunction, so a copy was not available.

Piero's agent was a very sharp person and wanted to see the truck and record the mileage it had done. The employee now became very cooperative and remembered he was surprised to see the truck had done less than one hundred miles and he asked the Viking if he was not satisfied with the truck. The Viking had rudely told him to mind his own business and pulled out a one hundred Euro note, which silenced the employee.

The agent asked about the passenger car and was told it was a gray four-wheel drive Jeep Renegade and got its license plate number. The car rental employee was summoned to the police station and asked to work with a police artist to create an image of the Viking, which he was doing at that very moment.

David asked Umberto what he thought about the new information and what he proposed to do with it.

Umberto said he had discussed the matter with Piero, and they concluded that obviously, the device must be within less than one hundred miles from Padova and probably stored temporarily somewhere close.

Piero had already sent his agents to the warehouse and by now they were questioning everybody in the area about a truck equipped with a crane.

In addition, they sent an all-points-bulletin alerting police about the gray Jeep Renegade and the Viking driving it, but were not very hopeful considering the timeframe and the fact that it was quite a common vehicle in northern Italy.

The vehicle, in addition, to a sketch of the suspect, might be a long shot, or might be the edge they needed.

CHAPTER 11

May 19, Trieste and Rijeka

Ollie had arrived in Trieste the previous evening after making the short drive from the farmhouse near San Giorgio delle Pertiche.

He stopped at one of the rest-areas on the A4 highway between Venice and Trieste and under the cover of darkness removed the license plates from a car that was parked farthest from the restaurant and replaced the Renegade's plates.

He knew that crossing through Slovenia into Croatia with the rented car would not be possible, especially if the car registration and license plates did not match, so he left the car in a large parking lot and checked in to a small family run hotel.

In the morning, he boarded a bus to Rijeka, where he intended to find a ship that would take his container with the device inside it to the Haifa port in Israel. The bus ride went smoothly, and no one gave his passport a second look when he crossed into Croatia after a short fifteen-mile stretch through Slovenia.

When he reached Rijeka and talked to a few shipping agents, he found there was no direct shipping line from Rijeka to Haifa but that a container could be transshipped through

Bari in Italy and Limassol in Cyprus and reach Israel three or four weeks later.

Although not happy with the delay, he thought this would give him time to arrange for the release of the container from the Haifa port and its shipment to the target area in Jerusalem. So, he made the required preparations, and the accompanying necessary cash transaction, to ensure his container with its marking as 'agricultural machinery' would be loaded on a ship that was to leave Rijeka heading for Bari four days later.

He still had to figure out how to transport the container to Rijeka and decided the best way would be to hire a Croatian company to collect the container from the farm near San Giorgio. This way, even if the truck was stopped, Ollie himself would remain untraceable.

The manager of the Croatian company said for a suitable fee he could make sure the container arrived in Rijeka safely and without delay, meaning without being opened. The 'suitable fee' quadrupled the original price but Ollie willingly agreed to pay half in advance and half upon delivery. He gave the manager instructions for getting to the farm and they arranged for the pickup to take place the next day in the evening.

After that, Ollie took the bus back to Trieste, retrieved the Renegade from the parking lot, and drove back to the farm.

May 20, Padova and San Giorgio

Ollie spent the night sleeping soundly in the bedroom of the farmhouse.

He had arrived late the previous night and after checking

that the container had not been tampered with, parked the Jeep Renegade in the barn next to the container.

He saw Andreas's body in the living room but was too tired to do anything about it at night. In the morning, he managed to move the heavy body to the barnyard and dug a shallow grave in which he placed Andreas's body. He cleaned the living room to the best of his ability since he feared the Croatian truck driver might want to enter the house on some pretext. He then settled down to wait for the truck.

**

Meanwhile, back in Padova, Piero summoned all his agents and told them one of the neighbors who worked not far from the Astraea warehouse had seen a truck equipped with a crane enter the warehouse garage and leave a few minutes later with a standard shipping container. He did not notice the writing on the container but was sure there was a sign or emblem on it. He wasn't sure about its color either but said the truck itself bore the name of a local rental company.

This information was not very helpful as Piero already knew about the truck and knew that it had been returned to the rental agency. The same neighbor also said that a short while after the truck departed about a dozen men also left the warehouse.

When he was shown the photo of Modena, he said he had seen him several times, but did not recognize Doctor Smalley's photo. However, when he saw the artist's image of the blond man and the Viking, he said they were the two people that had been in the truck's cabin.

Once again, Piero's elite troops set out on a search of storage facilities and farmhouses in the area surrounding Padova.

Umberto managed to arrange for a couple police helicopters to carry out an aerial survey while the rest of the agents scanned the roads.

The agricultural area contained many places in which a container could be easily hidden out of sight.

Piero supposed the container may have been transported to the holding area near the port of Venice and sent half his men to search for it among the thousands of containers awaiting shipment.

They were all equipped with radiation detectors but were told to focus on the containers listed as having arrived for shipment during the previous twenty-four hours.

In addition, he placed several roadblocks on the roads leading out of Padova but did not have enough radiation detectors for all of them.

***

The Croatian truck driver was stopped a couple times for examination, but his papers were in order and he had all the necessary documentation for a merchandise pick-up in Italy that was to be transported to Rijeka for shipment to Bari.

The policemen that checked him asked him why the container could not be shipped directly from Venice to Bari without leaving Italy but in broken Italian the driver grumbled he was only a truck driver and not the manager of the company.

In the evening, he arrived at the farm near San Giorgio where Ollie offered him a cup of coffee, which the driver declined. They used the truck's crane to load the container on the platform and secure it with straps.

The driver told Ollie he had been stopped a couple times by police, but Ollie told him not to worry as all the paperwork was in order. The truck with Croatian plates heading back to Rijeka with agricultural machinery equipment was only stopped once before reaching Venice but was quickly allowed to continue its way by the tired and bored policeman after its documentation was examined and found to be in order.

As soon as the container was on its way, Ollie got in the Jeep Renegade and drove south to Bologna, where he abandoned the Jeep Renegade at the railway station parking lot and checked in to a cheap hotel near the station.

The following morning, he boarded the train to Rome and from there he took a flight to Ljubljana. He rented a car at the airport and drove to Rijeka, contacted the shipping agent where he made sure the container had arrived and was to be loaded on the ship for Bari and paid the second half of the transportation fee.

He knew he had to get a new identity as he was sure the truck with the crane and the container would be traced to the farm, and he feared that Andreas's body would be discovered pointing a finger at him.

He decided to drive the rented car from Rijeka to the highway connecting Zagreb with Dubrovnik and then cross into Montenegro, ditch the car in Podgorica, and from there use public transportation to cross in to Albania, the only truly

Muslim country in Europe, not counting Turkey, of course. From Shkoder near the border he took an Albanian bus to Tirana and found a place close to the Tirana International hotel that had a room-to-rent sign.

***

The helicopters had been called off as soon as it got dark, but the ground survey continued and Piero's people worked through the night going from one farmhouse to the next.

It was after ten pm when one of the teams arrived at the farmhouse near San Giorgio, and although they found no one at home they opened the gate and wandered around the house and the barn. They noted the tire marks of a heavy vehicle on the ground and in the barn and called in for assistance.

Piero himself arrived with a sensitive radiation detector and they found slightly elevated radiation levels in the barn. A closer look in the barnyard showed signs of freshly dug soil and within minutes Andreas's body was discovered in the shallow grave Ollie had buried him.

Piero immediately identified the body that fit the description of the large Viking and he called Umberto with the news the hen had flown the coop.

There were no documents on the body and all they could do was take mug shots of the face that had not been too distorted after being buried for two days.

Upon hearing this, Umberto almost lost his cool and murmured a juicy Italian expletive before calling David in Vienna.

After hearing Umberto's report, David said they should

try to identify the Viking and suggested the photos they had taken be sent to all European police departments and to Interpol. The description of the exceptionally large body was also attached to the post-mortem photo.

David thought there was a high likelihood the man was from one of the Scandinavian countries and Umberto concurred and said he would personally contact the police chiefs in Denmark, Norway, Sweden, and Finland and ask them to give top priority to the investigation.

May 20, Vienna

David and Orna were just having a nightcap in her apartment when he received the phone call from Umberto.

David realized they kept getting close to finding the device and the mysterious blond man, who appeared to be the moving force behind the project, yet he was always one step ahead of them.

He told Umberto their top priority should be to find the man as he was definitely the leader of the project and he would call for an urgent meeting of the task force for the following morning to let them know the device had been moved again and they had to call for all the help they could get to find the blond man.

He then called all the ITF members and summoned them for a meeting at nine o'clock the next morning. David next called Haim Shimony, the Deputy Director of Mossad, and gave him a brief update on the situation. Shimony asked David to return to Israel after his meeting in Vienna.

By the time he had done this neither he nor Orna were in the mood for anything but cuddling. David didn't mention Ramona and the night he spent with her in Barcelona and Orna didn't enquire where he had been.

May 21, morning in Tirana, Albania

In the morning, Ollie went to the central mosque and asked to see the Imam.

Several eyebrows were raised when the blond man asked for the Imam, but he was granted an audience after the morning prayers in which he participated.

In stilted Arabic, Ollie told the Imam he was a Swedish convert to Islam and was in trouble with his country's authorities and needed a new passport.

The Imam was reserved and suspicious at first but when Ollie told him a little about his adventures with the Islamic State forces in Syria, the atmosphere changed dramatically, and the Imam offered his help and told him to return in the evening.

Ollie wandered around the city and was impressed by the difference between Stockholm and Tirana, both on the same continent while appearing to be worlds apart.

In the evening, he returned to the mosque and after prayers was introduced to Immad, a tall, thin man that would supply him with a passport.

The man looked him over, murmured it would be difficult because of his Scandinavian features. He said that if Ollie grew a French style beard and cut his hair short and dyed it brown, he would be able to arrange something that would not be easily recognized as a false identity.

Immad said it would take a week to make these changes and arrange a Swedish passport as there were not many Swedish young men that were tourists in Tirana.

Ollie felt he had no alternative but to wait for the fake passport and settled down for an extended stay in Tirana, not exactly his first choice for a vacation.

May 21, morning in Vienna

The members of the international task force were gathered in the conference room and anxiously followed David's summary of the events that had taken place in Italy.

He started by describing the physical evidence found in the warehouse—the mock-up model of the core that consisted of natural uranium, the radioactivity detected in several places in the laboratories that were used to produce U-233 and purify it, the 'missing' gamma radiation sources, and the irradiation chamber with the reactor in its center.

He asked the U.S. and Russia to send their best forensics analysts to try and determine the implications on the predicted performance of the improvised nuclear device.

They agreed and Thomas proposed to also invite the scientists from the Institute for Trans Uranium Elements (ITU) from Karlsruhe in Germany, who were famous for their work tracing the origin of smuggled nuclear materials in Europe.

David expressed everyone's frustration that although they had gotten very close to finding the device and the perpetrators, both had slipped out of their grasp once again.

He proposed they start a continent-wide manhunt for the blond man and alert all national police and intelligence organizations in Europe, warning them about the danger this man posed.

In order to minimize the panic that would surely erupt if it were known an improvised nuclear device had been constructed, he suggested the official reason given would be a strong suspicion a radiation dispersion device was ready to be detonated.

David also repeated his argument against involving Interpol and the IAEA because both were rife with politics and the latter included several member-states that would even condone such an act if it were carried out in what they considered a 'colonialist state.'

After some further discussion, it was agreed that only Interpol should be informed, in order to use the large database of convicted and wanted criminals to try to identify the mysterious blond man. The proposals were accepted unanimously.

Next, they discussed the measures that should be taken to locate the nuclear device, if it was indeed concealed inside a standard shipping container. The problem was that at any given moment there were several thousand containers being moved on Europe's roads to and from the main ports. Searching for a particular one, without details on its color, markings, or number, would be a formidable task, not to mention the delays such a project would cause and the cost of these delays to the economy.

A more practical solution would be to install radiation

detection portals at each port from which containers were shipped, and to ascertain each container be monitored. Several ports already had installed these portals but not all containers were examined, while many others had no such facilities and it would take months, if not years, to install the portals in those ports, even if funds for that were available.

While many containers were shipped from ports, there were many more transported from European manufacturers to clients via surface roads without any serious control and only superficial inspections that focused on documentation alone.

Finally, they discussed the possible scenarios for use of the device. Most of the participants thought the device would not be detonated without warning, especially if only a single device was produced. They believed it was more likely it will be used for blackmailing to achieve financial or political gain, or both.

Another possibility would be using it to create a viable threat, without making any demands, to install public panic at a level that would disrupt normal life. According to this scenario, the panic would not be limited to a single country and the economic and sociological effects would be tremendous, even if not a single life was lost.

David said he was not so sure the device would not be detonated because the logical analysis presented by the analytically-minded members of the ITF would not necessarily appeal to a group of fanatics—racists, religious, or self-modeled idealists, or even anti-colonialists bent on revenge.

He asked them to prepare for worst-case-scenarios

according to which the device would be used to precipitate an international conflict.

He was particularly worried that the detonation of the device in one country might invoke retaliation in the form of conventional acts of war or even a nuclear response, against historic adversaries or new real or imaginary enemies.

As the meeting adjourned, the participants left the conference room with a heavy load on their minds.

Thomas, the British member of the ITF, was charged with informing the intelligence organizations of the Western European countries.

Vassilly, the Russian, said he would make sure the former USSR European republics were informed.

Eugene was asked to enlist the assets of the U.S. and its closest allies.

The French member, Nicolas, would serve as the contact with Interpol presenting the tale of a blond man suspected of being involved in large-scale criminal activities, without any mention of nuclear or radiation devices.

David was to maintain close contact with the Italian police since Italy was the epicenter of the current activity, and with the Spanish police due to the involvement of Professor Modena and possible connections with the Catalan separatists.

CHAPTER 12

May 21, evening in Tel Aviv

David was surprised to see the head of Mossad and all the senior staff were already gathered in Shimony's office where the meeting was to be held.

After hearing David's update about the futile operation of Umberto's people in Italy and the decisions of the ITF meeting in Vienna, the Mossad head asked David to speak frankly.

Without further prompting David expressed his fears the device would be used and there might be far-reaching consequences resulting from its deployment, well beyond the immediate loss of life and damage to property.

He also said if it were simply to be used for blackmail purposes, then it would be only a matter of time before it was discovered and possibly rendered safe and neutralized. He added that the perpetrators would also be aware of this and would make sure it would be detonated one way or the other.

Shimony then asked all the participants if this device posed a threat to Israel's security, directly or indirectly.

His question was met by a long silence, broken only by the humming of the air conditioner. No one could give a logical, evidence-based answer.

Gideon, the representative of the Israeli Security Agency, who had also been invited to the meeting said they all had to make an operational assumption Israel may be targeted, although his gut feeling was that it was mainly an internal European problem.

David strongly objected, saying that eventually almost everything concerned Israel, one way or the other, so they should increase the security measures in all three ports, Haifa, and Ashdod on the Mediterranean coast, and even Eilat, on the shores of the Red Sea.

The Mossad chief directed the division heads to concentrate their efforts on finding any of the people that had worked on the Astraea project in Padova and interrogate them, starting with the two known scientists, Professor Modena and Doctor Smalley. Therefore, the Mossad's assets in Spain and the UK should be enlisted for the task.

David decided he would go to Barcelona to try to trace the professor through his contact with Ramona and requested the local Mossad agents be available to help him. He also proposed to make a stopover in Rome to discuss with Umberto further steps toward locating the container, or at least getting a better description of it that may help in tracking it.

May 22, afternoon in Rome

David landed at Fiumicino-Leonardo da Vinci airport in Rome and was escorted by a plain-clothes policeman to a private VIP room at the airport.

Umberto Stefano and Piero Adriano welcomed him and

offered him some refreshments that he declined saying he had had his share of airline food.

The Italians informed him there was no trace of the container or the blond man and they were quite sure that both were no longer in Italy.

They had had a small breakthrough with the description of the container as the same person who witnessed the truck with the crane leaving the warehouse recalled under hypnosis the container was painted brown and appeared to be quite rusty. He also remembered that the word 'machinery' was written on the container.

Despite this helpful information the container had not been found in any of the ports in northern Italia. Umberto excitedly said the body of the Viking had been identified by the Swedish police as being that of Andreas Harald Nordholm, also known as the 'head cracker,' who was the leader of a notorious racist Stockholm street gang.

David suggested that Umberto contact his colleagues in the Stockholm police and ask them to carry out a full investigation of Andreas and his buddies in order to try to find out the identity of the mysterious blond man, who was the key person to the whole operation and probably responsible for the murder of Andreas.

He also asked Umberto to make an introduction to the Swedish police in anticipation of his own visit to Stockholm. David forwarded all the new data to the ITF members in Vienna and to Mossad headquarters in Tel Aviv.

May 22, evening in Barcelona

David called Ramona and arranged to meet her for dinner at a Brazilian restaurant near the Girona metro station and close to her apartment.

The restaurant was quite crowded, so they relaxed, had a couple chilled glasses of Caipirinha as an aperitif and enjoyed the assortment of grilled meats consumed with good wine.

Ramona told him that seeing him every two months suited her as she did not want to commit to a long-term relationship and was quite satisfied with his undemanding presence.

He agreed this arrangement suited him as well, without saying anything about Orna in Vienna. They returned to her apartment and simply enjoyed each other's body, first with great passion and urgency and then in a more relaxed and patient mode.

David gingerly brought up the subject of progress with her doctoral research work and asked her if her advisor, Professor Modena, had returned to the university.

She told him he was officially still on a leave of absence and she had decided to switch to another advisor and changed the subject of her thesis, so was not too seriously affected by his absence.

David asked her if she knew where he had gone and whether he had a taken up a different academic position and Ramona said she had not seen him since he had left the previous summer. She only heard from him once when he said he was in Padova to prove to the world his theory and experimental work could be validated. She had no idea where he intended to do this and if he had succeeded.

David tried to remain calm after learning this information and asked her if she knew anything about Modena's personal life and she said he was divorced with no children and was now something of a recluse. Once again, she did not admit her affair with him and refused to share with David any intimate details about her relationship with the professor, but he was quite convinced their relationship was beyond the regular student-advisor affair.

May 23, Vienna

David flew from Barcelona to the meeting in Vienna for purely business reasons and from Ramona to Orna for a combination of business and pleasure.

At the meeting with the ITF members, the general feeling was that a pattern was emerging from the connections of the nationalistic racist movements, as personified by Doctor Smalley in Britain, and Andreas in Sweden, and the separatist movements represented by Professor Modena, and the north Italian separatists' involvement exemplified by the fact the laboratory was established at the heart of the Veneto separatists' stronghold in north Italy. To most ITF members, this indicated the target would be in a major European city.

Nicolas speculated that Brussels or Strasburg would be the preferred targets as they were the seat of major institutions of the European Community.

Colin Thomas suggested the City of London or Buckingham Palace could be targets because of the involvement of

Doctor Smalley in the production of the device.

Eugene and Vassilly believed their countries were relatively safe but raised their fear that Madrid may have been selected by Professor Modena.

David stated they needed solid evidence before making such assumptions and suggested they follow the best lead they had—the connection of Andreas with the project. He also emphasized the manhunt for the mysterious blond man should be intensified and it was time to appeal to the public for help.

The rogue nuclear device was a clear and present threat to normal life not only in Europe as racists may seek to use it in other places, such as Asian and African countries from which the immigrants came to Europe, as a deterrent and punishment.

He informed them he would be leaving for Stockholm in the evening to follow up on any information about Andreas. Orna was disappointed to learn he wouldn't be spending the night with her, but he promised he would be back in Vienna in a week or so.

Upon arrival in Stockholm, David checked in to a hotel in the city and arranged to meet the chief of police the next morning.

May 24, Stockholm

The Swedish Police Service, called Polisen in Swedish, was a relatively small force of less than thirty thousand employees, under the Ministry of Justice. The elite unit, Piketen, was set up to be deployed as an emergency response team for crisis management.

When David arrived at the headquarters of the Stockholm police, the chief was already waiting for him after being alerted by Umberto.

He had been given the cover story that a 'dirty bomb' may be in the hands of extreme nationalists and there was a strong involvement of local Swedish street gangs.

The chief told David that Andreas was someone the Polisen had been trying to convict unsuccessfully for some time and had a thick file on him and his street gang. They did not mourn his gruesome death and believed he got what he deserved. He said he had assigned a Piketen squad to help David in this investigation and introduced the squad leader as Jorgen.

David and Jorgen hit it off immediately, recognizing each other's combat experience and training and together devised an operational plan.

David and Jorgen left the police headquarters in an unmarked car followed by two other unmarked cars with six of the elite unit fighters. They went straight to Andreas's apartment, quickly neutralized the bodyguards who had been busy playing cards and entered the apartment.

They found Alva sleeping in the master bedroom and when they woke her up, she was completely disoriented probably because of too much alcohol still in her system. When they asked her about Andreas, she swore she had not seen him or even heard from him since he left Stockholm a week earlier and was quite upset he hadn't even called her. She said he was usually not absent for more than a couple days, but this time was different as he appeared to be very excited before leaving.

She said she did not know where he was but suspected he had gone to Italy once again. She added he never told her where he went but she figured out it was to Italy as he had returned from his recent trip with bottles of Chianti and Parma sausages they had devoured together.

David showed her the gory photographs of Andreas's body and told her about the way he was slaughtered with a serrated knife.

Alva broke into tears and said Andreas was her true love and she would do anything to help find his murderer. David told her they suspected a colleague of his and showed her the photo image of the mysterious blond man. Seeing the image of what had to be Ollie's familiar face, Alva flew into a rage and between sobs, swearing, and cursing and told them everything she knew about Ollie and how he had become Andreas's closest friend.

She said the two of them had travelled together frequently and Ollie was probably overseeing some big project she knew nothing about except it involved many people from other countries. She said her twin sister, Agda, had had an affair with Ollie and perhaps she would know more about him, and offered to call Agda and ask her to come over to the apartment.

When Agda arrived, Alva went to her and tearfully showed her the photos of Andreas's body and told her Ollie was the prime suspect in the ruthless murderer. Agda also burst out crying, and sniveling through her tears said she hated the

Polisen but would do anything to help bring Ollie to justice. She told them everything she knew about Ollie—that his full name was Olaf Gunther Andersson and he grew up in Malmo, where he was assaulted by Muslims which explained his hatred of all foreigners and particularly Muslims.

She also told them they had been lovers and Ollie had taken her on a trip to Athens in January, where he had some meetings with local Greeks at the marina in Piraeus. She said she thought they were top rank officials in the Golden Dawn movement and described the place where the meeting was held. She also told them about Ollie's unexplained disappearance and then with some hesitation mentioned her affair with Niko during Ollie's absence.

David and Jorgen thanked her for her cooperation and as an afterthought asked her if she had any photographs of Ollie and Niko. She showed them her cellphone and a selfie photo of Niko and herself smiling at the camera. When she handed Jorgen her phone, he downloaded this photo and then found a couple of more photos of herself with Ollie and with Niko. These, too, were downloaded.

When they all returned to the police headquarters Ollie's photo was edited with photoshop and the Polisen database was searched for matching pictures. They got several possible hits, but their attention focused on a photograph from three years ago of a young man suspected of murdering an unconscious patient in a hospital in Uppsala. Apparently, the dead patient had driven a motorcycle that slammed into a car killing the suspect's newly wedded wife. The suspect, one Oscar Gunar Axelsson, had converted to Islam and was on his way to his honeymoon when the accident took place.

He disappeared after the cyclist's body was discovered but the case was never brought to trial and the investigation was not completed so the case was left open as a possible homicide. There was no record of Oscar Gunar Axelsson ever leaving or entering Sweden or even of his living in the country. The comparison of the three-year-old photograph with the current photo of Ollie showed some similarities but the confidence level of a match between the two was below eighty-five percent.

David thanked Jorgen and the chief of police and headed to the airport where he caught a flight connecting to Tel Aviv.

May 25, Uppsala

A special investigation was initiated in Uppsala to gather more information about the whereabouts of Oscar Gunar Axelsson and his ties with Islam. The small Islamic community center had been transformed into a mosque, and the Muslim population of the town had increased threefold since the accident and the suspected murder of the cyclist in the University Hospital.

The old man that had been the head of the community center had passed away two years previously and the police officers did not find anyone in the Muslim community that admitted having known Oscar. However, when they checked the records at Uppsala University, they found a student with the name Oscar Gunar Axelsson had attended classes at the department of mechanical engineering but left just before graduating.

The police asked to see the list of his classmates and located some that still resided in Uppsala. However, only a few of them remembered Oscar at all, and none of them seemed to know anything about his present whereabouts.

One of the women said she'd had a crush on him and when her husband was out of the room admitted they had a short fling, a one-night-stand, in their second year at university but he was not interested a long-term relationship with her, and to the best of her knowledge with any other student.

She said she had seen him around during their third and fourth year at the university and he became more aloof toward graduation. She mentioned she had occasionally seen him in the company of two Arab students but did not know their names.

One of the nurses at the University Hospital remembered the incident of the suspected murder of the motorcycle driver. She said she had noted it especially because the bereft honeymooner appeared to be Scandinavian, while the family of the bride was typically Muslim and at the time intermarriages of this kind were not common.

The disappearance of the man immediately after the cyclist was found dead in his hospital bed seemed to be more than a coincidence and the police questioned the staff about this. The nurse could not provide any more details about the groom but said there was probably a medical record of his examination after the accident as he was in shock and suffered superficial wounds when he was brought in by the ambulance that also carried his bride.

The hospital required a court order to release the medical records but once this was presented and the records were examined no further information was obtained.

Examination at the Swedish passport control authority of all people leaving the country in the three-week period following the disappearance of Oscar Gunar Axelsson yielded nothing. The police concluded he either had assumed a new identity and remained in Sweden, or more likely, had managed to slip out of the country without being registered.

Jorgen forwarded all this information to David, who was on his way to the Mossad headquarters in Tel Aviv.

May 25, Tel Aviv

Once again, David Avivi presented the latest developments and new information to the Mossad head, the Deputy Director and the division chiefs.

He reported it was highly probable Oscar Gunar Axelsson was the mysterious blond man that had coordinated the work of Professor Modena and Doctor Smalley and the efforts to produce fissile materials for an improvised nuclear device.

Furthermore, if this was the case then his ties with the radical Islam could mean his true target could be in Israel rather than in Europe.

This stunned all the participants and they discussed the significance of this new information and the potential implications on Israel's security.

Next, they discussed the countermeasures that should be deployed to minimize the risk and divided the problem into two parts: finding the device and finding the blond man, preferably before they entered Israel.

The data they had on the improvised nuclear device was quite limited. They knew it was probably quite large as it had to be transported in a standard container and had to be lifted with a crane.

They had some information about the container but could not be sure it had not been painted over or the device was not moved into another container.

They also figured if they could locate Modena or Smalley, or any of the people who had worked in the Padova laboratory they would be able to get more details about the device.

The key personnel would also know about the mechanism used to detonate the device, which would be helpful for rendering it safe if they got hold of it.

The information they had on the blond man was also quite limited although now they did have a recent photograph of him, taken by Agda in Athens. They did know the name he assumed in Stockholm, Olaf Gunther Andersson or Ollie for short, and the name he used in Uppsala, Oscar Gunar Axelsson or Ossi for short, which was probably his real name.

They were sure he would not use any of these names in his travels, yet they thought it was highly likely he would still maintain a Swedish passport, or perhaps a Finnish, Norwegian, or Icelandic passport, as it would be quite difficult for him to pass an official check as being of any other nationality.

They also speculated he might try to change his appearance but had no idea what form he might choose.

The countermeasures at the Israeli borders were to alert

188 | C<small>HARLIE</small> W<small>OLFE</small>

the passport control officers to closely examine all tall, well-built, blond men travelling with Scandinavian passports, with special emphasis on men travelling unaccompanied.

The three seaports were also alerted to scan all suspect containers with radiation detectors but considering the volume of such containers' traffic this would cause serious delays that would infuriate customers.

The Mossad head also called for a continent-wide effort of all agents to try to trace the man and the container and said the information would be passed on to all friendly countries in Europe and asked David to update the international task force.

There was no decision whether to inform the public about this threat, or even about the 'dirty bomb' cover story, as this was more of a political decision than a professional security one.

The Mossad head said he would inform the Prime Minister, Minister of Interior Security, the Chief of Staff of the IDF, the head of the Israeli Security Agency and the Chief Inspector of the Police and ask them to decide how this serious, unconventional threat should be handled.

CHAPTER 13

May 26 and 27, Athens

David took the morning flight from Tel Aviv to Athens and was met by an agent of the Greek National Intelligence Service (NIS), who drove him straight to the director of the service.

Although the director was appointed by the Minister for Citizen Protection and could be fired by him, the current director was a professional intelligence officer and not a political appointee.

The head of the Hellenic Police, in charge of counter-terrorism, was also present.

Both were aware of the dangers posed by Golden Dawn to Greek democracy and were determined to protect it.

David showed them the selfie photo of Niko and Agda and told them she had informed the Swedish police about the meeting with Golden Dawn functionaries she thought took place at, or near, the marina in Piraeus, although she wasn't sure about the exact location.

They called the local head of the political surveillance section and he instantly recognized Niko as Nicodemus Alexios, an activist in the Golden Dawn movement, a prominent TV persona, famous for his smooth talking.

Niko had also been frequently interviewed by foreign TV networks due to his good English and apparent moderate presentation and rationalization of the movement's principles.

David accompanied the two detectives from the Hellenic Police sent to pick up Niko and bring him to the station.

They found Niko at a café in Exarchia sipping a cold beer and chatting up a blonde tourist who appeared to be hypnotized by the handsome Greek man.

When the detectives approached him, Niko who was used to being harassed by the police, made an apology to the disappointed lady, and accompanied them without protest.

At the police station, he said he was willing to cooperate as he had nothing to hide but initially claimed total ignorance when he was asked about Agda and the blond man. However, when he was shown the selfie photo with them, he quickly had a vague recollection of meeting the two tourists when they asked him for directions and then requested to be photographed together.

Niko was taken to one of the interrogation rooms and David could watch the progress of the questioning on a closed-circuit TV. As he did not understand Greek, an interpreter sat next to him and gave a live translation of the discussion in English.

After Niko's memory was 'refreshed' by recounting the highlights of Agda's testimony about the wild affair they had carried on in her hotel room, he suddenly remembered he was simply asked to take the couple to a private meeting at the marina. After a little more none-too-gentle-prompting he even recalled the address of the club and the name of the person he brought there as Ollie. After some further hours of interrogation, he recollected the Greek person at the club was called Guido, no last name, and described him as a man with fine aristocratic features.

The detective doing the questioning left the room and joined David next door and told him he knew who Guido was and where to find him. He added that Guido was well connected to senior politicians and could not be brought in for questioning without a magistrate's order, which would be impossible to obtain in view of Guido's influence.

David said all he needed was the name and address of Guido and he would take care of everything. The detective pretended not to understand the meaning of this statement and simply gave him the information as requested. David thanked him and left the police station.

It appeared that Guido lived in an isolated villa in an upper-class neighborhood just outside Athens.

David called the local Mossad resident, Doron, and asked for an emergency meeting in one hour, telling the agent to prepare for a 'hot' operation after midnight.

David met Doron and briefed him regarding his plan to snatch one of the senior Golden Dawn politicians and interrogate him—no holds barred—and probably should eliminate him after that. The resident agent was not happy with the plan and said they needed to survey the ground, come up with an operational plan, and make arrangements to quietly kidnap the person. Then they would need to bring him to an isolated place for the interrogation. He suggested they postpone it to the following night after reinforcements were sent by Mossad in Tel Aviv.

David was worried about word leaking from the police or that Niko would be able to send a warning to Guido and insisted on carrying out the operation that same night. Doron had no choice but to obey as he had been forewarned by the Mossad chief himself to do whatever David required. He only wanted to be on record and to get David to understand that this was a breach of standard operating procedures, but David repeated the importance of carrying out the operation without delay and Doron promised to cooperate fully.

David asked Doron about his assets in Athens and was told he only had three other operatives. Two were involved in intelligence gathering rather than in field work and the third, Yakir, was a fresh graduate of the field training course had never seen action outside Israel though he had some military experience in an elite unit of the IDF.

They had three cars at their disposal; one was a closed van, and the other two were regular economy size cars. They also had a couple encrypted phones for communication purposes.

Mossad had a safe house in Athens, but it was located in an apartment in a residential area with thin walls and many neighbors. This apartment was only suitable for providing a temporary residence for an agent or two that needed to disappear from public places. Doron explained they had a small yacht berthed in the Piraeus marina which he took out for a short trip on weekends to help maintain his skipper's certificate.

David knew that the risks of being exposed or complete

failure of the mission were immense but the alternatives—postponement or cancellation—were worse. There was no time to gather information on Guido's household staff or even if he had a family, so David knew they had to find a way to call him away from the house under some pretense and hope to grab him when he was on the street.

He then hit upon the idea of posing as Ollie and asking for Guido's help in an extreme emergency. When he presented Doron with the idea, and gave him some background information about the situation, he found a skeptic audience. However, Doron liked the part that they would not have to break in to Guido's house with so many unknown factors and trying to entice Guido to leave the villa reduced the risk of exposure considerably.

By the time they had finished discussing the details of the plan it was close to midnight. The two of them took a short drive through Guido's neighborhood and found there was very little traffic at that time of night.

They drove back to Doron's apartment where the three agents were already having a strong cup of coffee served by Doron's wife. Doron quickly introduced David, who briefed them on the operational plan. The female intelligence gathering agent was dispatched to the marina to prepare the yacht and obtain permission to sail before dawn.

The other intelligence agent and Doron were to take the van and wait on a quiet side street just outside Guido's villa.

David and Yakir were to take one of the small cars and stage an accident near the villa's gate. The agent was to smear himself all over his face and body with red ink and pretend to be the victim of a traffic accident caused by the car driven by David.

David was to make the call to Guido from his cellphone posing as Ollie and then wait over Yakir's body in the middle of the road and flag down Guido as he left the villa's grounds.

As soon as Guido stopped to find out what was going on, David was to neutralize him with an injection of a strong tranquillizer that was stored in Doron's refrigerator. Then they would call the van, stuff the unconscious Guido into the van driven by Doron with Yakir watching over him, and drive to the marina followed by David in the small car.

The intelligence agent would take Guido's car and leave it in a busy parking lot in the center of town and then return to his home. There were so many loopholes in this improvised plan they all hoped they would not end up, before morning, in a Greek jail, or worse.

After they were all in position, David pulled out his cell phone and called Guido. When Guido answered, he sounded very angry and a bit confused at being woken up in the middle of the night.

David spoke English with an imitation of what he considered a light Swedish accent, identified himself as Ollie and told Guido he was being held by a couple police officers in Athens and they threatened to expose the 'big plan.' He urged Guido to come immediately to the police station near Syntagma Square and get him released from custody.

Guido asked to speak to the police officers holding him and David cut the connection. Fifteen minutes later, after the Israeli team had almost given up and left, they heard a car engine starting and the villa's electric gate opened slowly.

A black Mercedes emerged and upon seeing the accident scene the driver stopped the car and slowly opened his window.

Within a second, David pounced on the open window and stuck the syringe needle into Guido's exposed neck removing the car keys from the ignition with his other hand.

Guido collapsed on the steering wheel and the car's horn blasted for an instant before David pulled back Guido's unconscious body.

The van driven by Doron came around by the time David and Yakir had pulled Guido out of the Mercedes and none too gently threw him on to the mattress that had been placed on the van's floor.

Yakir got in the van and started cleaning off the red ink while Doron drove the van toward the marina.

David drove the small car and followed the van while the intelligence officer got in the Mercedes and headed to a parking lot near the town center.

So far, the operation had gone very smoothly, and David started to worry that unpleasant surprises lay ahead.

***

The van and the car arrived at the marina without a hitch and the passengers boarded the yacht, with Guido supported by Doron and Yakir, and David following.

They asked the female agent, who had prepared the yacht, to drive the van away from the marina and park it near her apartment. They were not worried about the economy car as it was frequently seen in the marina's parking lot whenever Doron took his yacht out for a spin.

Doron carefully steered the yacht out of the marina and dropped anchor in a shallow area a few miles south of the marina after making sure no one was around.

David injected Guido with adrenalin to wake him up and before the captive was fully conscious, he put a black mask with a green banner of the Islamic State over his face and in Arab accented English started questioning him about Ollie's visit in January.

Guido was still confused and asked David and Doron who they were, and they told him they were from ISIS and pointed at Yakir who was similarly dressed and held a long knife in his left hand. David told Guido he was the notorious executioner, John the Beheader, a cousin of the infamous, John the Jihadist, who was seen on global TV broadcasts.

When Yakir grabbed Guido's hair and exposed his neck, he started shaking, sniveling, and cried that he would tell them everything if they spared his life. Yakir appeared to be testing the sharpness of the blade and started growling in a low voice promising death to the infidels and placed the blade on Guido's neck.

Guido wet himself in his pants and begged David to dismiss the executioner so he could speak without the knife on his neck.

David motioned for Yakir to leave the cabin and without further prompting Guido told them everything about Ollie's visit and the plan to manufacture an improvised nuclear device to blackmail several governments to expel all foreigners.

He also explained that the project was a joint venture by many nationalist and separatist movements who shared a common cause.

David asked him what Ollie wanted in Greece and Guido said he wanted more money for the project but agreed to settle with enlisting two Greek scientists instead of cash. Guido claimed he did not know the location of the laboratory but said the two scientists were supposed to meet with the project chief scientist, a Spanish professor Modena, in Milan.

David asked who they were, and Guido gave him their names and addresses. When David prompted him for more information, Guido said that one of them, Panos, had a family and lived in a small villa while the other one, Stavros, was a divorced engineer who lived alone in an apartment building.

David realized that Guido had no more relevant information and decided they could spare his life as he did not pose any danger to them in their assumed ISIS identity. They blindfolded him, gave him another dose of the tranquillizer, set him ashore on a deserted beach, and returned to the marina just as the sun began to rise.

David, Doron, and Yakir returned to Athens and arranged to meet at noon after a short rest and try and find at least one of the scientists. They were not worried that Guido would be able to warn them as they expected him to remain unconscious at least until late in the afternoon.

***

When the three of them met at noon in Doron's apartment they decided to use the same ploy to extract information from one of the scientists. They thought it would easier to do that with the older of the two, the divorced engineer called Stavros.

The two intelligence officers had already located the address given by Guido on Google Earth maps and Street View photos, but the team still had to find a way to seize Stavros in broad daylight without setting off alarms. So, they pulled out the oldest trick in the book—seducing Stavros with a woman that presented him with an offer he couldn't refuse.

Finding a willing and able woman proved to be quite simple and just a matter of offering the right amount of money to the right type of woman. They invited a high-class call-girls, Alexis, who came to Doron's apartment and after hearing their proposal, a little haggling took place and an agreement was reached on the price for her services.

Her part was very simple—she was to knock on Stavros's door pretending to be lost while looking for a person who had called for her special services and asking for permission to use his toilet as she suddenly felt unwell. Then she would ask him if she could lie down for a moment. The way she looked, no red-blooded Greek man could refuse her request.

A minute later Yakir would ring the bell and when the door opened, he would see Alexis and fly into a rage saying he had called for her services. He would then overpower Stavros and inject him with the tranquillizer, pay Alexis and send her on her way.

Doron and David would then come to the apartment and

replay the ISIS executioner scene and get Stavros to speak. Once again, the plan was fraught with holes, but they knew that Guido might warn Stavros to disappear and time was of the essence.

Surprisingly, the plan worked, and they quickly had Stavros trussed up on a chair and gagged in his own apartment. The, John the Beheader, act worked wonders and Stavros was more than willing to cooperate.

David was mainly interested in two things: if Stavros knew the intended target of the device, and more importantly if he could describe it. Stavros said that to the best of his knowledge, as he had been told by the professor, the device was to be used only for blackmail purposes and never to be detonated. He understood, without being expressly told, that it would serve to purify Europe of unwanted foreign elements and would be shared by several likeminded organizations.

The description of the device matched the implosion bomb model and the dimensions he gave confirmed it was like a stripped-down version of the 'fat man' unsophisticated atomic weapon. His information about the container did not add anything new as he only saw it for a moment when the device was placed in it and he did not remember the exact name painted on it. He could not provide any new details about Ollie beyond the fact he visited the lab in Padova quite frequently and often with a large Viking-type called Andreas.

When questioned about the workforce he told them there were about a dozen employees from different countries and the only people he knew were his Greek colleague and Professor Modena. When he was shown a photo of Doctor Smalley, he recognized him immediately as the man called Doctor Jay.

David figured that the nickname was derived from the initial of his first name, Jason. Stavros said that all the employees kept pretty much to themselves and were warned not to relate any personal details. After warning him that if he called anyone about the interrogation they would get to him and cut his head off with a dull knife, the Israeli team left the apartment after giving Stavros another dose of the tranquillizer that would keep him quiet in wonderland until the next morning.

May 28, Tirana, Albania

At the central mosque, Immad looked at Ollie and smiled when he saw the French beard he had grown during the past week. He then took a Swedish passport out of his pocket and looked at the photograph of the previous owner from which it was stolen in Dubrovnik.

Apparently, there were no suitable Swedish tourists that even remotely resembled Ollie or were approximately the same age and with the same build in Tirana, or for that matter in Albania. Immad told Ollie that the price would be higher than expected due to the extra costs involved in getting this passport. He also explained that Ollie would have to make some further changes with his hair style but would not have to dye it, as he had previously thought.

When he handed over the passport, after a substantial sum of money was transferred, Ollie opened it and looked at the photograph of Andreas Nester Burkhart, age thirty-three, five feet ten inches, blue eyes, balding blond hair, with a little

French goatee beard, and a small scar on his left cheek partly covered by the beard.

The irony of being called Andreas was not lost on Ollie. Immad said he would take Ollie to a local barbershop where his appearance would be slightly altered to match the photograph. When the changes had been made, Immad told Ollie he should use the passport quickly and sparingly as it might soon be reported as stolen.

Ollie had heard that getting into Israel as a lone traveler could be problematic since the border control officers were automatically suspicious of young single men arriving in Israel, regardless of their nationality and appearance.

He figured the best way to enter the country without drawing unwanted attention to himself would be to join a church group on a pilgrimage to the holy places. He decided to take a flight from Tirana to Oslo, in Norway, and then cross into Sweden by train and book a sightseeing trip to the Holy Land with one of the many church groups.

He was sure his Swedish passport would not be scrutinized scrupulously in Oslo, as it may have been in Stockholm or other airports in Sweden where perhaps an alert for a missing passport may have been issued.

According to the schedule of the Rijeka shipping agent, the container would be due to arrive in Haifa between June 10 and June 17, so Ollie decided he should join a group that would set off for Israel around the middle of June.

The Rijeka agent had arranged all the documentation and paperwork for the 'agricultural machinery' to be delivered to the Khodori Institute in Tulkarm, near Nablus, one of the two agricultural schools in the Palestinian Authority territory. He had given Ollie the name of the addressee as Doctor Anwar El-Alami, who was the dean of research at the institute.

Ollie knew little about the relations between Israel and the Palestinian Authority (PA) beyond the articles he had read in the popular press but was aware that slipping into the PA from Israel, or in the opposite direction, would not be difficult with the right contacts as thousands of Palestinians did this every day.

May 29, Vienna

The teams of nuclear forensics analysts from the U.S., Russia, and the ITU in Germany had finally managed to agree upon the factual evidence found in the Padova warehouse but had some major differences of opinion on their interpretation.

They all agreed the findings indicated that pound quantities of U-233 were produced by bombarding a mixture of thorium and beryllium oxides by gamma radiation from the stolen medical and industrial sources found in the warehouse.

They also conceded the quality of the product was high and the level of the bothersome U-232 was below the threshold that would prevent the device from working properly but high enough to impose a safety hazard due to the intense radiation from its thallium-208 decay product.

They considered the implications on the health of the employees that may have been exposed to unsafe doses of radiation and concluded those that had been in close contact with the radiation sources for extended periods might develop symptoms of radiation sickness sooner or later. Their estimates of the expected yield of the device spanned a large range because they did not know the details of the implosion mechanism, but based on the weight of the mock-up model of the core and its diameter, they finally agreed that, at the maximum, it would probably be like the Nagasaki plutonium atomic bomb that was also based on an implosion mechanism.

Namely, something like a device with an explosive power equivalent to fifteen to twenty kilotons of TNT. Imperfect implosion or design artifacts would reduce this yield, but it was anyone's guess what the actual explosion would be like.

The most significant finding arose from the particles of organic matter they found in the metal cabinet that was positioned in the corner of the laboratory. Meticulous analysis showed these originated from a block of a conventional explosive with a unique composition only found in nuclear devices made in North Korea.

The link between the lab in Padova and North Korea was very disturbing in the minds of the scientists as that could also mean that a tested bomb design was at their disposal.

After getting confirmation that the objective of the Astraea project was to construct an improvised nuclear device, based on U-233 as the fissile core and an implosion type mechanism, David called for a meeting of the international task force.

He updated the team on the information he had gathered in Athens, without going into any details about the methods used to obtain it. He repeated his suspicions that the plot of using the device only for blackmail purposes was a clever cover story concocted by the blond man they now knew as Oscar Gunar Axelsson, or by his more recent alias Olaf Gunther Andersson or Ollie.

They had also discovered his ties to Islam from the incident in the hospital and from the testimony of some of his friends from the university days in Uppsala.

David expressed his fear that the ultimate target may not even be in continental Europe and could be practically in any city or other location to which containers were shipped.

The information they got from the Greek engineer, Stavros, and the Golden Dawn operative, Guido, did not get them any closer to finding the device, the intended target, or the chief perpetrators.

The French member of the ITF, Nicolas, told the team that Interpol had received many calls about seeing a blond man that matched the description and image and all had turned out to be false alarms, so they stopped responding to these calls.

He added that with the photo from Agda's cell phone they might have a better chance of finding the blond man known as Ollie.

Thomas, the former MI6 operative, said that the search for Doctor Smalley in the UK had not provided any leads, and suspected he had gone underground somewhere in Europe.

There was no trace of Professor Modena, or any of the other people who had worked with him.

Eugene and Vassilly had no news and suggested the task force draw up a contingency plan in case the device left Europe and arrived in their own country.

May 30, Gothenburg

Andreas Nester Burkhart, the name Ollie now used, did not want to be seen in Stockholm, so after his plane landed in Oslo, he travelled by bus to Gothenburg in Sweden.

Since he intended to join a tour group going on a pilgrimage to the holy places in Israel, he bought the local newspaper, Göteborgs-Posten—Gothenburg Post—looking through the classified ads for a suitable tour group.

He found an advertisement of the Israel Christian Tours agency that organized eight-day tours devoted to seeing modern Israel and Holy sites, that was scheduled to depart on June ninth. The itinerary included two nights in Tel Aviv, two nights in the Galilee in a Kibbutz hotel, and three nights in Jerusalem.

This would give him an opportunity to survey the intended target area in Jerusalem and make preliminary arrangements with Sheik Khalil in Umm al-Fahm, the head of a faction of the radical Islamic movement in Israel, the contact person that Ibn Tutta had specified.

Meanwhile, he wanted to use the ten days before departure to arrange a new identity and a new passport as he feared the Andreas Burkhart cover might be compromised soon.

He had to avoid the two groups he was acquainted with. The Muslim community in Gothenburg was quite strong but the mosques were under police surveillance for two opposing reasons.

On the one hand, the police offered the Islamic community protection against right-wing extremists that harassed foreigners in general and dark-skinned people, especially Muslim women wearing burkas. On the other hand, the police kept an eye on the leaders of the Muslim community, especially the sheiks in the mosques that served as recruiting agents for volunteers that wanted to join ISIS.

Ollie's other connections were with racist nationalists like the group he had joined in Stockholm and these elements were also targeted by the police to prevent them from causing trouble.

So, Ollie looked for the regular criminals, those that had no political agenda and were willing to do business with whoever paid them. The experience he gained in the seedy quarters of Stockholm served him well and within a couple days he came across a shady former Estonian, called Kermo, who dealt in bogus passports.

After agreeing on the price and delivery date, Kermo did not ask any questions and only requested a recent photograph.

Two day later, after five thousand Euros exchanged hands, Ollie received a well-used Swedish passport with his photo and the name Hugo Elias Jacobsson, a thirty-five-year-old male from Gothenburg, whose profession was listed as an architect.

Ollie went to a travel agency and found out there was still a vacancy for the Israel Christian Tour group. The female travel agent was very pleased a young man would join the group that usually consisted mainly of retirees. She told Ollie there was a single girl in her late twenties who would be thrilled a handsome young man was also booked on the tour.

Ollie saw this as an opportunity to blend in with the group and get through the Israeli passport control without raising suspicion.

CHAPTER 14

June 9, Tel Aviv

The Swedish tour group arrived at Ben Gurion airport outside Tel Aviv. Ollie, or as he was now called, Hugo, managed to be seated on the flight from Stockholm next to a plain looking girl by the name of Lena, the only other young person in the group.

He had turned on the charm and she was flattered by the attention of this good-looking man.

When they stood in line at the passport control, they were already holding hands and together they approached the border security officer seated in her booth.

She had been briefed to keep an eye open for a Scandinavian-looking, single, young man and knew pilgrimage groups from Sweden seldom included young men. She looked at the couple and saw a handsome man with a rather plain woman. She saw that their passports were under different names and the stamps on the passports indicated they had not travelled together previously. So, she went through the usual routine of asking them what the purpose of their visit was and where they intended to stay and for how long.

She was satisfied with the answers but still a bit concerned about the couple, so she politely asked them to step aside. They were escorted to a small room and invited to sit down and wait for the supervisor.

By now Ollie thought that hitting on Lena was a bad idea and was quite sure his cover was blown. However, he knew that in the waiting room they were probably being monitored by a video camera, so he started chatting with Lena as if he did not have a worry in the world.

Lena was a bit uptight, but he managed to allay her concerns talking about the places they would see and the things they would do in Israel. They were speaking in Swedish, of course, but Ollie was sure their conversation was translated and understood.

After about ten minutes, a grim looking man entered the room with their passports in his hand. He said that Lena could leave the room and handed over her passport. She was hesitant about leaving Ollie, but he told her everything was in order and asked her to tell the tour group leader he had been delayed for questioning by Israeli authorities.

The supervisor asked him in English what he had said to Lena and Ollie translated what he had just said. The supervisor enquired about Ollie's travels, based on the entry and exit stamps on his passport, and as he had prepared for this in advance, he supplied details of his former trips.

This seemed to satisfy the supervisor, who told Ollie he was also free to go and gave him his passport. As Ollie was about to leave the room the man said in Arabic, 'Salaam Aleika,' and Ollie caught himself at the last moment before automatically replying, 'Aleika as-salaam,' and instead said he did not understand.

The man smiled and let him go to collect his luggage. By the time Ollie picked up his small suitcase, the whole group was waiting to board the bus that was to take them to their hotel in Tel Aviv.

After the group checked in to a large hotel on the beach front they were to meet in the lobby and headed to old Jaffa for a taste of the lively city's nightlife.

Ollie and Lena were in adjoining rooms but intended to spend the time together. This part of the tour was to give them a taste of modern Israel—there were no holy places in Tel Aviv—only a bustling city that never rested.

***

The supervisor, who was a senior officer in the Israeli Security Agency, smiled to himself and called his boss at the ISA telling him he was sure that the man they knew as Ollie, was travelling with the passport of Hugo Elias Jacobsson.

He said that while he had Ollie's passport in his hand, he had managed to insert a microchip tracker that would enable the ISA to track Ollie, or more accurately Ollie's passport, even from a distance.

***

The information was passed on to the head of the ISA and to Mossad headquarters, and 'Hugo' was placed under close surveillance. The instructions given by the head of Mossad were to find the improvised nuclear device and disarm it and

'Hugo' was to be followed but not arrested until they were sure he would lead them to the device.

The ISA had the schedule of the tour group so two agents were posted in the lobby of the hotel in Tel Aviv with orders to follow 'Hugo' if he departed from the group.

***

David received the information with mixed feelings. He was glad the mysterious blond man he had been trying to catch was within the grasp of Israeli security agents but was worried that this 'Hugo,' whom he preferred to call Ollie as this was the name of the person he had been chasing, would manage to evade his 'babysitters' and get hold of the device.

He already knew that Ollie was exceptionally cunning and ruthless and feared he may have contacts with local Arab extremists in Israel or the Palestinian Authority that would assist him if he tried to go underground.

He was especially concerned that if the device was detonated in a populated center in Israel the collateral damage would be intolerable for such a small country. David expressed his uneasiness to Shimony, the Deputy Director of Mossad, but was told the best ISA agents were on the case and that a blond man like Ollie would stand out among the Israelis.

He also said that without knowledge of Hebrew or Arabic Ollie would find it difficult to get around unnoticed. David said he wasn't sure that Ollie did not speak Arabic as no one knew where he had spent the time between disappearing in Uppsala until he re-emerged in Stockholm several years later.

David asked for permission to share the information about Ollie's presence in Israel with the members of the international task force and was instructed to wait until they determined what Ollie was up to.

Shimony said he worried that Ollie would somehow become aware of the fact his cover was blown and take evasive action if he noted he was being followed. Furthermore, he said, if all the extra security measures deployed in the major European cities because of the 'dirty bomb' threat were suddenly removed, it might alert Ollie.

David was not pleased with this decision but knew he had to obey, so he asked when the international task force could be informed about Ollie's whereabouts and Shimony told him that would be only after the device and Ollie were seized.

June 9, Girona, Catalonia, Spain

Professor Matias Antonio Modena had quietly returned to Spain after leaving Padova in May and rented a small apartment in Girona under an assumed name. He now called himself Santiago Guaman and posed as a retired university professor, who was writing a fictional thriller.

Ironically, the apartment was in an old section of the town on a narrow street near the Museum of Jewish History.

He had no idea Ollie had taken charge of the device and had made shipping arrangements to transport it to Israel. He was concerned he had not received any word from Andreas or Ollie, and the media was not full of the reports he had expected of policy changes toward 'unwanted elements' or the revival of separatist movements all over Europe.

He began to worry and wanted to contact Delgado through the local branch of the Catalan separatist movement but was afraid his true identity would be uncovered and that would compromise the whole plan. He decided to call the only person he trusted, his former graduate student and sometime lover, Ramona, and ask her to come to Girona to meet him.

He was not sure how she would react as he had severed all contact with her for almost a whole year when he left Barcelona and moved to Padova.

***

Ramona was surprised to hear from the professor after all this time and was relieved when he told her he was well as she feared his health could be affected by his quite careless handling of radioactive materials.

She did not acknowledge to David that she and the professor were more than a student and a mentor but did not deny it. She greatly respected Modena for his intellect, intelligence, and dedication to Catalan independence and that made up for the considerable difference in age between them.

She admitted to herself the sex with him was not all that exciting for her but patiently accepted his attempts to please her physically as well as intellectually. She readily agreed to meet him in Girona, and they arranged to have dinner in a small restaurant near the famous cathedral.

When she entered the restaurant, she was taken aback by the professor's appearance. He had lost several pounds, looked quite emaciated, and, at least, ten years older than she had remembered him. She refrained from making a comment on his looks and kissed him on both cheeks as he rose to greet her.

They sat down and Modena gently held her hand and caressed it while she smiled at him. Without being asked, he told her he had fulfilled his life's ambition and had proven that a fissionable material could be produced without a neutron source or nuclear reactor.

He boasted that soon the whole world would recognize his genius and the Nobel Prize was as good as his as he had succeeded in fulfilling the alchemists' dream of transmutation of a low value material into a precious commodity.

Ramona was in a state of shock upon hearing this and was speechless for several minutes. The professor did not even notice her expression and continued to boast about his scientific achievement. By the time he had finished his self-aggrandizement, she found enough courage to ask him how he would prove that he had made uranium-233 by his innovative method.

The professor said that he could provide a sample of the material for analysis to satisfy the skeptics, and then looked at her and enigmatically added that the further proof would become evident when the cause of independent Catalonia would be advanced thanks to his work.

Ramona asked him what he meant by this comment, but he said they should eat their dinner and talk about other things. They had a couple of drinks after dinner and the professor shyly invited her to spend the night in his apartment rather than drive back to Barcelona.

She felt sorry for the professor and pitied him in his present state and she also wanted to learn more about the meaning of his last statement, so she agreed. She had to support him up the stairs to his apartment as the last drinks had taken their toll on him. She undressed him and put him in bed and lay next to him and gently caressed him until he fell asleep.

He murmured something unintelligible in his sleep and all she could make out were the words, "free Catalunya," "not detonate," "Doctor Jay," and "Andreas."

In the morning, the professor was deeply embarrassed to find himself in bed listening to Ramona singing to herself while making coffee in the apartment's little kitchenette. When she saw that he was awake she smiled and offered him freshly brewed coffee.

They set their coffee mugs on a small breakfast table on the balcony overlooking the narrow street and the professor bashfully asked her if he they done anything the previous night.

Ramona smiled and answered he had fallen asleep as soon as his head hit the pillow and that he mumbled some incoherent things in his sleep she did not understand.

Professor Modena said that his sleep had been full of strange disturbances lately and he had no idea what he said or if the words had any meaning.

Ramona realized that now, completely in control of his senses, he would not be as forthcoming as he had been the night before. When he asked her about the separatist movement, she told him she had not been in contact with the movement since he had left as she was afraid she would be interrogated about his disappearance. She also told him that she had had to switch her research topic to a new supervisor.

Both of them became aware of the fact that their relationship had changed and would not be as close as it was before his departure so when Ramona said she had to return to Barcelona he stood up and kissed her cheeks and offered his hand for a farewell shake.

June 9, Ibiza, Spain

Doctor Jason Smalley had just finished a liquid dinner consisting of a variety of alcoholic beverages in a bar overlooking the busy main street of the frantic resort town of Sant Antoni di Portmany on the western coast of Ibiza.

He did not want to return to his empty hotel room so moved on to one of the many nightclubs that catered to the hordes of young, fun-seeking tourists, mainly from the affluent countries in northern Europe. As he decided to cut down on his alcohol consumption, he ordered a bottle of red wine with only twelve percent alcohol that was a lot less than the forty percent alcoholic drinks he had been gulping earlier.

He looked around and saw a couple hundred youngsters, none of which appeared to be over twenty-five years of age dancing, singing, and making out as if there was no tomorrow.

He was disgusted to see several interracial couples that consisted of a blond girl and a dark-skinned man. He smiled to himself with the knowledge that this abomination would we wiped out from Europe soon, thanks to his own handiwork.

Doctor Jay walked up to one of the scantily dressed girls, whose short, strapless white dress contrasted beautifully with her dark skin. The dress was practically molded to her full figure so when she turned to him, he did not need to use his imagination to guess what lay beneath the dress.

He invited her to join him for a glass of wine, or a drink of her choice. She laughingly said her name was Veronica and she would gladly join him if his intentions were serious as she was a working girl who needed an income and asked for a glass of expensive Remy Martin.

He ordered the drink for her and told her she could call him Jay, and that he was very serious about her if she was willing to try some kinky stuff.

Veronica said she was ready for anything if the price was right and the deal was sealed with her giving him a peck on his cheek while her right hand patted his backside to make sure he carried a stuffed wallet.

She said she had a fully equipped room reserved in a hotel next to the club and its price was included in the deal. She sensed that although he professed to like her, he kept looking around the bar and his glance lingered on some handsome guys, so she told him that for some extra cash she could arrange for a threesome of any variety he chose.

Jay was excited by this new twist but said he would tell her later what he preferred.

Jay and Veronica left the nightclub and walked to the hotel. Jay was already quite inebriated but did not refuse the drink she offered him in the room. He drank it quickly and said he had to use her bathroom. When he didn't come out after a few minutes Veronica knocked on the bathroom door and softly opened it to see that he had passed out on the floor.

She smiled to herself, thanked the manufacturers of the chloral hydrate 'knock-out' drops, took the wallet out his pocket, and found that it was indeed stuffed with fifty and one hundred Euro bills. She also saw the plastic key card to the room in his hotel in a small holder with the room number and the name of the hotel.

She called her partner on a cell phone, told him she had a parcel to deliver, and asked him to arrive quickly.

Juan knocked on the door and without a word she let him in and showed him Jay's wallet, the hotel card, and the gentleman himself on the bathroom floor. They decided to leave him on the floor until the drug's effect wore off and meanwhile go through his room in search of anything of value.

Veronica said the wallet contained enough cash for her and Juan to disappear for a few days until Jay hopefully would leave the island. The search in Jay's room did not yield much besides a British passport in the name of Jason Smalley. They left the passport in its place because they figured he would need it to travel from Ibiza, and as far as they were concerned the earlier he left the island the better for them.

When Doctor Smalley regained conscious, he found himself on the bathroom floor in a strange room. After a few moments, he managed to stand up, lean on the bathroom sink and wash his face with cold water. He immediately realized his wallet, cell phone, and watch were missing. He shook his head as he left the bathroom and entered the bright bedroom area and was shocked to see the time on the clock-radio in the room was eleven fifteen.

He left the room after noting the room number four six-ty-eight on the door and took the elevator down to the lobby. He went to the front desk and asked who was checked in to room four sixty-eight. The desk clerk took one look at the disheveled man and understood what had happened.

He told Jay he could not disclose this information and offered to call the police. Jay did not want to get involved with the police and be questioned by them, so he said he would go to his own hotel and lodge a complaint from there. He slowly sauntered to his own hotel and presented himself at the front desk and asked for another key card to his room. Here, too, the clerk realized what had happened, did not ask any questions, and handed him a key card.

Jay entered his room and saw it had been ransacked methodically and professionally. He was pleasantly surprised to see his passport still on the table; it had not been taken.

He considered his options and knew he urgently needed to get money, and the quickest way would be to contact his bank in the UK and have money transferred to him in Ibiza. He also realized he had to block the stolen credit card and obtain a new one.

He knew that a risk was involved in doing these things as his temporary shelter in Ibiza might be exposed, so he decided to wait for the money transfer to arrive and then move to a new location. He even considered travelling to London and personally collect the funds and new credit card but was worried he would be arrested the minute he set foot on British soil.

Then another thought occurred to him—contact Paul

Dooley, who Jay held responsible for his dire situation, and ask for his financial and organizational help, despite the directive to avoid contact with him. After giving the matter some further thought, he decided to contact the bank to cancel the stolen credit card and block it, without disclosing his whereabouts. He next called Dooley and threatened him with exposure if he refused to deliver financial support. He would give Dooley an ultimatum to transfer the money within twenty-four hours, then leave Ibiza and find a new sanctuary.

The call to the bank went smoothly and after identifying himself and answering the usual 'security questions' he was told that no cash had been recently drawn from his account nor any new transactions made and his request for cancellation of the credit card would be immediately honored.

The call to Paul Dooley's cell phone was another matter. Paul refused to take the call from an unidentified foreign number. Jay used a simple trick and called Dooley's office pretending to be a consular officer at the British Embassy in Madrid. He said he was instructed to notify Mr. Dooley that a man called Doctor Jason Smalley requested his help as he was in a local hospital after being badly injured in a traffic accident in Ibiza.

Paul said he did not know anyone called Jason Smalley but after some prompting added that if a compatriot of his was in distress, then he, as a Good Samaritan, would help. So, a money transfer was arranged. Jay received the money later that afternoon and took a ferry to Palma de Mallorca, where he established himself in another busy tourist resort.

Palma was traditionally, even from the 'good old days' of

Franco's regime, a strong Nationalist stronghold and Jay was sure he would feel comfortable there as long as he did not express his true opinion of Spaniards.

He wondered where Ollie and Andreas took the device and why there was nothing in the press or TV on the change of immigration policy he had expected. He suspected that no government would disclose that it was being blackmailed but thought there would be some low-profile actions against 'undesirable foreign elements.'

He wanted to contact Paul Dooley again and ask him about this but considering the cold shoulder he received when he tried to speak to him recently, he knew he would be rejected again. So, he decided he would use the money he received and have a good time and when it ran out he would force Dooley to fork out some more.

June 9, Athens

Guido took more than a week to recover from the traumatic experience of his 'near execution' at the hands of the fake ISIS operatives.

He had lost his appetite and thus also a few pounds, which was an unexpected, and unwanted, blessing. He was not certain whether Stavros or Panos suffered a similar fate or if Niko had been the one responsible for their situation although he suspected as much. Yet, he had a feeling he was not the only one who had suffered the rough treatment and suspected his torturers had followed up on the information he gave them about the two scientists.

He invited Niko to come over to his villa and bring the two scientists with him for an urgent meeting. When the three guests entered the house, Guido took one look at Stavros and from his cowed expression knew he had also been visited by the ISIS gang. He saw that Niko had a guilty expression on his face, but the other scientist appeared to be completely at ease and relaxed.

Guido offered them coffee and some pastries, and they talked about the Golden Dawn party and its aspirations. Niko wondered what the hurry was and why Guido had mentioned an emergency but kept his thoughts to himself. When Guido thanked them for coming the three of them stood up ready to leave, but Guido asked Stavros to stay for a few minutes and dismissed the other two.

Stavros would not meet his eyes even when only the two of them remained in the room. Guido wanted to know what exactly Stavros had told the ISIS people and knew that to get a complete and frank account he had to make Stavros feel comfortable.

He did not want to admit to Stavros that he was the one who had revealed his address to the ISIS people, so asked him if he had been under some stress recently as he looked kind of disconsolate.

Stavros, who was no fool, said that Guido himself did not look well and admitted he had received an unwelcome visit that turned in to a life-threatening situation.

The shrewd look on Guido's face unveiled he knew exactly what he meant, and Stavros said he would tell all if Guido did the same.

Each recounted the frightening visit and intimidation, and both felt somewhat relieved they were not alone in their total acquiescence and submission.

Stavros's account of the information he gave the ISIS gang was news for Guido who was not aware of the technical details of the construction of the device and knew only that building such a thing was being considered.

He asked Stavros if he knew where the device was, and Stavros told him he had last seen it loaded into a standard container on a rental truck with a crane and that the truck was driven by Ollie and Andreas.

When he gave Guido a description of the two Swedes, Guido said he had met Ollie and that although he did not personally know Andreas he knew of his reputation as the organizer of the meetings in which the Astraea project was conceived.

Stavros departed after they promised each other not to share the traumatic incidents with anyone else.

June 9, Vienna

The international task force convened again in the small meeting room at the IAEA headquarters.

David was still in Israel and joined them via a video conference-call. He was under strict instructions not to reveal that Ollie had been spotted in Tel Aviv and was under surveillance.

The discussion evolved around the plausible targets of the device and a lot of speculative ideas were presented. Naturally, the biggest concern of each participant was that his own country would be the prime target, but none could show any evidence that the device or Ollie were in their country.

The European delegates reported the excitement they had earlier sensed in the local nationalist movements had abated and thought this may be indicative of the fact the device was not to be used in their country. However, they all said the state of enhanced security was to be maintained until the positive identification and capture of Ollie and the container.

David felt uncomfortable about being the only one who knew Israel was the target and that the extra security measures in Europe were a waste of money and time, but reluctantly adhered to the orders he had received and disclosed nothing.

June 12, Palma de Mallorca and London

The Spanish police received an anonymous call telling them that a British tourist was involved in an international plot to detonate a radiation dispersion device in Barcelona. The tip off originated from a public phone in the heart of the City of London and the caller had an upper-class English accent.

At about the same time, a similar call was placed to MI6 public relations department informing them that a UK citizen was about to be arrested in Palma for planning to use an RDD to disrupt normal life in London.

The anonymous caller said that the person in question was Doctor Jay Smalley, a former employee of the Aldermaston Atomic Weapon Establishment (AWE).

The information was forwarded to Colin Thomas, who immediately got the Foreign Office to demand that Doctor Jay Smalley be extradited to the UK for crimes committed on British soil, including treason and violation of the Official Secrets Act 1989.

The Spanish police had no difficulty in locating Doctor Smalley and arresting him as he was too intoxicated to resist or even understand the charges against him.

Before he sobered up, he was already on a plane to London under heavy guard.

When confronted by Thomas he was shocked to hear that the man he knew as Ollie was a convert to Islam and not the racist, rabid hater of Muslims and foreigners, as he had presented himself.

Jay broke down and confessed all, except the connection with Dooley whom he believed remained his only ally. He felt he had been led on by Ollie and played as a fool by him, and he sought revenge, so he told Thomas all about the laboratory in Padova.

Thomas already knew about the laboratory, about the professor, and the device, but wanted to get more technical details concerning the device from the very person who had manufactured it.

Doctor Jay described the device and mentioned all the difficulties and potential pitfalls. He said the core of the improvised nuclear device consisted of a sphere containing about twenty-five pounds of U-233 metal. The core was surrounded by an array of shaped, high explosive charges.

The explosives were provided by Ollie who said they were

purchased from a North Korean official, who also supplied them with fast detonators of the type used in nuclear devices. Each shaped charge had a small slot drilled into it to provide a hole into which the detonators were to be inserted. All the detonators were wired to the timing mechanism.

Smalley proudly told Thomas that it was designed by him based on his experience in AWE, in a way that would assure simultaneous activation of all the detonators. He explained the detonation of the high explosives would compress the U-233 core to a supercritical configuration, just like the implosion bomb developed by the U.S. during WWII.

The whole system weighed a few hundred pounds and was packed in a thin, steel shell with inserts for the detonators. Thomas asked how the device was armed and Smalley said the detonators had to be inserted in the slots, connected to the timing mechanism and a car battery, and could be dismantled by simply disconnecting the battery.

Thomas then asked whether there were any health hazards and Smalley laughed and said no one would feel comfortable sitting next to a few hundred pounds of high explosives or if the device fell on someone's foot it could be painful.

Thomas was not amused by this answer and asked if there was any radiation emitted from the U-233 core and Smalley replied there was a slow build-up of decay products from the U-232 impurity, and particularly one of those, thallium-208 had a nasty energetic gamma ray that easily penetrated through the layer of high explosives and thin steel shell.

This radiation could be detected from a distance of a few feet. He also added that during the production of the U-233, the workers at the Padova laboratory would have been exposed to gamma radiation and the longer they worked with the material the higher the risk. He stated he had noticed some symptoms of radiation sickness in Professor Modena's behavior but thought the other workers would not be at a serious risk because of the short duration of the project.

Thomas thanked him for the information and said that his cooperation might help reduce his prison sentence or at least allow him to get better treatment in jail.

Smalley said he would like to know what happened to Ollie and wished him to burn slowly in hell.

Thomas then conveyed all the information provided by Jay to the members of the international task force and mentioned it corroborated the information given by Stavros under duress.

CHAPTER 15

June 12, Haifa

The Panamax class cargo ship from Limassol arrived at the port of Haifa with three thousand five hundred sixty-eight standard shipping containers on board.

The unloading was routinely executed, and the ship was quickly ready to take on a new load of containers with goods exported from Israel.

All the offloaded containers were placed in the port's holding area until custom officials examined their documents and cleared them.

Since the portal with the radiation detectors was closed for periodic maintenance, once the containers cleared customs they were loaded on trucks and transported by land to their destinations without any further checks.

The rusty container marked as 'agricultural machinery' was placed on a truck and transported to the Khodori Institute in Tulkarm. Crossing over from Israel into the territory of the Palestinian Authority involved a long delay at both checkpoints but no special examination of the container's content was carried out.

Doctor Anwar El-Alami, the dean of research at the school,

had been told that a container with agricultural machinery would be delivered to the institute but he was not to open it until the technician, whose job was to install the equipment, arrived.

El-Alami was not used to having containers delivered to his poorly equipped school and was even more surprised by the directive not to open it. He inspected the container and saw it was closed with a stamped, tamperproof seal, so had no option but to abide by his orders.

He tried to enquire from the driver when the technician was expected, but the driver said he did not have any information. He then looked through the shipping documents and saw that Rijeka was the port of origin and the container had been transferred from one ship to another in Bari, Italy, and again in Limassol, Cyprus, before reaching Haifa.

He went back to his office and tried to locate Rijeka on the map and found it was in Croatia, but that did not give him a clue about the contents of the container.

June 14, Jerusalem

Ollie was pleased the tour group had reached Jerusalem after two days in the Tel Aviv area and two days in the Galilee.

In Tel Aviv, he felt the pulse of this vibrant city, where traffic near the promenade along the beach at two in the morning was almost as busy as in the middle of the day. The cafés, restaurants, and beaches were full of people laughing, singing, and having a good time. The beaches were crowded from morning to night and he saw so many good-looking girls of all ages wherever he cast his sight, that he started to imagine the seventy-two virgins awaiting the faithful who died as *sha-hids*, only he wasn't quite sure whether there were that many virgins among the beach goers.

The group was taken to old Jaffa to get a taste of the night life, quite unexpected for a pilgrimage tour of the Holy Land.

His tried to chill his relationship with Lena once they settled in their hotel room since he didn't need the cover of a lover anymore. But Lena would not let this handsome man slip away so easily and to avoid having a big public row that would raise the suspicion of the rest of the group he had to play along.

He particularly detested spending the nights in their king-size bed, as he quickly found out that below her plain surface, she had a voracious sexual appetite that had probably not been satisfied too often.

Her plain looks belied the fact she was very playful and inventive in bed. Ollie thought about the wild times he had spent with Agda and tried to blow off steam and vent his anger and frustration with Lena the same way, but she would have none of that rough stuff in bed. When he tried slapping her gently, as he had done with Agda, she turned red and became so indignant she threatened to go to the police.

Ollie accepted this unexpected form of punishment and after the second night started to enjoy her enthusiasm in love making. He recalled a saying of one of his friends from the days at Uppsala University about plain looking, even ugly, fat women. The friend had said that they were so grateful to whoever slept with them they were willing to do anything and everything to please their mate.

Lena's behavior provided good testimony of this—for a kiss, a hug, or a smile from him, not to mention more passionate contact, she was ready to practically become his slave and worship him. Ollie thought that this could become useful for carrying out his plans and meanwhile made the most of her eagerness and fervor in bed.

In the morning, he told Lena he wanted to wander around the Old City of Jerusalem on his own, without being forced to follow a guide leading the group like a flock of sheep.

Lena offered to join him, and he agreed, knowing that her presence would help him blend in as a young couple with the many tourists that visited the city.

He collected a tourist map of the Old City from the hotel's front desk and got some advice and instructions from the concierge. Ollie and Lena set off on their own and walked down the narrow streets that led from the Jaffa Gate towards the center of the Old City.

The narrow streets were just one large colorful open market and after a few hundred feet they left the busy bazaar and veered toward the Church of the Holy Sepulchre. They stood in line with the other tourists waiting to enter the crowded church.

Lena, who was wearing a short-sleeved top and short pants that did not flatter her figure, had to cover herself with a scarf they purchased from one of the many vendors outside the church.

Ollie was more interested in the security in the city, and particularly near the church, than in the church itself and kept looking around.

Lena was impressed by the fact that the church was divided between several different Christian sects: the Greek Orthodox, Eastern Orthodoxy, Oriental Orthodoxy, and Roman Catholics, who all jealously watched over their part of the church.

Fortunately, the Anglicans and other protestant groups believed the true burial place of Jesus was in the Garden Tomb outside the walls of the Old City, so they posted no claims in the Church of the Holy Sepulchre. From the cool church, they returned to the hot narrow bazaar streets and followed the crowds of tourists to the Wailing Wall, or Western Wall, the most sacred place to the Jews.

The open space in front of the Wall which was separated into two segregated parts—one for men and one for women—was crammed full of people. While some were busy praying near the Wall, many other tourists stood a little further away and concentrated on taking photographs of the Wall and colorful worshippers.

There were many police officers and soldiers among these onlookers. Lena was impressed by the size of the stones at the bottom of the wall and wondered how they were carved to exactly fit each other more than two thousand years ago. She admired the Dome of the Rock Shrine with its glittering golden roof located on top of the Temple Mount, considered the third most holy site for Islam, while Ollie gazed at the security measures.

Lena and Ollie entered the large open space near the Dome of the Rock, but non-Muslims were not allowed to enter the mosque during prayers. Ollie had to accept this since in front of Lena he could not admit he was a devout Muslim.

Israeli soldiers and police forces were stationed at the entrance to Temple Mount but not in the space between al-Aqsa mosque and the Dome of the Rock. Ollie had heard they only entered this area if the Muslim worshippers started throwing stones and rocks at the Jewish worshippers down below.

This tour of the Old City alarmed Ollie and rattled him, since he realized it would be impossible to drive a large truck with the shipping container into the heart of the city. The narrow streets were not traversable for vehicles that were large enough to carry a container, so Ollie knew he had to have the device transferred to a smaller vehicle, which would not be easy considering its weight and size, and disguising it would be a real challenge.

He told Lena he wanted to walk back to the Church of the Holy Sepulchre from the Lions Gate that was near Temple Mount—following part of Via Dolorosa in the footsteps of Jesus. He was more interested in the width of the streets than in the fourteen stations on Via Dolorosa, but Lena was impressed by his sudden burst of religious zeal.

The two ISA agents had followed Ollie and Lena the whole time keeping a safe distance from the couple and in the bustling crowd were not noticed by Ollie.

In the evening, Lena and Ollie joined the group for dinner and their guide promised them a special treat—walking on the ancient walls of the Old City at night and seeing all the holy places illuminated by special lighting.

After the tour of the walls, Ollie went to one of the few remaining public phone booths, which were hard to find in a country that had more cellular phones than residents and called the private number of the shipping agent in Rijeka.

He was informed the container had already been delivered safely to the agricultural institute in Tulkarm. He then placed another call to a randomly selected number in the Tel Aviv area and hung up a few seconds after it was answered without saying a word.

The two ISA agents who had been trailing Ollie since his arrival in Tel Aviv were a bit surprised when he left the group and wandered around the Old City with Lena during the day. They did not see anything unusual in the fact he had visited the holy places of Christianity, Judaism, and Islam and did not suspect he had been planning how to place an atomic bomb amidst the Old City.

So far, he had behaved like a typical tourist and the signal from the tracking device planted in his passport was strong and continuous. The agents followed him to the phone booth and entered it as soon as he left and then redialed the last number. The call was answered by an old woman who sounded confused when they asked her who had just called, and she said she didn't know as the caller hung up without speaking.

They recognized this simple ploy immediately and called the telephone company. After speaking to the shift supervisor, the agents got the list of numbers that had been called from that booth, and by the timestamp identified the number in Croatia that Ollie had called. A quick search revealed it belonged to a shipping agent.

They passed the information to the ISA headquarters who forwarded it to Shimony at the Mossad. Shimony decided to send the resident Mossad agent from Zagreb to interrogate the shipping agency so he instructed him to find the shipping agent and discover everything about his connections with Ollie, and especially whether he had made a shipment of a container and its destination.

June 15, Jerusalem

Ollie told Lena he had called his mother from the phone booth the previous day and that due to an emergency involving his aging mother in Sweden he had to depart immediately. When he started packing his bag, Lena burst out crying and pleaded with him to stay another couple days and return to Gothenburg with the group but he insisted he had to leave right away and promised her he would get in touch with her in Sweden as soon as his mother's health improved. He then asked her to inform the group's guide about his plans and left fifty Euro as a tip for the guide.

Ollie made his way to the main bus station just outside the walls of the Old City that catered to the East Jerusalem Arab population and in English asked at the information counter how he could get to Umm al-Fahm.

A fast exchange in Arabic took place between the man at the counter and a taxi driver and since Ollie had spent enough time in the Middle East with the ISIS forces and understood basic Arabic, he knew they were planning on charging him double the regular exorbitant rate.

He said something quite rude about cheating tourists so once they realized he spoke Arabic, they managed to negotiate a price that was only slightly over the normal rate. He then got in the taxi and told the driver in English to make it fast.

The two-hour trip was uneventful as the taxi had the Israeli orange colored license plates and was not stopped by any police or military roadblock. When they reached Umm al-Fahm Ollie asked the driver to drop him off at the central mosque, tipped him generously, and to the driver's surprise entered the mosque as if he belonged there and not like a Christian tourist.

The few worshippers who were in the mosque suspiciously eyed the tall blond man, and when he asked in English to see Sheik Khalil he was ignored and no one responded. Ollie switched to Arabic and that only increased their distrust as they had all encountered ISA agents who spoke the language. Ollie got down on his knees and prayed—an act they had also seen done by ISA agents posing as true believers.

Ollie tried to restrain himself but under his breath he let out a scandalous curse in Iraqi accented Arabic and only then did one of people in the mosque get up and tell Ollie to follow him. The man led Ollie to a house that was right next to the mosque, told Ollie to wait outside and entered the house after knocking on the door.

He reappeared after a couple minutes and invited Ollie to enter. He escorted Ollie to the living room where a young man was sitting at a bare table sipping dark, black coffee from a small decorative glass. The young man introduced himself as Sheik Khalil, the sheik of the Umm al-Fahm mosque and head of the radical—he used the word "true"—Islamic movement in the north.

Ollie stated he brought a message from the brave brethren in Syria and clearly pronounced the code words "al tahrir al Islami."

Sheik Khalil asked Ollie's escort to leave the room, invited Ollie to sit down and offered him coffee, which Ollie gratefully accepted.

Sheik Khalil asked about the holy warriors of ISIS and Ollie told him that despite the fact many good brothers had been killed fighting for the cause of the new Caliphate, many volunteers flocked to the organization to fill the ranks of those lost in battle.

Ollie said that the new Supreme Commander Abu-Alli was especially pleased with the young men and women that came from Western European countries and had come to receive military training, ideological indoctrination, religious fervor, and experience fighting for ISIS in Iraq and Syria. Those that survived and excelled in their work for Allah would then return to their home countries and either act on their own instilling terror in the hearts of the *kefirs* or lay low until called upon to carry out special operations.

He mentioned as examples the acts that were carried out by El Qaeda trained fighters in Madrid, London, Paris, Brussels, Copenhagen, and the United States and said that in the future each of these would be regarded as a promo for the real thing—the globally coordinated actions carried out on behalf of ISIS. Sheik Khalil was duly impressed but asked what ISIS was doing to forward the cause of the Palestinians.

Ollie explained that the Palestinian were just the tip of the iceberg and there was a plan for an operation on such an immense scale that would free all Muslims, including the Palestinians, from the infidels forever. Those that accepted the true faith would be allowed to live and those who refused would be summarily eliminated.

Finally, they got around to the matter at hand. Ollie told Sheik Khalil he needed his assistance in getting to Tulkarm and transporting a container to a safe place in which he could prepare the device for operation.

When Khalil asked about the nature of the device, Ollie told him it was a device that will disperse deadly radiation among the Jews. He knew that if he told Sheik Khalil about its true intended target in Jerusalem and the objective included destruction of the mosques on Temple Mount then the sheik would probably refuse to help.

He also told Sheik Khalil he would need a pick-up truck capable of travelling through narrow streets and of carrying a weight of several hundred pounds. The sheik said the second part was not a problem as trucks of this sort were available from his Arab supporters.

When Ollie said the truck would probably be destroyed by the bomb, the sheik said they could easily steal a truck from a Jewish settlement rather than wreck a truck of a true believer. Sheik Khalil invited Ollie to stay at his house for the night while he made the necessary arrangements to comply with Ollie's requests.

The ISA agents that had been following Ollie had no trouble

locating the taxi driver as soon as he left Umm al-Fahm and bringing him to one of their safe houses for questioning. It didn't take long for the driver to admit he had dropped Ollie off at the central mosque.

The agents already knew this as the tracking device in Ollie's passport led them there but as they were reluctant to wander around the hostile village, they did not approach the mosque itself. They asked the taxi-driver what Ollie had said about the purpose of his trip and what they talked about and the driver truthfully said they had not talked at all and when they departed Ollie gave him a nice tip.

The chief interrogator did not believe him but after deploying some more pressure and persuasive measures with no results, he was finally convinced the driver knew no more than he had already admitted.

June 16, Several European cities

The increasing number of terrorist attacks in major Europeans cities had become the focal point of all intelligence agencies and police forces.

Although the violent acts did not seem to be coordinated by a central command, they did have one thing in common: they were all carried out by Muslims. A closer scrutiny showed that the perpetrators were almost always young men or women, who had returned to their home countries after fighting for ISIS in Syria and Iraq.

Some of them came from Muslim families and were second or third generation residents in Europe while others were fresh converts to Islam. The attacks included planting bombs in crowded areas, especially in public transportation stations, buses and trains; suicide bombings by single or multiple young men and women; shooting of policemen, soldiers, innocent civilians, and school kids; and random acts of gang violence.

They specially targeted newspapers that published derogatory cartoons, photos, or articles about the prophet Mohammad or Islam in general. In addition, several acts were aimed at Jewish schools, stores, people, and synagogues. These were the acts of a small minority of Muslims but reflected on the whole community.

One cynical politician said, "Not all Muslims are terrorists but almost all terrorists are Muslims." And that was a good enough excuse for the nationalist movements in these countries to increase their harassment of Muslims and all other immigrants. Street riots broke out between the two groups, and as usual, the victims were mainly the innocent bystanders who were unfortunate enough to be in the area.

The authorities were helplessly trying to break up the riots, separating the gangs of violent European racists from the no-less violent Muslim youth. The police in the democratic countries had their hands tied by the courts and the frustrated law enforcement personnel often had an itchy trigger finger that resulted in the shooting of rioters from both sides.

Very few police officers were ever prosecuted, even fewer were convicted, because witnesses seemed to disappear and the number of people who saw nothing, heard nothing, and remembered nothing increased dramatically when they were summoned to testify.

Such chaos in the streets was helping the racist parties, or using the euphemistic term: "nationalist movements," thrive and prosper. Everyone knew the next election in any country that had a sizable Muslim minority, such as France, Sweden, the UK, Germany, Holland, or Belgium, would see a rise in the power of these extremists.

There was a very real fear that all this could be the beginning of the end of democracy in Europe. The barrel of dynamite was ready; the fuse was inserted inside the dynamite, and the match needed to ignite the fuse was already out of the box and ready to strike it.

On this very day, Ollie held the ultimate match in his hand and was within inches of striking it against a rough surface to ignite it.

CHAPTER 16

June 16, Umm al-Fahm, Israel and Tulkarm, the Palestinian Authority

Sheik Khalil made the necessary arrangements to smuggle Ollie across the line that separated Israel from the territories controlled by the Palestinian Authority (PA).

Although Israel had constructed a wall that was twenty-seven feet high along a large part of that separation line with several official and closely monitored checkpoints, there were many places where the wall could be crossed with a minimal risk of being discovered. The sheik and his people knew these places and Ollie's escorts headed toward a dirt road that led from the Gilboa Ridge inside Israel to the Jenin area in the PA.

Ollie was dressed as one of the local peasants and he had a cover story in case they were stopped by an Israeli roadblock or patrol. He was instructed to say he was returning to his village near Tubas after seeking employment, illegally, in the town of Afula in Israel. He left his bag, European clothes, and fake passport in the sheik's house in Umm al-Fahm.

The sheik had promised him he would deliver the bag to Ollie when he returned with the device, 'the birthday parcel' as they had agreed to call it, to Israeli territory.

Three of the sheik's men escorted Ollie in a Jeep and two of them were to guide him across the border on foot where he was to be met by another local supporter of ISIS, who would take him to the agricultural school in Tulkarm.

Sheik Khalil had given Ollie a cell phone with a new SIM card with an Israeli number and told Ollie to use it only in case of an emergency as he was aware that all cellular communications were probably monitored by Israeli intelligence agencies. They had agreed on a simple code word that was to be repeated twice in case Ollie was being followed or three times if there was imminent danger. The code word they chose was an apparently innocent phrase, 'the coffee is ready.'

The Jeep passed the Meggido Junction connecting the highway leading north to the Haifa area and south to Jenin with the roads that led east to the Sea of Galilee or west to the Mediterranean coastal town of Netanya.

Ollie's escort pointed to the mound that rose above the junction and said it was Tel Meggido, known to the *kefirs* as Armageddon. Ollie smiled to himself as he heard this and thought that Doomsday was much closer than any of them imagined.

***

The ISA agents with their receiver tuned to the signal emitted from the chip planted in Ollie's passport, did not take notice of their mark, only one of many Arab garbed passengers in one of the many cars that left Umm al-Fahm every morning toward Meggido Junction.

They did wonder what Ollie was doing for such a long time in the sheik's house, but no alarm bells had gone off in their minds. They called their headquarters every two hours, as instructed, just to give a status report that nothing had changed yet. By noon the controller at ISA headquarters called Mossad and said he was worried something had gone amiss.

The Mossad duty officer called Shimony and informed him that Ollie himself had not been seen all day and that the beacon in his passport was still signaling from the sheik's house.

Shimony asked to be connected directly with the ISA agents on duty and instructed them to pay a cordial visit to Sheik Khalil and sniff around. He told them to have a police backup nearby in case things got nasty and to report to him personally about their findings.

As soon as they saw a Border Patrol Jeep with four police officers drive to the village central square, the two ISA agents knocked on the door of the sheik's house. It was opened by one of his attendants who told the agents the sheik was at the mosque and would be able to see them after prayers.

The agents said they were in a hurry and the attendant advised them not to interrupt the prayers, and in a menacing tone said if they did so and a riot broke out then it would be their responsibility. The agents wanted to avoid a riot and said they would wait for the sheik, so the attendant suggested they have coffee at the café on the corner. He added that he would ask the sheik to come as soon as possible to the café.

The agents did not like the way things were developing but did not want to cause a disturbance with such a small police force at their disposal so they updated the police officer and suggested he call in for reinforcements just in case they had to make some arrests.

After they had drunk three cups of strong, bitter coffee Sheik Khalil entered the café with an entourage of six young men. No one smiled when the two agents stood up and asked the sheik if they could have a word in private.

The sheik looked around and saw that by now there were three vehicles loaded with fully equipped Border Patrol riot police and invited them to his house saying they would have more privacy there than in the cafe.

They left the café and once inside the sheik's house, they congregated in the modest living room and the agents followed the Arab custom and asked about life in general, the sheik's family, the economy, and other irrelevant matters before getting to the point and asking him if he had any guests staying with him.

The sheik told them he'd had a surprise visitor the previous day, but the guest had left in the morning without saying where he was heading.

They pretended to believe his story and showed him a photo of Ollie and Lena taken a couple days earlier in the Old City of Jerusalem.

Sheik Khalil took a long look at the photo and pronounced this was his guest but that he did not know the girl. When asked how come this guest had taken a taxi from Jerusalem specifically to meet him, Sheik Khalil said he had no idea and he thought the Swedish man was slightly '*majnoon,*' meaning a bit crazy, in Arabic.

The agents realized the sheik was playing them for fools but although they wanted to take him to one of their cellars for a more thorough interrogation, they needed authorization for that. So, they thanked him politely and said they may be back quite soon.

Naturally, they knew that Ollie's passport was in the sheik's house and assumed he would be back to pick it up or it would be sent to him. They couldn't confront the sheik with this information as that would give away the fact they had Ollie under surveillance, beyond the visual shadowing.

***

As soon as they left, the sheik summoned his attendant and told him to use a one-time phone and call Ollie repeating twice the phrase, 'the coffee is ready.'

He knew the call would probably be picked up but thought the message was important enough to alert Ollie. He also understood that Ollie's intentions were taken seriously by the ISA and wondered whether he would be able to pull this off.

***

Ollie was riding in a small pick-up truck with the local guide who came from Jenin when he received the short phone call warning him he had been followed.

One of the Israeli Arabs from Umm al-Fahm left them after

he saw Ollie handed over safely to the Palestinian guide and returned across the border the same way he had infiltrated it a couple hours earlier.

The other Israeli Arab, a young intelligent follower of the Islamic movement called Nasser, stayed with Ollie as ordered by Sheik Khalil.

Ollie assumed the ISA would not be able to follow him inside the territories of the Palestinian Authority, so his top priority remained the same: find the container and check the device. After confirming that everything was in order, he would plan how to transport it to Jerusalem and arm it while allowing himself enough time to get away. He told his Palestinian guide to continue to Tulkarm and the school.

They arrived at the school in early afternoon and Ollie immediately saw the familiar container in the backyard. When they reached the gate, the guard called Doctor Anwar El-Alami as he had been instructed after the container was unloaded from the truck that brought it from the Haifa port a few days earlier.

Doctor El-Alami was curious about the contents of the container but took the warning he had received seriously and did not even try to tamper with the seal.

Ollie thanked him for his cooperation and said he would open it to check the merchandise after the school was closed for the day and requested that no students or school personnel be present, except Nasser, his Palestinian guide, and El-Alami himself.

He also asked El-Alami to prepare a flashlight and a new metal band to replace the seal. El-Alami invited Ollie and the guide to his office and offered them coffee.

Ollie called his guide aside asking him to procure a small crane to lift the device on to his pick-up truck and a large tarpaulin to cover it. The guide drove to the nearby town of Tubas to find the items requested.

Ollie had enjoyed the coffee and pastries El-Alami served and during their little chat learned that El-Alami had received his doctorate in education from the Birzeit University, located north of Ramallah, but had also studied modern agricultural techniques at the Israeli Faculty of Agriculture in Rehovot, and spoke fluent Arabic, English, and Hebrew.

El-Alami tried to understand what was concealed in the container and Ollie told him the cover story about a 'dirty bomb,' saying it was only to be used to threaten and terrorize the people in Tel Aviv and it was not to be detonated.

El-Alami, who was no fool, was not quite convinced this was the whole story, but he kept his misgivings to himself.

By the time the guide returned, the school day had ended and following Ollie's instructions everyone else left the school's property, expect the guard that opened the gate to let the pick-up truck in to the school's backyard.

Ollie asked El-Alami to send the guard away for a couple hours and wait at the gate to make sure no unexpected visitors arrived. He then took the flashlight and went to the container and broke the seal on its door. He opened the double doors carefully not knowing whether the precious cargo was intact and was relieved to see that every item was exactly in the same position it had been when loaded in Italy.

The improvised nuclear device looked like a strange type

of bomb, which indeed it was, and any intelligent person who looked at it would realize that instantly. It certainly was nothing like any known type of agricultural machinery. On the other hand, the metallic box containing the triggering device, detonators, and timer looked just like any other metal suitcase, and would not arouse too much suspicion unless it was opened.

With the help of Nasser and the Palestinian guide with the portable derrick that he had brought, the three of them managed to maneuver the device out of the container and load it on the pick-up truck's platform. They used the tarpaulin to cover the device and tied down its corners to the hooks in the platform. Ollie was not pleased with the way it looked with the tarpaulin cover—it reminded him of a giant egg or of a large bomb.

He searched the school's backyard for some wooden poles that he inserted under the tarpaulin to break the egg-like contours of the odd bundle. It now had an unrecognizable shape—still bizarre but at least not obviously like a bomb. The metal case was carefully placed in the cabin of the pick-up truck. There was no room for the portable crane and Ollie summoned El-Alami and told him to return it to the garage in Tubas it was borrowed from.

By the time they had finished, the guard had returned to the school's gate and Doctor El-Alami wandered back to the container that was now empty and resealed with the new metal band.

Ollie ordered him to forget everything that had ensued that afternoon under the penalty of death to his entire family and say no word to anyone no matter what happened.

El-Alami's distrust grew stronger but there was nothing he could do.

Ollie and the two escorts drove away and headed toward the Balata refugee camp in Nablus where there were many devoted supporters of ISIS.

They parked the truck in a closed garage and, at Ollie's request, two guards were posted outside the garage door with strict instructions not to enter the garage.

Ollie and Nasser were offered a hot meal of skewered lamb and rice and given two beds to sleep in. Before turning in for the night Ollie asked his host if they could get him a minivan with dark windows and Israeli license plates.

The host asked him if he had any preference for the model or color. When Ollie said his only concern was that it would be able to travel one hundred miles without breaking down, his host smiled and said there were plenty of suitable vans, waiting in Israel to be recruited for the Palestinian cause and one would be ready for him in the garage in the morning.

June 16, Tel Aviv

In the evening, after Ollie had slipped the surveillance of the ISA agents and had not been seen since the previous day, the Mossad Deputy Director, Shimony, called an emergency meeting.

The ISA director of operations, known as the 'Fish,' summarized the day's events. In an untypical apologetic tone, he admitted his agents had made a huge blunder by allowing

Ollie to evade their surveillance.

Shimony also felt he had made an error of judgment by not ordering Ollie's arrest when he had been in their grasp and called the participants' attention to the fact they now did not have any idea where Ollie or the device were hiding.

His greatest fear, he added, was that Ollie had the device in his possession and would be able to detonate it somewhere in Israel. The Israeli authorities had no way of knowing whether the device was already inside Israel or was, as they believed, still in the territory of the Palestinian Authority.

Unprecedented measures were to be implemented all along the border, with special attention given to any vehicle that can carry an object the size of the device. The forces manning all the border checkpoints were to be doubled and every truck, pick-up truck, bus, or minivan that could carry a load of several hundred pounds was to be thoroughly searched.

Trucks carrying agricultural produce were to be particularly thoroughly inspected as the container was marked as 'agricultural machinery.'

The Chief of the Israel Police, who was also present at the meeting, assured the participants the Border Patrol units would be briefed, and the number of patrols would be doubled. He expected that by noon the following day all the extra personnel would be in position at all checkpoints.

The head of the IDF intelligence department promised to coordinate with the Air Force and send up special patrols of unmanned aerial vehicles (UAVs), or drones, to fly along the border and cover the sectors in the Palestinian Authority close to the border.

Shimony pointed out they would obviously receive hundreds, if not thousands, of false alarms as there were so many trucks and buses that crossed the border every day. He informed them he had considered the possibility of completely closing the border, but this required the Prime Minister's approval and since there was no information on a delivery date this situation could be extended indefinitely with irrevocable implications on the economy and on Israel's position with the world.

He emphasized the top priority of the ISA should now be to use every one of their informers and collaborators to obtain information on the location of the device and Ollie.

The 'Fish' said that Sheik Khalil would be arrested and interrogated as soon as a court order, signed by a judge, could be obtained. He added he expected the arrest would be done around three in the morning, a time favored by police forces and intelligence agencies all over the world as the mental capacity and physical resistance of suspects was at its lowest at this hour.

David sat quietly throughout the whole meeting and thought a completely different approach was needed. He tried to put himself in Ollie's shoes and considered the options. If Ollie and the device were already in Israel, then the only practical mode of operation was to try and deduce the potential targets and to position the extra security measures around them.

The targets that came to mind were the major government facilities, mainly in Jerusalem and Tel Aviv, with particular attention on the Prime Minister's office in Jerusalem and the headquarters of the IDF in the Kirya complex in the heart of Tel Aviv. Other attractive targets would be at the holy places to Judaism and Christianity in Jerusalem, but he thought that the proximity of the Wailing Wall to the Dome of the Rock mosque would make this less likely.

He considered a few other prime targets like the center of Tel Aviv or perhaps the Haifa harbor, or even Israel's main international airport—Ben-Gurion airport near Tel Aviv—or a large army or air force base but thought these would be only fallback positions. He then gave some consideration to the logistics of transporting the device in to one of those target areas, arming, and detonating it while allowing Ollie enough time to get away safely.

He knew it was impossible to disrupt life in Jerusalem or Tel Aviv by searching every vehicle large enough for carrying the device and concluded it had to be stopped before getting close to the prime target areas.

He raised his hand and asked for permission to speak and when that was granted, he presented his thoughts and concluded by saying the key could be Ollie's departure from the tour group when he and Lena wandered around Jerusalem on their own. He asked the 'Fish' to summon the ISA agents that had followed Ollie and Lena in Jerusalem and once again go over the detailed report they had submitted.

The meeting was adjourned, and David and the 'Fish' had another cup of coffee while waiting for the agents that had followed Ollie in Jerusalem.

The two ISA agents arrived half an hour later and were asked to retrace Ollie's movements in Jerusalem step by step.

The two agents took a moment to refresh their memories and with the help of a map, sketched out Ollie and Lena's route through the Old City. There appeared to be nothing unusual in their visit to the Church of the Holy Sepulchre, the Wailing Wall, and the Dome of the Rock mosque.

One of the agents mentioned that while Lena appeared to be moved emotionally by being at these holy sites, Ollie looked less interested in the details inside the church, for example, and was more concerned with the surrounding area and seemed to be studying the security arrangements at the sites and around them.

He had only glanced at the Wailing Wall itself but looked all around at the police and soldiers in charge of the protection and security. The same attitude was observed when they entered the large open space on Temple Mount and saw the Dome of the Rock and al-Aqsa mosques. The agent also noted that Ollie appeared to inspect the narrow streets leading to these places as if he was making an estimation of the size of vehicles that could travel through them.

The other agent concurred but said that he didn't think this was unusual as many tourists were kind of disappointed by the historic sites and more interested in the current life in the Old City.

However, in David's mind, alarm bells were ringing loudly. According to the reports from the ISA agents that had followed him, this was the only time that Ollie had left the group and wandered around on his own.

David thanked the two agents and asked the 'Fish' to remain for a few more moments.

When they were left alone, David told the 'Fish' his gut feeling was that the real target had to be in the Old City of Jerusalem and not, as he had assumed earlier, in Tel Aviv or at the Prime Minister's office.

The 'Fish' agreed that Ollie's irregular and uncharacteristic behavior was indeed suspicious and security in that area should be increased. Fortunately, he said, there was relatively little traffic of large vehicles inside the Old City and even those could only enter the heart of the old city through seven quite narrow gates. The most direct routes to the Church of the Holy Sepulchre and Temple Mount were through the Lions Gate or Damascus Gate and to the Wailing Wall through the Dung Gate or Zion Gate.

The 'Fish' said he would make sure that security at these bottlenecks would be doubled starting the next afternoon.

David called Shimony, who had already returned home and gone to bed to update him.

June 17, Both sides of the border between Israel and the Palestinian Authority

The improvised nuclear device had been transferred from the pick-up truck to the black Savana van 'borrowed' from the Israeli settlement of Barkan, just a few miles from the Balata refugee camp in Nablus.

The experienced car thieves had no trouble breaking quietly into the owner's house and stealing the original car keys hanging from a hook just inside the door. They did use a spray containing a strong tranquilizer to make sure the owner and his family would not wake up and confront them—a messy situation they were anxious to avoid.

The people in the house would wake up mid-morning with a strong headache and it would take them a while to figure out what had happened and report the theft. The van was designed to hold fifteen passengers, but Ollie and his host removed most of the seats, leaving only the front seat.

Ollie made sure the device was covered with the tarpaulin and the space in front and behind the device was filled to the van's roof with cheap merchandise that was supposedly being transported to the market in Netanya—a popular beach resort in Israel.

The van was driven by Nasser, Ollie's guide from Umm al-Fahm, who had an Israeli identification card and driver's license. Ollie had discarded his Arab garments and was dressed in the uniform of an Israeli reservist soldier supplied by his hosts in Nablus.

They planned to cross the border early in the morning before the van was reported as stolen. The plan was that Ollie would pretend to be asleep if they were stopped—quite a common sight for reservists that were often on duty most of the night. This would help hide Ollie's inability to speak Hebrew.

The fallback plan, in case the police or soldiers manning the border checkpoint wanted to speak to him, was that he would say in bad Hebrew he was a new immigrant who had just been enlisted for *miluim*—reservist army duty.

As they approached the roadblock, Nasser drove straight to the lane reserved for Israelis who lived in the Samaria settlements, and not to the lane that served the local Palestinians who wanted to cross into Israel for work, medical treatment, school, or for any other reason.

Misha, the Border Patrol police sergeant manning the post took one look at the black Savana van and saw the license plates and the sleeping reservist soldier and waved them through without even asking for the driver's papers.

Nasser nudged Ollie, smiling broadly, and asked him where he wanted to go.

Ollie asked to be taken to Jerusalem, with a stop somewhere quiet and out of the way so he could check the device once again.

Nasser explained he had relatives in Tira, a large Arab township in Israel which the police did not enter frequently. Ollie asked him to call Sheik Khalil and have his bag and passport sent to the family in Tira but did not tell Nasser this was in preparation for leaving the country after planting the device in Jerusalem.

After a short drive, they arrived at the house belonging to Nasser's relatives. The house did not have a closed garage, but like many houses in Arab towns, it was surrounded by a corrugated iron fence that was seven feet high. Several families, all related to one another and to Nasser, lived in the large house that was more like a complex than a single residential building.

Nasser quietly told Ollie that some of them were also supporters of Hamas or ISIS but most of the family members were neutral or even loyal Israeli citizens who enjoyed the benefits of social security and excellent medical insurance plans. He assured Ollie that none of them would unveil Ollie's presence if he kept to himself.

Nasser suggested they wait until the evening before working on the device, and while they waited he would get a new set of license plates in case the van had been reported as stolen.

Ollie agreed since he preferred to take the van to Jerusalem after dark. Ollie asked Nasser to park the black Savana close to the corrugated iron fence and cover it with a sheet of fabric taken from the back of the van.

***

Meanwhile, along the border between Israel and the Palestinian Authority, the orders from the ISA and police to reinforce the checkpoints were implemented. The soldiers and police officers manning these posts were instructed to search all vehicles that were larger than private cars, regardless of the identity of their drivers. This was expected to cause some vociferous protests from the Jewish settlers used to driving through these checkpoints as if they were above the law that in their opinion applied only to Arabs.

In addition, a list of all sizable vehicles stolen in the Israeli sectors close to the border was distributed throughout all the checkpoints. The list included several pick-up trucks that were very popular in those areas, a couple full-size trucks, and a handful of other vehicles like passenger minivans and cargo transporters.

Misha, the soldier that had been manning the checkpoint

through which Nasser and Ollie had entered Israel a few hours earlier, saw that a black Savana was mentioned as one of the vehicles stolen the previous night. He recalled it had Israeli license plates and it used the lane reserved for settlers and for that reason was not inspected closely.

Misha also remembered that besides the driver, there had been a man, dressed in IDF army uniform, asleep in the passenger's seat and since Misha did not want to wake him up, he had decided not to delay the vehicle. This information was passed on to the 'Fish' at ISA headquarters and he alerted David this could be the vehicle they had been looking for.

The 'Fish' and David arrived just before noon at the checkpoint and asked to interview Misha. Misha, who had immigrated to Israel from Kazan in Russia when he was ten years old, still had not quite gotten over his inbred fear and distrust of the authorities and cooperated hesitantly.

David and the 'Fish' used the "good cop/ bad cop" approach. David promised Misha that no harm would come his way if he fully cooperated with them while the 'Fish' threatened him with a long prison sentence for treason if he did not disclose every little detail of the Savana.

David gently asked Misha to describe the driver and passenger while the 'Fish' huffed and puffed right behind Misha's back. With David's gentle guidance and leading questions, Misha recalled that the driver looked like an Oriental Jew, or perhaps an Arab, and the reservist was wearing military-issue uniform, but his head was not completely covered so he could see he had short blond hair.

Before allowing Misha to leave, the 'Fish' asked him if he

remembered anything about the vehicle. Misha thought for a moment and then said it appeared to be carrying a heavy load in the back as it was slightly tilted backwards but he could not quite see what it was carrying because of the tinted windows.

Upon hearing this David and the 'Fish' exchanged a look of comprehension and concern.

They called the control center of the police and alerted all patrols to stop every black Savana van and search it, but to approach it carefully as the people inside were dangerous and possibly armed. They also issued a warning the passenger may be posing as an IDF reservist and he was not to be trusted.

Within thirty minutes' traffic blocks were positioned on all highways in the area close to the crossing point and on the main highways leading to Tel Aviv and Jerusalem. In addition, unmanned drones and police helicopters were dispatched to survey the whole vicinity in search of a black Savana.

Traffic delays were caused all over the center of Israel and the public was informed this was due to a surprise exercise intended to test the readiness of the police forces and simulate an incident in which a terrorist element penetrated Israeli security at the border.

***

Nasser's cousin who was sent to steal license plates, saw the commotion and called Nasser informing him that some unusual police activity was taking place in their vicinity.

Nasser switched on the radio and heard the announcement

about the surprise exercise and skeptically murmured to Ollie this was a typical ploy of Israeli security and their vehicle was probably compromised.

Ollie said they shouldn't take any unnecessary risks and asked Nasser if they could transfer the device to another vehicle and not rely solely on the switch of license plates.

Nasser proposed to call a friend of his who had a garage in which pick-up trucks were serviced and repaired and ask him if he could borrow one of the trucks.

Ollie liked the idea and Nasser made a few phone calls until he located a suitable pick-up truck. Ollie didn't inform Nasser the truck would be destroyed as he feared this would discourage him.

They agreed to bring the truck to the house in Tira in the evening and arrange a small derrick for transferring the device from the Savana to the pick-up truck.

When they stepped out into the yard to survey the van, they could hear a noisy police helicopter circling over and around Tira. This increased their conviction that the Savana's crossing into Israel had been reported and word of its deadly cargo had been spread.

Nasser knew this flurry of activity could not be due to a simple theft of a van and started to suspect the device he had helped transport was more than a simple bomb, or even a 'dirty bomb,' but he did not broach the subject with Ollie whom he began to regard as an extremely dangerous person.

Ollie's bag, including his forged passport, arrived from Umm al-Fahm with a short note from Sheik Khalil wishing him luck with his endeavor and warning him the ISA was trying to locate him.

Little did he know the very act of delivering Ollie's belongings gave the ISA the key to find him.

After dusk, an Isuzu pick-up truck was driven to the yard and parked close to the black Savana and the derrick was set up to enable the transfer of the device.

Ollie had planned to arm the device before taking it to Jerusalem but was not keen to drive from Tira to Jerusalem, using back roads and possibly bumpy dirt roads with a few hundred pounds of armed explosives four feet behind his back.

He also wanted as few people as possible to witness his actions, so the device was simply moved to the Isuzu and the metal suitcase was placed behind the passenger seat where Ollie's belongings were also positioned.

The shock absorbers of the old Isuzu groaned under the full weight of the device and would have complained bitterly if they could speak. The device was still covered with the same tarpaulin and its unique shape was camouflaged with the wooden poles.

Nasser, who had a lot of experience in dodging police road blocks from his career as a car thief, suggested that one of his cousins drive a few miles ahead of the Isuzu and warn them about police roadblocks, allowing them time to find an alternative route to circumvent the roadblock.

Ollie liked the suggestion and the initiative and patted Nasser on his shoulder.

***

The ISA agents that had remained at their post near Sheik Khalil's house picked up the change in the signal emitted from Ollie's passport and reported this to the officer in the control room.

He ordered them to follow the signal at a safe distance and alerted the 'Fish,' who in turn called David and informed him that the passport was in motion.

The agents reported they were following a dark green Mazda and were on route 57 from Umm al-Fahm toward Netanya but then the car took a sharp turn south on a secondary road leading to Tira. They were following it but knew that going into Tira would expose them and suggested that a drone be used to follow the Mazda in case it entered Tira.

The 'Fish' had been in direct contact with his agents and said that a drone would be overhead within five minutes and they must stick with the Mazda until relieved from duty.

Just before the green car entered Tira, the agents received a message the car was now in the sight of the drone and were ordered to remain alert on the outskirts of the village, so they parked on the side of the road leading from Tira to Highway 6.

The 'Fish' and David went directly to the ISA control room to be at the 'nerve center' at this crucial stage of the operation to seize Ollie and the deadly device.

The drone following the green Mazda sent live photographs of it entering the walled yard of a large house in the center of the village. The drone operator then said he only had fuel for another fifteen minutes until it had to return to its base.

The 'Fish' called for a replacement drone, preferably one equipped with a receiver for the signal sent from the chip in Ollie's passport but was told the proper equipment was not on hand, and the best alternative was to use a drone equipped with infrared night vision.

David was not satisfied with the alternative but had no way of getting anything better.

June 17, evening, Tira

After dark, the small convoy consisting of an old, white Skoda Octavia driven by one of Nasser's cousins, Mahmoud, with his fiancée, Leila, riding shotgun and followed at a distance by the Isuzu pick-up with Nasser and Ollie left the house in Tira.

The ISA agents received the signal from the chip implanted in Ollie's passport and knew the target was on the move. They didn't take notice of the white Octavia that passed right by them, but Mahmoud who was on the lookout for any signs of unusual activity became aware of them and told Leila to call Nasser and warn him.

Nasser took evasive action and instead of heading toward Highway 6, the main route to the south and to Jerusalem, he switched off the Isuzu's lights and took a detour through a dirt trail in one of the many orange groves that surrounded the township and headed along a secondary road towards the town of Kfar Saba.

The ISA agents saw the change in direction of the beacon but did not manage to get a look at the Isuzu that was now travelling without lights. With growing concern, the agents saw the signal from the chip fade away as the distance between them grew. They completely lost the trail in the dirt roads that traversed the cultivated fields of Tira and the neighboring Jewish villages.

The agents called their control and informed the duty officer they lost the culprit. The duty officer ordered all police and Border Police patrols in the area to immediately set up roadblocks on all the roads leading south from Tira and informed David and the 'Fish' that were in the control room of this development.

The 'Fish' ordered his two agents to return to Tira and question all the people who were in the house pinpointed by the drone. He informed them that police reinforcements were on the way to meet them at the house.

The ISA agents, now with the backing of uniformed police officers, entered the house without knocking on the door and gathered all the residents in the large living room. They then took all the men out to the backyard and showed them the black Savana parked under a makeshift shelter and asked them who it belonged to.

The men knew that it was stolen property and suspected it was used in some high-profile criminal activity and soon realized they could be facing a serious charge, yet they were more afraid of Sheik Khalil and his religious zealots than of the police and refused to cooperate.

Two ISA agents took the youngest man, who was seventeen years old and looked more like a scared boy than a grown man and led him to a dark corner in the yard and intimidated him with threats of what would happen to him in prison. They didn't need to use physical violence as the young boy cracked and told them all about Nasser and Ollie and about the Isuzu pick-up truck to which some large object was transferred from the Savana van.

The ISA agents immediately forwarded the information to the control room. The police took the owner of the house and the young boy into custody, while cautioning all other men to remain in the house and not call anybody.

The men returned to the living room joining the women and children under the supervision of three tough looking Border Police officers.

***

The people manning the roadblocks were told to stop and search all Isuzu pick-up trucks but to allow all other traffic to continue. They were warned that the driver and passenger in the suspect vehicle could be armed and were extremely dangerous, so caution must be practiced when approaching the vehicle.

Furthermore, they were ordered to shoot only at the tires if the suspect vehicle tried to run through the roadblock as it probably had a large load of explosives that could be set off by a stray bullet.

Reports about Isuzu pick-up trucks started coming in, as this was a very popular vehicle, but none had caused any problems when ordered to stop or objected to being searched, and of course, nothing was found.

***

Nasser and Ollie did not have the means to monitor the police radio transmissions, but Nasser came up with the idea of using the live traffic information system to see where there were traffic hold ups that were probably due to the roadblocks.

He switched on his cell phone and used the appropriate application and saw that they were just a couple miles from the closest traffic obstruction.

He looked for a way to get off the road and spotted a narrow trail in an orchard that led to a deserted house swerving off the paved road to follow it. He suggested to Ollie that they should lay low for a few hours until things cleared up.

He then called his cousin Mahmoud only to learn he had been stopped at one of the roadblocks but as his papers were in order, and with Leila sitting next to him, he could continue his way and was now entering Tira.

Mahmoud excitedly said there were several police cars near the house of Nasser's cousins, and he was proceeding to Leila's house.

Nasser updated Ollie about these developments and Ollie said the police had probably traced the black Savana to the house.

Ollie asked Nasser to move the Isuzu to a spot that couldn't be seen from the road and they parked behind a deserted building. Ollie got out of the cabin, and with Nasser's help removed the tarpaulin that covered the improvised nuclear device, and started inserting the detonators into the slots that were drilled into the blocks of high explosives.

This operation took quite a while because there were a few dozen detonators that had to be correctly wired. In addition, it was tricky to place the detonators in the bottom part of the device because of the difficult access to those slots on the back of the pick-up truck.

It took Ollie about thirty minutes to complete the procedure and all he had to do now was to connect all the electrical leads to the battery and set the timer. Ollie did not want to commit suicide but dreaded failure of the divine mission he had undertaken, so he installed a direct triggering mechanism bypassing the timer that would detonate the device instantaneously when pressed.

He would set off the device if he thought he was about to be stopped and vowed he would do this as a last resort. Ollie told Nasser what he had done and instructed him to press the trigger if he himself were disabled.

Nasser watched the procedure for arming the device identifying it for what it was—he had seen the movies and realized they were travelling with a nuclear device. He commented that even if it went off in the middle of nowhere in Israel the physical damage and psychological ramifications would be a great victory for Islam over the Jewish invaders and the Western civilization and thanked Ollie for allowing him to be part of this heroic act.

June 17, late evening, at the deserted house and Kafr Kassem

Ollie's primal instincts set his skin tingling and his hair standing on end, so he spent a few minutes analyzing the situation and deduced that the performance of the ISA agents tracking him first to Umm al-Fahm and then to the house of Nasser's cousins in Tira could only be due to a tracking device planted in his belongings.

He discussed this with Nasser who agreed with him. They removed Ollie's luggage from the Isuzu, placing it behind the fence surrounding the deserted house and decided to leave the house immediately, realizing they would be sitting ducks if they stayed there any longer.

Without switching on the headlights, they returned to the paved road and headed back toward the network of secondary roads in the agricultural area looking for another dirt road that would take them to Jerusalem circumventing the roadblocks.

Nasser, who knew the area well, suggested they try to head to the densely populated area on the west side of Route 6 where Arab and Jewish villages coexisted side by side, and then try to switch vehicles again either with the voluntary help of an Arab supporter, or if necessary by coercion.

Using the cellular phone's navigation software to evade roadblocks, they managed to reach Kafr Kassem without being challenged. In this large Arab village, they looked for Palestinian flags painted on the walls or flown on poles and signs of support for the Islamic ultra-religious movement.

They didn't have to search for long before they saw a car repair garage with posters calling for donations to support Al Aqsa mosque. They parked the Isuzu in a dark corner of the poorly lit street and while Ollie remained in the truck to keep watch on the device, Nasser went to the large shuttered door of the garage and knocked on it.

After a couple moments, a male voice said in Arabic that the garage was closed until tomorrow morning. Nasser said he had come to make a large donation for the Al Aqsa fund and asked the man to open the door.

The garage owner was still suspicious as this ploy had been used by the Israeli police and security agency and it took Nasser a few minutes to convince him he was indeed a disciple of the famous Sheik Khalil of Umm al-Fahm.

Finally, a small side door was opened by the garage owner who introduced himself as Abdul Aziz and asked Nasser what he wanted as nobody had ever come late at night seeking to donate to the fund. Nasser said they needed a car to deliver some goods to Jerusalem.

Abdul Aziz saw that he winked when he said 'goods' and understood no good would come from these 'goods.' He smiled and said he had just completed the repair of a minivan that would probably be suitable for transporting the 'goods,' and showed Nasser a brand-new Honda Odyssey that had been involved in a minor fender-bender accident. He said the car was brought in by a wealthy Israeli resident from nearby village of Oranit, and the owner would not come back until the following week as he had gone on vacation to Paris.

Nasser asked Abdul Aziz to open the garage door as he had

to transfer the 'goods' from the Isuzu truck to the Odyssey and would need a derrick or winch to do that.

Looking around the fully equipped garage Nasser saw it was ideal for their purposes, so he went back out and drove the Isuzu in to the garage.

Abdul Aziz was surprised to see the blond man but when Ollie welcomed him in Arabic and praised Allah, he became enthusiastic that such a typical Scandinavian man had adopted the true faith.

The back seats of the Odyssey were removed, and the device was placed in it and covered once again by the tarpaulin. The windows of the minivan were of the dark type so no one could see into the car from the sides or back.

Abdul Aziz offered them coffee and pastries that they accepted with great joy as they were famished and tired. He noticed they looked haggard and invited them to stay at his house for the night saying they would attract less attention in the heavy daytime traffic than late at night when very few vehicles would be on the road.

Nasser exchanged a look with Ollie and agreed, but asked Abdul Aziz to cover the Isuzu until it could be returned to Nasser's family in Tira.

June 18, Jerusalem

Ollie and Nasser felt fully refreshed when they left Kafr Kassem, after thanking Abdul Aziz for his help and hospitality.

Nasser enjoyed driving the new Odyssey on paved highways after having driven the old Isuzu truck on dirt roads at night without lights.

They got on the busy Highway 444 that took them south and then headed south-east on Highway 443 flowing with the heavy traffic to Jerusalem.

There were a few roadblocks on the way, but the shiny Odyssey was waved through without a second glance. At each roadblock, there were several Isuzu trucks that were searched by armed soldiers, so they felt reassured the police and ISA were still barking up the wrong tree.

The mid-morning traffic on the outskirts of Jerusalem was moving at a slow stop-go pace so Ollie and Nasser started to relax and set into a fatalistic mood about their chances of success and their personal destiny. Their route took them through an array of Jewish suburbs and Palestinian refugee camps intermingled in a complicated jumble that displayed how difficult it would be to divide Jerusalem between Palestine and Israel, if a 'two states solution' were ever seriously negotiated.

Ollie thought to himself that if their plan worked that would be the least of the problems of the Middle East...

Ollie had rigged a cable from the instant detonation emergency switch of the device in the back of the minivan to the front seat so he could blow them both to smithereens together with everything within a radius of a few hundred meters. He jokingly told Nasser they would need more than seventy-two virgins in paradise as they would be atomized to a zillion parts each deserving its own share of virgins.

They passed very close to the headquarters of the Israeli police and then took the road circling along the walls of the

Old City until they reached the Lions Gate on the east side of the city. They entered through the gate that was only a passage through the massive stone wall without an actual gate and continued down the narrow street past the Church of Condemnation and Via Dolorosa.

The streets were barely suitable for motorized traffic, but Nasser told whoever enquired why they were driving on this narrow street he was heading to the market to unload his goods. Ollie realized their main problem would be to find a place where the car could be parked for a couple hours without being towed away allowing them time to get as far as possible from the 'ground zero' point.

Nasser suggested they park in the yard of the Austrian Hostel which was as far they could drive since at this point the streets became pedestrian lanes.

Ollie was supposed to play the role of a tourist looking for a place to stay and ask permission to park until he settled down in his room. So, Nasser drove to the hostel and Ollie went up to the reception desk and had no trouble charming the matronly lady in charge.

He booked a room for three nights and obtained permission to leave the vehicle there for a couple hours. The matron suggested he go to the roof terrace and observe the view of the Old City from there.

Ollie thought this was a good idea and he and Nasser climbed the three flights of stairs to the roof. Looking toward the south-east they could clearly see the Temple Mount with its mosques—one with the golden dome and one with the silver dome. Looking west they saw a few more mosques and several small churches including the top of the Church of the Holy Sepulchre. They couldn't quite see the Wailing Wall but knew it was on the west side of Temple Mount.

They agreed the location was ideally suited for their plan, walked down the stairs and out of the building. In the yard, Ollie set the timer of the device for two hours and both men walked out of the Old City using the Damascus Gate and hailed a taxi.

The Arab driver asked them where they were headed, and they said they had to get to Umm al-Fahm in a hurry. After some haggling, they agreed on a price and off they went.

CHAPTER 17

June 18, 17:21 local time, Jerusalem

The sound of the blast was heard five miles from Jerusalem by anyone who was not totally deaf. Those who happened to be looking toward Jerusalem, even with their peripheral sight, thirty seconds before the blast could be heard saw a strange flash of light from the direction of the town that served as the cradle of the Christian and Jewish religions.

Those whose eyesight remained intact could see a huge cloud rising rapidly to a height of several miles and it gradually gained the typical mushroom shape of an atomic blast seen so many times in news reels from the middle of the Twentieth Century and in horror movies that were harbingers of the end of the world.

The static air overpressure wave caused by the blast flattened many buildings within a radius of sixteen hundred feet, which more or less meant the entire Old City of Jerusalem.

The destruction of civilian buildings could have covered a radius of about one and a half miles while moderate damage would be observed even three miles away. But the colossal walls of the Old City built five centuries before, absorbed the pressure, thus reducing the range of the damage.

Among the few structures that remained standing were the massive walls surrounding the southern and western parts of the city that were relatively far from ground zero, the foundations of the Wailing Wall, and the Tower of David built by King Herod as a fortress two thousand years previously. Most of the excavations from the period Before Christ that were laboriously uncovered by generations of archeologists were once again covered by debris, only this time these were highly radioactive.

This was followed by dynamic waves of vacuum and over-pressure that pushed, tumbled, and tore apart any object in the path of the blast.

People who were not crushed directly by the blast or the collapsing buildings were fried by the intense thermal radiation in the form of the wave of heated air that followed the blast.

Fires broke out everywhere as the gas tanks of cars and cooking gas cylinders as well as wooden objects, carpets, and curtains caught fire. First degree burns were received by people who were several miles from the blast center while those who were less than two miles away suffered third degree burns that often led to excruciating death.

Some had their retinas burned out by the thermal radiation while others were blinded by the intense flash of light. Those a little further away, who happened to be in open areas, received a dose of ionizing radiation that killed them instantly if they were lucky, or agonizingly slowly if they were not.

The debris from the blast thrown sky-high fell back to earth. Some of the larger pieces hit people killing them straight away, others caused more collateral damage to property, but the worst part included highly radioactive fallout that covered a large area. Smaller particles of radioactive dust were carried by the dominant north-west winds toward Jordan and were deposited there by the unseasonal rain showers that also resulted from the blast.

Since the detonation took place at ground level, the amount of radioactive fallout was much higher than that created by the atomic bombs dropped on Hiroshima and Nagasaki that had been detonated two thousand feet above ground.

The larger pieces fell quite close to the epicenter, forming an area of intense gamma and neutron radiation. The overall visual effects were somewhat like the fourteen-kiloton test shot Charlie that was carried out in Nevada in 1951, where the top of the mushroom cloud had a red-orange color caused by ionization of oxygen and nitrogen air molecules forming nitrogen oxides.

People that saw the red color from a safe distance immediately associated it with blood and carnage, even without exact knowledge of the huge number of victims. Though the electromagnetic pulse caused by the bomb destroyed electronic devices within a radius of a few miles from the blast center, effectively cutting out all radio and electronic communications in the vicinity, a few landlines remained operational and conveyed the news of the devastation.

The first reports that an atomic explosion had taken place in the Old City of Jerusalem were sent almost simultaneously by satellites circling the Earth and by the network of seismic stations that monitored earthquakes and nuclear tests.

Within less than twenty minutes unmanned drones of the IDF were circling above the area of the blast. The live photos they sent to the underground control center in Tel Aviv were so shockingly clear that the normally vibrant atmosphere was replaced by a ghastly silence. After a few minutes, some of the battle-hardened officers wiped tears from the corner of their eyes and got down to business.

The first call of the day was to check whether the chain of command was still operating. The air force colonel in charge of the control center updated the emergency center in the underground bunker of IDF general command headquarters.

He was relieved to hear that the Minister of Defense and Prime Minister were on a tour of Israel's northern border on the Golan Heights and were accompanied by the IDF Chief of Staff and most of the senior officers of the General Staff.

Just before boarding the helicopter that would fly him back to Tel Aviv, the PM made a statement that was issued to all the local and international news agencies, denouncing the heinous crime perpetrated in the Old City of Jerusalem, the sacred site to all monotheistic religions. He particularly emphasized that the Wailing Wall, the holiest site of Judaism was targeted and expressed his grief the same fate had included the Church of the Holy Sepulchre and the mosques on Temple Mount and wondered out loud who would be behind such a sacrilegious act.

David and the 'Fish' were on their way to Jerusalem to check the extra security measures that were put in place after Ollie got away from the roadblocks the previous evening. They were listening to the radio when reception of the official radio station, the Voice of Israel from Jerusalem, was suddenly replaced by static noise.

They were near Latrun, about twenty miles from Jerusalem, when this happened and couldn't figure out what had occurred until they saw the mushroom cloud rise rapidly above the Judean Hills in the direction they were heading.

With great difficulty, David managed to control the car and pull up by the side of the road without being rammed by other motorists that headed for Jerusalem without understanding what lay ahead.

Without another word, the 'Fish' and David exchanged a glance and found an interchange on the highway that enabled them to turn the car around and head back to Tel Aviv, travelling at a high speed with lights flashing.

After a few moments, the two men recovered slightly from the shock and deliberated where they should go first—the Mossad, ISA, or directly to the Ministry of Defense and IDF headquarters that were both located in the Kirya complex in the heart of Tel Aviv.

By the time they reached the entrance to Tel Aviv the radio had come back to life informing all listeners about the detonation of an atomic bomb in Jerusalem and warning people to get as far away from the city as possible.

They noticed that all traffic heading for Jerusalem had stopped and the drivers were searching for a gap in the divider fence to turn around. The chaos was unimaginable and the situation got worse due to the number of accidents that blocked Highway 1, the main road connecting Jerusalem to the rest of the country, so traffic on the busy highway was essentially at a standstill and no police cars were on hand to control the traffic.

However, by then David and the 'Fish' had arrived at the Kirya and flashing their Mossad and ISA IDs were quickly allowed to enter the parking lot. They rushed to the tower of the Ministry of Defense and saw the officials running around like beheaded chickens.

They made their way to the fourteenth floor where the Minister of Defense had his office and were shown into the office of the Special Assistant for Unconventional Security.

The official told them that the PM, Minister of Defense, and Chief of Staff were already airborne in a helicopter that was expected to land on the roof of the building within minutes.

The three dignitaries, accompanied by a posse of bodyguards, entered the office and immediately summoned David and the 'Fish' for a report. They had already received several updates about the situation in Jerusalem and the emergency response teams were already set in motion, but they now wanted to know who was responsible.

The head of the ISA and head of Mossad had also arrived and stood peevishly with their subordinates knowing they were in the line of fire.

After hearing about the events of the last twenty-four hours and the futile manhunt to catch Ollie, the cynical politicians were already playing the 'blame game' and looking for a culprit. Unfortunately for them, this time they could not put the blame on their favorite scapegoats in the opposition political parties, so the obvious offender responsible for the catastrophe was now the ISA that oversaw the operation to stop Ollie and the bomb.

The attribution and disclosure of the people and organization that detonated the improvised nuclear device were important, of course, but secondary to considerations to political survival. The heads of government were now dividing their focus among three fronts: dealing with the extensive damage and the public panic was the top priority; next, came finding excuses for the terrible sloppiness of the security services and those responsible; and finally, designating the perpetrators and taking revenge.

Damage reports kept flowing in and the gravity of the catastrophe became evident. Although there were no precise figures of casualties at this early stage and only rough estimations, the specialists from the Israel Atomic Energy Commission appraised the damage as being somewhat less than the outcome of the atomic bombing of Hiroshima.

This was due to two main reasons—the fact that some of the blast and radiation were attenuated by the massive stone buildings and the fact that it was detonated at ground level. The significance was that the immediate loss of life and destruction were largely contained within the walls of the Old City—an area of about one square mile with less than thirty thousand people.

The population of the entire city of Jerusalem included about five hundred thousand Jews and three hundred thousand Muslims as well as twenty thousand defined as 'others,' meaning mainly Christians. Many of those residents would receive a dose of radiation directly or from radioactive fallout, and the expected number of casualties could reach about fifty thousand within the next couple months when radiation sickness took its toll. The loss of property, and more importantly the destruction of sites of cultural heritage and great religious significance, would be beyond anything in history.

Live updates from police and army forces on the ground and photos from airborne drones and helicopter crews showed great confusion and mass hysteria.

The medical services in Jerusalem had largely collapsed due to the influx of patients and the exodus of some members of the medical staff who wanted to save themselves and their families. However, most of the dedicated staff decided to stay and help those who could be saved. The triage—sorting those who could not be helped, those that didn't need any medical attention, and those that could benefit from medical treatment—was the most demanding position in the emergency wards of the hospitals.

Even the most hardened doctors who had seen mass-casualty victims during wartime, or because of terrorist bombing of buses and markets, could not stay at this post for more than an hour before arriving on the verge of suffering from a nervous breakdown. The real wounded, as well as the shock victims, continued to arrive in ambulances, private cars, buses, and on foot.

Fortunately, the two major hospitals in Jerusalem were a few miles west of the Old City and were not directly hit by the blast, heat wave, or by significant doses of radiation.

The roads leading out of Jerusalem looked like a large parking lot until the police managed to install some order and block all traffic going toward Jerusalem, turning the dual thoroughfare into a unidirectional highway. Cars that broke down were simply pushed off the road.

Emergency teams, equipped with radiation monitors were flown in to the Jerusalem region by helicopters and started surveying and marking the areas where the radiation level was above the hazard limit, and assisting people who could not get out of those areas, either because of physical injuries or due to shock and loss of orientation.

The entire Old City was announced as unsafe and as a radiation hazard and subsequently put off limits. A few looters were shot on sight which effectively stopped those that tried to take advantage of the misery of others. A curfew was imposed by armed patrols wearing protective gear to avoid exposure to radioactive dust and armored vehicles, which afforded some protection from radiation sources and 'hot spots' on the ground.

By the next morning, the government felt it had gained control of the situation and life was slowly returning to normal in the areas that had been declared safe by the radiation monitoring teams. Fortunately, the so-called "rule of seven" stating that after the first hour, every seven hours, ninety percent of the radiation abated came into effect, so that after twenty-nine hours the radioactivity was about ten thousand times lower than one hour after the explosion.

Many people who lived far from the ground zero site offered hospitality in their homes to the refugees from Jerusalem, although others were afraid of catching radiation sickness despite the assurances issued by the TV and radio that it was not contagious.

By now, the government was moving to the second phase—placing the responsibility on the head of the ISA, who readily submitted his resignation to the PM.

The resignation was accepted publicly, but in private the PM asked him to coordinate the hunt for the perpetrators. The information provided by Mossad, based on David's work, clearly indicated the extreme Islamic movement of ISIS was behind this dreadful act, but the PM wanted to use this opportunity to rid Israel of its worst enemies.

The list was long, but Iran, Iraq, and Syria were at the very top, and the PM called his military and civilian top advisors to propose plans for settling the account with the governments and infrastructure of these countries. The crucial meeting was set to take place the next evening, since they wanted to gauge the reaction of the world leaders.

June 18, 17:21 Umm al-Fahm

Ollie and Nasser paid the taxi driver and entered Sheik Khalil's modest house right by the mosque in Umm al-Fahm, just as the news about the atom bomb in Jerusalem broke out.

Within minutes the central square was filled with shocked residents who had mixed feelings. On the one hand, they felt the Israelis deserved to be punished for the occupation and the many crimes committed against the Palestinian people since the foundation of the Jewish state in 1948.

On the other hand, they realized that many of the victims were Arabs, and they also mourned the destruction of the Al

Aqsa and Dome of the Rock mosques. Except for the Sheik, no one knew the part played by their own young man, Nasser, and by the blond stranger who was the guest of honor at the Sheik's house.

The celebrations did not last long because in less than an hour the village square was surrounded by armed Border Police troops accompanied by ISA agents that had come to arrest the Sheik and the two perpetrators.

When the youths in the village demonstrated, and tried to stop the troops, warning shots were fired in the air above the demonstrators. When they did not disperse instantly, live ammunition was used indiscriminately by soldiers who already knew of the catastrophe that had hit Jerusalem. A few demonstrators were killed or wounded, and the rest fled the area.

Ollie and Nasser tried to disappear in the scuffle and sought refuge in the mosque with other villagers. The troops surrounded the mosque and ordered all the men to come out with their hands raised or they would demolish the mosque, killing everyone inside.

The blond man stood out in the crowd of worshippers and when a police officer approached him with handcuffs Ollie attacked him, hoping to be shot dead, but the sergeant who covered the officer zapped Ollie with his Taser. Ollie dropped to the floor, convulsing as the high voltage current swept through his central nervous system.

David was informed that Ollie was captured alive and arranged for his interrogation at the most secure prison in Israel. The interrogation was short and easy as Ollie proudly narrated his involvement in the planning and manufacturing of the improvised nuclear device and in placing it in the center of the Old City of Jerusalem. When he was told that most of the casualties were Muslims he shrugged and said they too would be *shahids,* who died for the cause of the true faith.

The whole confession was filmed for distribution to the world mass media.

A few days later Ollie was brought to a military court that after a short trial he was sentenced to death by hanging.

He was told the final act would be carried out by a Muslim woman, the widow of one of his victims who had gladly volunteered to deliver the punishment, so that he would never reach paradise and the promised virgins.

CHAPTER 18

June 18 to June 20, The World

The immediate reaction from the leaders of the Muslim world was to censure Israel for the destruction of the mosques on Temple Mount so that they could build the Third Temple on their ruins.

They put the blame on extremist Jewish factions that had gone on record and openly stated many times this was their objective.

The Arab leaders said they did not know if the explosion was a result of 'an accidental blast' or a premeditated act by these extremists, supported by the right-wing government of Israel, and added that in any case they held the government accountable.

The government of Pakistan, the only Muslim country officially in possession of atomic weapons, was under intense pressure by Islamic fundamentalists calling for revenge and urging the government to nuke Israel to complete the job the bomb in Jerusalem had started and destroy the Jewish state.

Iran, a wannabe nuclear power, threatened to launch missiles with unconventional warheads against Tel Aviv and Haifa.

The leaders of Iran claimed they were three months short of manufacturing missiles with atomic warheads and said, therefore, they could not get involved in an all-out war with Israel.

India, whose government had developed close ties with the Israeli defense establishment, threatened Pakistan that it would not sit still while Pakistan deployed nuclear weapons without even being directly attacked.

China, no great lover of Pakistan and Muslims, felt that it should deter India from using its own nuclear arsenal and issued a stern warning to India that China would not sit idly if weapons of mass destruction were used in Asia.

The Christian world did not hasten to blame the official Israeli government, but in a finely phrased diplomatic language stated that 'extreme religious factions, Jewish, and Islamic, stood to gain by removal of all Christian history in Jerusalem.'

The Vatican, the power broker of the Christian world, sadly recalled the saying, *How many divisions does the Pope of Rome have*? And settled for expressions of moral indignation.

Other self-acclaimed champions of Christianity including the New Evangelists in the United States, the Muscovite Patriarchate of the Eastern Orthodox Church in Russia, and even the Catholic Church in France, all called for unrestrained nuking of Israel and all Muslim countries in the Middle East. When asked about the morality of this action of indiscriminate slaughter of Muslims and Jews, they answered by quoting Pope Innocent III who headed the Albigensian Crusade of 1209 against the Cathar heresy: *Kill them all. Let God lord sort them out.*

The British government issued its own statement about 'fragile world peace' and made a plea to prevent a nuclear war.

Another cry for action against Muslims and Jews arose from the racist movements in several European countries from Greece, Spain, and Italy in the south to Sweden, Norway, and Finland in the north. Although not unexpected, the vehemence of these cries for revenge was surprising. Only those who knew how the leaders of these movements felt once they realized they were duped by Ollie, who had turned out to be a renegade Aryan Swede who converted to Islam, could understand the source of their wrath.

The racist movements urged their governments to expel all 'unwanted elements,' as these were involved in acts of terror against Christian assets and set a challenge to 'all civilized people.'

In Europe, only France and the UK possessed nuclear weapons, so the pressure from these groups came through the Parliament of the European Union in which the racist factions were represented disproportionately compared to their strength in each country's own parliament.

June 21 to June 28, North Korea and the Rest of the World

The traces of the conventional explosive materials found in the Padova warehouse that undoubtedly were of a North Korean origin pointed a smoking gun to that country.

The U.S. President and both houses of representatives, that

had been insulted by the repetitive violations of nuclear agreements signed with Democratic People's Republic of Korea (DPRK), seized the opportunity and called for a decision of the United Nations Security Council to punish the DPRK for its involvement in the Jerusalem explosion. They suggested imposing severe sanctions that would effectively boycott all trade with that country and bring it beyond the verge of starvation—which was not far from its current position.

China opposed this proposal and vetoed it, claiming there was not enough evidence for involvement of the DPRK government and the explosives could have been stolen by a renegade *agent provocateur* planted in North Korea by the West.

The U.S. threatened to carry out an independent operation with its NATO allies, and China answered by declaring a state of emergency and put its armed forces and nuclear facilities on a highest state of alert.

North Korea started moving troops to the Demilitarized Zone (DMZ) along its border with South Korea and threatened to invade it unless the U.S. and NATO stood down. It also launched three short-range missiles off its east coast as a warning sign.

The U.S. kept a close watch on the DPRK troop movements with its satellites and sent an unmanned drone to fly along the southern side of the DMZ. North Korea saw this as a blatant provocation and shot down the drone that fell on a building in the village of Kijong-dong killing a whole family of five who lived there.

South Korea responded by shelling DPRK positions near the demarcation line.

The U.S. and Japan supported this act by sending troops to the DMZ and making sure these troop movements were shown on all TV stations.

From here the situation deteriorated rapidly when these troops were immediately met by DPRK artillery fire. The South Korean response was to send a squadron of F-16 fighters to fly north-west toward the Sea of Japan and then head directly east along the thirty-ninth parallel passing over the center of Pyongyang at supersonic speed, before crossing in to the Korean Bay and returning to their base in South Korea.

Windows were shattered all over Pyongyang but the DPRK air defenses managed to shoot down two of the F-16s and capture one of the pilots alive. In response to this provocation, four missiles armed with small tactical nuclear warheads were fired by the North Koreans—two short-range missiles targeted Seoul and two long-range missiles were aimed at Tokyo.

The devastation in both large cities was beyond description and the total number of casualties exceeded half a million human lives lost in a blink of the eye.

The leaders of DPRK left Pyongyang and dispersed around the sparsely populated countryside just hours before a megaton retaliatory nuclear strike by the U.S. hit the city.

The Chinese could not accept the loss of face of their close ally and launched a missile with a thermonuclear warhead at Honolulu, practically destroying the entire island of Oahu.

The U.S. answered by taking out Shanghai and its surroundings with one of their own five Megaton nukes.

The Pakistani government was toppled in a bloody *coup*

d'etat by the Islamic Fundamentalists that seized control of the country's nuclear arsenal. Their first target was the long-disputed state of Jammu and Kashmir that had been under control of India since 1947.

The population in the Kashmir valley included about four million residents, mostly Muslim people, but that did not stop the Fundamentalists who were mainly out to make a point.

India struck back by sending a couple aircraft equipped with small nuclear bombs to fly below the Pakistani radar and drop their bombs in Karachi, obliterating the entire seafront of the city.

The Fundamentalists also tried to launch a Taimur experimental long-range missile from Islamabad toward Israel, but due to a malfunction of the missile's engine it fell on Esfahan, Iran, and fortunately for the residents of this beautiful city, the nuclear device did not work properly and only spread some radioactive contamination over a small area.

The Iranian Revolutionary Guard attributed this attack to Israel, despite the clear Arab lettering on some of the debris of the missile and its unique features, that clearly identified it as a Pakistani Taimur missile. They launched an all-out attack sending missiles and aircraft directed at the Jewish state.

Most were intercepted in mid-flight by the Israeli anti-missile Arrow missiles and the aircraft were shot down by Israel's F-15 and F-16 jetfighters. Nonetheless, a few got through and caused havoc in Tel Aviv and Haifa—there was nothing of significance left to hit in Jerusalem.

Israel retaliated by destroying all the main cities in Iran and seized the opportunity to do the same in Iraq and Syria sending those countries back to the Stone Age.

Lebanon was spared because the French government appealed to Israel to let it be.

In Turkey, the Islamist government was sent in to exile by the army that seized power in a bloodless military coup, and so they managed to keep Turkey out of the nuclear conflict although some fallout did reach it.

The Egyptians, Saudis, and the small Gulf states offered no public statements but in private assured the Western nations, and Israel indirectly, they would not mourn the annihilation of Iran, Iraq, and Syria. They quietly added they certainly would not grieve over the eradication of the Islamic State movement they perceived as the most serious threat to their governments.

The European governments called upon all sides to stop the fighting before it became an all-out nuclear conflict that would destroy all civilization and perhaps humanity itself.

Thanks to the persistence of the Russian and U.S. governments, and the self-control of the Chinese, a full-scale World War III was prevented. However, the loss of life in one week from the handful of nuclear weapons that were deployed, was comparable to the total number of casualties in the five and a half years of the Second World War.

September, the Aftermath

A new world order was established. The five 'official' nuclear powers, that also happened to be the five permanent members of the UN Security Council—in the order of becoming nuclear powers—the U.S., Russia, the UK, France, and China, agreed to reduce the number of nuclear warheads they each kept operational.

They also approved to continue to blend down the weapon grade fissile materials and convert them in to fuel for nuclear power plants. All other countries that had demonstrated and tested nuclear weapons were allowed to maintain a single item—to preserve their honor but to prevent them from starting a nuclear war.

The terrorist movements, especially those motivated by religious fanaticism, were banned and any governments that gave them asylum or support of any kind, were to be punished by trade and economic sanctions. If that did not stop them, then armed intervention by a UN multi-national force would be carried out.

The reconstruction of Jerusalem would have to wait a few more years until the radioactivity abated to a safe level. Plans for rebuilding the churches, mosques, and Jewish temples were discussed in the General Assembly of the United Nations but the funding was not found as the countries in which nuclear weapons were exploded were busy taking care of their own losses.

This solved one of the major problems of the Middle East—the question of who would control Jerusalem and its holy places. Neither Israel nor the Palestinian Authority wanted sole responsibility for rebuilding the city, so it was divided between the two with each side accountable for reconstructing part of the city that would eventually serve as its own capital.

ACKNOWLEDGMENTS

First and foremost, I would like to thank you for reading this book. I hope you enjoyed it despite the scientific jargon, that I tried to minimize.

I dearly appreciate your comments, so please send them to: Charlie.Wolfe.author@gmail.com

This book would not have been possible without the help of Doctor Wikipedia and Professor Google. I also found a wealth of information in the eight volumes of, *Swords of Armageddon—U.S. Nuclear Weapon Secret History* by Chuck Hansen, in Carey Sublette's chapters on, "Nuclear weapons," and in the book entitled, *Nuclear Forensic Analysis—Second edition* by K. J. Moody, P. M. Grant, and I. D. Hutcheon from the Lawrence Livermore National Laboratory. I also learned about the development of nuclear devices from Richard Rhodes' two books, *The making of the atomic bomb*, and *Dark Sun*.

Any misinterpretation of the technical and geographical information from those sources is my own responsibility. I have also found inspiration in several other scientific publications and textbooks, but I alone can be held accountable for any conclusions that I may have drawn from them.

Needless to say, no one has produced fissile uranium-233

by gamma irradiation of thorium and any serious physicist would immediately tell you it is impossible in the real world. However, in a book of fiction, anything is possible as you have witnessed. As a chemist, a real one not an alchemist, I am happy the dreadful alchemist turned out to be a physicist and not one of us.

Professor Modena, the fictitious alchemist, can be tagged as a naïve "mad scientist" but certainly not as "dreadful." This dubious title is rightfully owned by people who would detonate a nuclear device in the heart of a city that is the cradle of monotheism and among a local population that includes Muslims, Jews, and Christians.

I have visited an elk farm at Bjurholm, and liked it, as well as many other locations mentioned in the book, and am aware of no improper activities in these nice and friendly places. On the whole, I strongly recommend a visit to these places.

It is unnecessary to declare that this book is a work of fiction and any resemblance to real events or people is not to be understood as anything but a coincidence. I apologize in advance in case any person feels offended by the plot.

Finally, I am grateful to my good friend Debbie Zelnik for editing this book, to Nira Bar for designing the original cover used in the first edition of this book.

To my family and friends who read the manuscript and enabled me to improve the text, thank you for their astute comments.

Printed in Great Britain
by Amazon

48087983R00177